A thud, a blinding flash: the explosion, remarkably unimpressive after the previous upheavals, shook the old submarine's hull. He was deafened momentarily by the sound of cascading water in the engine-room as the bulkhead door slammed shut on its hinges, torn from its clips. He picked himself up at the foot of the bulkhead, reached up and swung off on the quick-acting wheel, watching the dogs dig home into their sockets. Gasping for air, he fought his way upwards to the for'd door of the control room, fell through it, grasped at the outstretched hand reaching for him. . . .

30 p

RHONDDA BOROUGH LIBRARIES

LENDING DEPARTMENT

1. This book must be returned within 3 weeks of the date of issue. The loan may be renewed on personal application or by telephone if not required by another reader.

2. Overdue books will be charged at the rate enforced by the Authority at the time of issue.

3. Borrowers will be charged for lost or damaged books.

4. **One** set of tickets may be issued to a borrower. The tickets may be used at any Library except the Mobile.

5. Please notify of change of address.

6. The Librarian may suspend or cancel tickets of borrower who fail to comply with these regulations.

Susan Scott, F.L.A.
Borough Librarian

Submarine

JOHN WINGATE

SPHERE BOOKS LIMITED

SPHERE BOOKS LTD

Published by the Penguin Group
27 Wrights Lane, London W8 5TZ, England
Viking Penguin Inc., 40 West 23rd Street, New York, New York 10010, USA
Penguin Books Australia Ltd, Ringwood, Victoria, Australia
Penguin Books Canada Ltd, 2801 John Street, Markham, Ontario, Canada L3R 1B4
Penguin Books (NZ) Ltd, 182–190 Wairau Road, Auckland 10, New Zealand

Penguin Books Ltd, Registered Offices: Harmondsworth, Middlesex, England

First published in Great Britain by
Weidenfeld & Nicolson 1982
Published by Sphere Books Ltd, 1982
Reprinted 1982, 1988

Reproduced, printed and bound in Great Britain by
Hazell Watson & Viney Limited
Member of BPCC plc
Aylesbury Bucks
Set in Baskerville

When a nation, whose very existence depends on overseas trade, spends so much on its social services that it allows its navy to shrink to a coastal defence force and hands over control of its vital sea routes to its potential enemy, that nation is undoubtedly in a state of grievous decline.

Blackwood's Magazine, January 1978

Freedom is the sure possession of those
alone who have the will to defend it.

Pericles

Acknowledgements

The task of writing these three novels of the Royal Navy –
Frigate, Carrier and *Submarine* – has been demanding but
immensely satisfying because of the friendship and help so
spontaneously extended to me by those who 'drive' the ships
and those who train the men and administer the Fleet. And it
is the lives of the men who today serve in the Royal Navy and
in the Royal Marines that I have tried to reflect in these
books. It would be invidious to single out individuals for my
gratitude, but I wish to mention some of those to whom I owe
special thanks: the Commanding Officer, Officers and Ship's
Companies of HMS *Hermes*, HMS *Phoebe*, HMS *Birmingham*, HM
Submarine *Spartan*; HMS *Seahawk*, Royal Naval Air Station,
Culdrose; HMS *Dolphin* and the Commander, Royal Naval
Submarine School, for his guidance and care in the checking
of the manuscript.

The work has absorbed three years: without the encouragement and counsel of Admiral of the Fleet Sir Edward
Ashmore, GCB, DSC and of the Naval Staff of the Ministry of
Defence the trilogy could never have been written. I am
grateful for their continuing help.

My acknowledgements would not be complete without
thanking Kay Forster for her boundless cheerfulness and
stamina while typing and assembling the manuscripts, and
Marcia Fenwick, my indefatigable editor, for her patience and
endurance during the production of the novels.

JOHN WINGATE

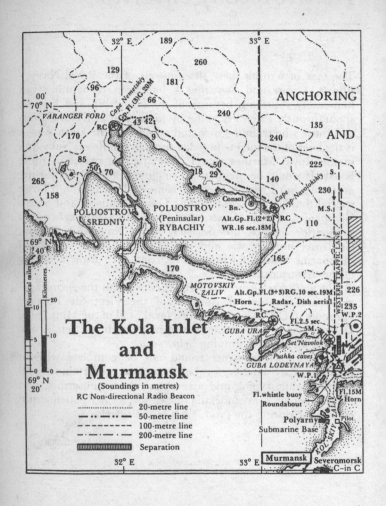

The Kola Inlet and Murmansk

(Soundings in metres)

RC Non-directional Radio Beacon

```
.................  20-metre line
— - — - — - —    50-metre line
— — — — — —      100-metre line
————————          200-metre line
▥▥▥▥▥▥▥▥          Separation
```

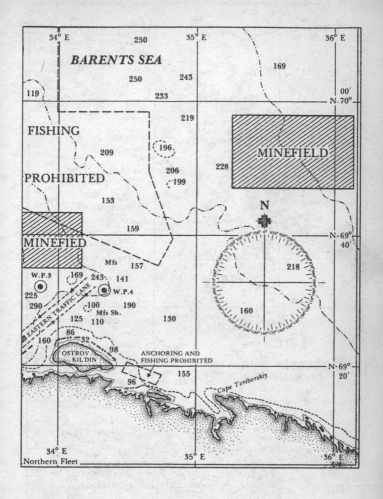

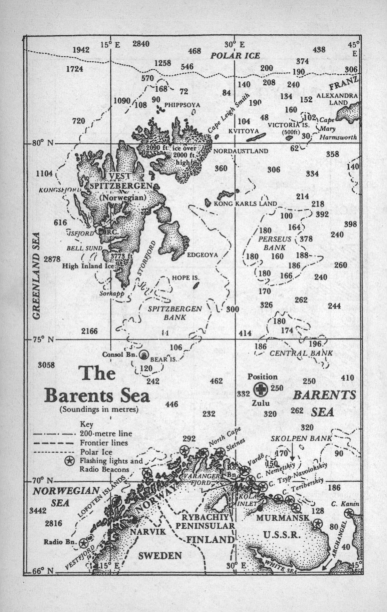

15° E   2840   POLAR ICE
1942   468   438
                1258   546   374   306
1724   200   190
        570   208   240
    168   72   140   FRANZ
1090   90   84   ALEXANDRA
   108 PHIPPSOYA   134 152   LAND
720   190   160
              104 48   VICTORIA IS. 102 Cape
        Cape Leigh Smith KVITOYA (500ft) 30 Mary
80° N   NORDAUSTLAND   62   Harmsworth
        2090 ft ice over   358
        2000 ft high'   306   334   140
1104 VEST   214
   SPITZBERGEN   KONG KARLS LAND 218
KONGSFJORD (Norwegian)   100 392
                        180 164   398
616   PERSEUS 378   240
   ISFJORD RC.   180 160 BANK 188
   BELL SUND   186   260
2878   3773   180 166 240
High Inland Ice EDGEOYA   180
        HOPE IS.   170
   Sorkapp   326 262   244
            SPITZBERGEN   300   180
            BANK   174
75° N   2166   11   414   186   196
        106   CENTRAL BANK
   Consol Bn. BEAR IS.   186 196
3058   120   Position
         242   462   332 ✚ 250   250 410
The   Zulu
Barents Sea   446   320   262 BARENTS
(Soundings in metres)   232   SEA
        Key   320
--- 200-metre line   292 North Cape SKOLPEN BANK
--- Frontier lines   Slettnes   170   90
··· Polar Ice   Vardo 150
⊛ Flashing lights and   VARANGER C. Nemetskiy
   Radio Beacons   FJORD Bn. C. Tsyp-Navolokskiy
70° N   KOLA C. Teriberskiy 186
NORWEGIAN   NORWAY INLET
SEA   LOFOTEN ISLANDS   128   C. Kanin
3442   RYBACHIY   80
2816   NARVIK PENINSULAR MURMANSK 40
Radio Bn. ⊛   FINLAND U.S.S.R.
   VESTFJORD SWEDEN   WHITE SEA
66° N   15° E   30° E   45° E

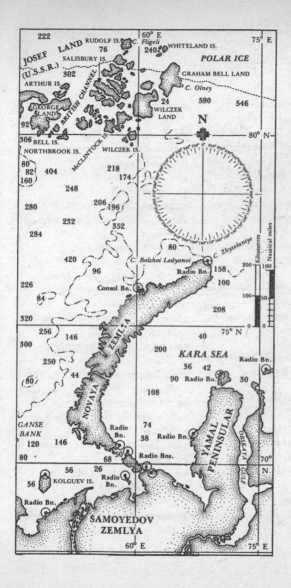

Glossary

AIO *Action Information Officer*

ASW *Anti-Submarine Warfare*

CEP *Contact Evaluation Plot*

Chief Ops *Chief Petty Officer (Operations)*

Chief RS *Chief Radio Supervisor*

CINCEASTLANT *Commander-in-Chief Eastern Atlantic*

CINCPAC *Commander-in-Chief Pacific Fleet*

CINCSUBEASTLANT *Commander Submarine Forces Eastern Atlantic*

CINCSUBPAC *Command Submarine Forces Pacific (US)*

CVN *Aircraft Carrier, Nuclear*

D/F *Direction Finding*

DR *Dead Reckoning*

DGI *Director-General of Intelligence*

DSRV *Deep Submergence Rescue Vessel*

EP *Estimated Position*

ECM *Electronic Countermeasures*

EW *Electriconic Warfare*

FCO *Fire Control Officer*

FOSM *Flag Officer Submarines*

HE *High Explosive*, also *Hydrophone Effect*

HP *High Pressure*

ICBM *Intercontinental Ballistic Missile*

JCS *Joint Chiefs of Staff (US)*

Jimmy *The First Lieutenant*

JR *Junior Rating*

LOP *Local Operations Plot*

LP *Low Pressure*

LRMP *Long Range Maritime Patrol*

MBU *Multi-Barrelled Underwater Weapon*

MEAOW *Marine Engineering Artificer of the Watch*

MEM *Marine Engineering Mechanic*

MEO *Marine Engineering Officer*

SCC *Ship Control Console*

SCOW *Ship Control Officer of the Watch*

SINS *Ships Inertial Navigation System*

SLBM *Submarine-Launched Ballistic Missile*

SR *Senior Rating*

SSBN *Submarine, Strategic Ballistic Missile Nuclear*

TASO *Torpedo and Anti-Submarine Officer*

TCC *Torpedo Course Calculator*

VDS *Variable Depth Sonar*

WEO *Weapons Engineering Officer*

Wrecker *The CPO in charge of the panel in the control-room*

1

England, 24 April. The coastguard officer replaced his cup to add
another tannin circle on the battered tray. His keen eyes had
detected through the early mist what he had been expecting,
but he picked up the binoculars to confirm his sighting. He
glanced at the brass clock on the wall: yes, that must be her, HM
Submarine *Orcus*. She was dead on time, an indistinct blur
where her fin floated in the haze sealing the sky to the glassy
sea. The stream was easing as the time of high water
approached and tide lines snaked mazily upon the mirror-like
surface of the muddy bay of Hilpsford Point: the morning was
turning out to be one of the few decent days of spring since the
equinoctial gales which had struck so late this year.

In the circle of his binoculars he could see her better now, the
black outline of her casing showing when she turned at the
buoy. The after edge of her fin, sticking up like a matchbox on
end, was slightly raked, and he could make out her periscopes
and masts. Her square fore-planes were turned in and stuck
upwards like the dorsal fins of a fish. Her fine lines were spoilt
by the ugly bulb on her bows – presumably her sonar. A light,
tinged red in this dawn mist, was blinking from her bridge: that
was her, flashing her identification now that wartime radio
restrictions were in force. The coastguard picked up his lamp
and, moving outside to the small parapet, flashed back his
acknowledgement. He returned to the warmth of the room and
picked up the telephone.

'That you, pilot? Yes, Hilpsford Point coastguard here: *Orcus*
is off the channel buoy.'

Ten minutes later the submarine was sliding up the channel,
with only her wake ruffling the surface as she proceeded on her
electric motors. Sinister, mysterious lone wolves, submarines
always produced a tingle at the back of his neck when they
appeared out of the mist, silently like thieves in the night.
Submariners were a special breed, he knew that: not only
because his father had served in 'the Trade' but also because

these submarines and their men were part of Barrow-in-Furness. Vickers had been building submersibles for the Navy since the beginning of the century, from the tiny Holland boats to the huge nukes which were the capital ships of today's fleet. The coastguard officer returned outside to his parapet and waved back at the figures on *Orcus'* bridge. She must be in from patrol: patches of paint had flaked from her fin and there was a jagged gash in her after casing. Her White Ensign flapped lazily from a wartime staff erected on the fin; her sailors were breaking rank to man their wires. The poor sods, the coastguard thought. The Navy and the RAF were bearing the brunt of this bloody war. Up here, many of the Barrow girls had married sailors. But the public knew little about the struggle taking place out there in the Atlantic: the climate would change, he reckoned, when the appalling casualty figures were released. He gave his final wave. *Orcus* was end-on now and would be docking within the hour.

'Thanks, sir, for fixing everything,' said Lieutenant-Commander Julian Farge, as he banged shut the carriage door. 'I'm unused to travelling first-class sleeper.'

The ageing commander peered up from the platform of Lancaster station. 'I'll do all I can for you,' the Resident Naval Officer for Barrow said. 'Make the most of your leave.' He returned Farge's salute and strode towards the ticket barrier.

Farge extracted his pyjamas and sponge-bag from his pusser's grip which he then slung up to the rack above his bunk. He had had enough today and his Northwood visit tomorrow could be a drawn-out affair: the sooner he got his head down, the better.

The face peering back at him from the mirror of the toilet cabinet did not really reflect the exhaustion he felt, though there were grey half-moons beneath his tired, dark eyes and the lines at the corners of his mouth were more accentuated than usual. He always needed a shave at the end of the day, and his thinning black hair and the fuzz at the sides needed cutting. He did not like what he saw: he was twenty-nine and already beginning to look older than his years, beginning to show the pinched, anxious look of an officer reaching the end of the zone – not many more chances before being passed over for commander, when he'd have to join the shore brigade.

Tomorrow, if he could get away from Northwood, he might be able to reach home in time for dinner. He could do with Exmoor air on his week's leave: his hollow cheeks were pale, his scraggy frame needed filling, and his father usually managed to organize a meal, provided he was given warning. Farge dried himself and crawled between the sheets, the first clean linen he had known for weeks. He lay on his back, arms crossed beneath his head, going over for the hundredth time the events of the last fourteen days.

While the convoy battles were raging in the Atlantic, *Orcus*, Farge's old diesel submarine, was maintaining her patrol and covering the gaps 250 miles north-east of Shetland. The battered HX–OS 1 convoy carrying the survivors of the Canadian Division to Oslo had fought its way through on 18 April but had almost been caught by the Soviet Northern Fleet, saved only at the last minute by Carrier Striking Group Two's resolute attack. In *Orcus*, Farge had listened in to the battle. Sifting the enemy reports, he itched to be down there with the other Nato boats; they were taking their first crack at the enemy submarines who were harassing the convoy as it turned at Position Juliett. But nothing had come *Orcus'* way, as perhaps intended by COMSUBEASTLANT: *Orcus* was one of the last of the Oberons and in peacetime would have been consigned to the scrap-yard long ago.

So it had been a surprise when, during that savage gale, Farge had stumbled upon a lone Russian Fleet replenishment ship with its Kashin escort. The destroyer was weaving ahead of its consort and Farge, allowing the Kashin to pass ahead, had taken *Orcus* in sixty degrees off the Russian's bow. He had not been enough off-track when he fired his salvo; in his mind's eye he could still see the shiver in the large ship's hull when the torpedoes struck, the hump of sea and then the heave upwards as she blew asunder. She must have been carrying ammunition, for she literally disintegrated into the darkening twilight. Chunks of metal, glowing red and hissing, plunged steaming into the sea. Even though *Orcus* was at periscope depth, there was the clanging shock, the trembling throughout her hull as something struck her aft – then the cry from the motor-room, the water streaming in, the fire in the switchboard. The Kashin began her counter-attack immediately while they tried silently to cope with the emergency, but knowing that she too was vulnerable to the lurking submarine, the Kashin had broken off the hunt to pick up the replenishment ship's survivors.

A strained hinge on the after escape hatch was causing the leak in the pressure hull and, in spite of the chief's efforts, could not be dealt with in the foul weather of the Norwegian Sea. Then, as Farge was making out his signal to COMSUBEASTLANT, the recall to Barrow came through, and two days later, the general signal re-imposing the rules of engagement and reporting truce negotiations with the Soviets.

All had gone well, until approaching the Butt of Lewis. The ship's company had been good news – not surprisingly, with Bill Bowles as their cox'n. And, though Tim Prout lacked experience and was inclined to stand on his dignity as *Orcus'* first lieutenant he had done well. And so had all the others, especially Eddie Foggon, the other two-and-a-half and the boat's MEO. He was a first-rate engineer officer and had done his best on that suicidal after casing, trying to repair the torn plates. Farge was lucky with his officers: his taciturn WEO, Davis Powys, was a Welshman, totally unperturbable, as the impeccable running of his torpedoes had proved. Alastair Murray, the Third Hand, was a competent navigating officer, steady and reliable, experienced with SINS and the new gear.

Farge's Fourth Hand, Chris Sims, the youngest lieutenant, was slightly built, a year junior to Alastair and a very different character. Born within the sound of Bow Bells and proud of the fact, he injected spice into what could have been a prosaic wardroom. When things were gloomy, the sight of Chris' jovial, freckled face cheerfully grappling with his sonar problems was infectious. The Fifth Hand, Sub-Lieutenant Bertrand Halby, was the TASO; he was a conceited and tactless young man whom the cox'n was gently trying to guide in the art of dealing with sailors ten years the sub's senior.

The lurching of the train across the points brought Farge back to his present surroundings. He was whacked but could not sleep: he was exhausted, but his mind relentlessly pursued the problem of Woolf-Gault. A last-minute, enforced addition to his wardroom before going on patrol, Denzil Woolf-Gault was a senior lieutenant, four years senior to Tim Prout, the first lieutenant. For some reason, Woolf-Gault had remained a spare squadron Jimmy for longer than his contemporaries; he had been unable to get an operational boat and the experience necessary for recommendation to his 'perisher' and command. With Tim Prout's agreement, Farge had reluctantly accepted Woolf-Gault for two patrols as a passenger, an understudy to *Orcus*' first lieutenant.

From the first day, Woolf-Gault had proved a menace. Supercilious and omniscient, he criticized Tim Prout's every decision until, half-way through the patrol, Prout registered a protest. Farge told Prout to lump the situation, because there was precious little that he, the captain, could do about it in the middle of the Norwegian Sea. 'But I'll allow him to do a bridge surface-watch on his own,' Farge said. 'That'll get him off your back for a bit, Tim, when we reach the Minches.' *Orcus* was to make her landfall off the Butt of Lewis . . . Farge stretched out on his bunk, relived the incident, every detail of it.

Due to problems with the controlled leak in the motor-room, *Orcus* was running late for her ETA Barrow on 24 April. Approaching the Butt, and being within the RAF's protective umbrella, Farge obtained permission to proceed on the surface to make up time. *Orcus* surfaced at morning twilight and, after reassuring himself that the officer of the watch on the bridge, Woolf-Gault on his own for the first time, knew his orders and was happy, Farge went below for his first decent sleep in days.

He was woken minutes later by two klaxon blasts, and the sudden silence following the stopping of the diesels. When he reached the control-room, the mike connection on the bridge had already been yanked out; through the voice-pipe, he heard someone with a Geordie accent diving the boat. In the gloom of the red lighting, the hands were scurrying around him to their diving stations; the telegraphs were already at half ahead, grouped up; the main vents were opened; the planes were at hard-a-dive and the snort induction shut. *Orcus* was taking on her bow-down angle and, trimmed-down as she was, in less than two minutes she would be fully dived.

'First clip on!'

Farge heard the cry from the tower, shouted by the same Geordie voice. It wasn't Woolf-Gault's voice, the oow.

5

Number One had the dive well in hand and Farge let him get on with it – but something was wrong, Farge sensed it.

'Second clip on!'

As he watched the pointer on the depth-guage, he was aware of the rustling behind, where the first of the lookouts was dropping through the lower lid to the control-room deck.

'Thirty-five feet, sir,' Number One reported.

'Blow Q!' Foggon shouted, getting shot of the water in the emergency diving tank.

'Forty, sir.'

'Seventy feet,' Farge snapped. 'Back to fifty-eight.' He had to be sure, by giving the boat a bow-up angle, that all air was expelled from the ballast tanks.

Then, to his astonishment, he saw that the first man to emerge through the lower hatch was the oow, Woolf-Gault.

'What the hell's going on?' Farge snapped, glaring at the passenger. Then the second man appeared, white-faced and silent.

'A riser, sir,' Woolf-Gault reported aggressively. 'Green 60 at four hundred yards. I saw its periscope.'

The third man, Thomas, the Geordie signalman, dropped through the lower hatch, his heavy-weather gear dripping into pools at his feet. He stopped at the ladder for a moment, his gloved hand on the upper rung. He stared, speechless, at Woolf-Gault; he glanced at his captain, meeting his eyes. Then he turned his back and shuffled for'd to shift from his sodden clothes.

'Fifty-eight feet, sir.'

'Up search periscope,' Farge snapped. 'Anything on sonar?'

Farge took his time during the all-round sweep to make up his mind. Full daylight had not yet arrived and there was nothing in sight.

'Wait for me in my cabin, Lieutenant Woolf-Gault,' he ordered brusquely, trying to smother the anger seething inside him.

'Nothing on 187,' the sound-room reported.

'Surface,' Farge snapped. 'Number One, relieve the officer of the watch.'

During the post-mortem, which Farge immediately instituted during the run through the Minches, the issue of the possible periscope sighting was irrelevant – it was the duty of the oow always to dive the boat. It was obvious to every man jack in *Orcus* that an officer had failed. But it was Woolf-Gault's reaction which most troubled Farge.

The officer had remained unrepentant, as arrogant and as self-opinionated as ever. Farge sighed in the seclusion of his night sleeper. He had told Tim Prout to send Woolf-Gault on first leave; tomorrow, Farge would ask FOSM that Woolf-Gault be relieved forthwith.

Julian Farge reached up for the bunk light, flipped off the switch and for a few minutes lay awake in the blue gloom from the night light. It was not only the Woolf-Gault incident that was disturbing: why was FOSM summoning him to headquarters in such a hurry?

2

Northwood, 25 April. The sleeper express stopped for over forty minutes outside Euston. Julian Farge, shaved and hungry, waited in the corridor with the other passengers, impatient at the delay: if he did not catch the tube by 0700 he was bound to be late for his appointment with FOSM. The hold-up was galling after all the Resident Naval Officer had done for him in Barrow to ensure that he caught the train.

He had never seen such congestion in any main-line terminus: the queues of trains were crawling like caterpillars into the station. As his own train began slowly to creep forwards, he watched the packed crowds jostling good-humouredly along the Euston platforms. Lugging their bursting suitcases, thousands of children, pale-faced and tearful, labels tied around their necks, milled in confusion while distraught women shepherded them towards the barriers. When a roving inspector elbowed his way past the carriage door, the man ahead of Farge asked what it was all about.

'They're beating the gun, coming home,' the man said. 'The Russians have had enough, mate. Haven't you heard?'

It was 0640 by the time Farge reached the queues for the phone-boxes. The only hope for finding change was in the buffet where tired staff were doling out plastic cups of coffee. When finally Farge pushed into the phone-booth, the automatic tape blandly mocked that the lines were choked. In exasperation he fought his way down to the ticket office of the Metropolitan line: he would ring through on arrival at Northwood.

The platform was packed and he had to wait twenty minutes before the Amersham train appeared. He stood until Wembley Park, his pusser's grip between his feet. It was strange to observe the new Britain, self-conscious in its wartime garb. Farge was hemmed in by uniforms, some of which he had not seen before, light-blue, green . . . volunteer services, nuclear defence wardens.

After Wembley, he found a seat. The rows of suburban houses flicked by the windows, many of the gardens scarred by nuclear shelters and fresh earthworks: the human animal was contriving to conserve its species by digging holes to survive the terror from the skies. Farge tried to relax before what was most certainly going to be an eventful day.

Though Farge had been Jake Rackham's Number One in *Osiris* it was unusual for a more junior co to be summoned before the FOSM. Rackham was half-way through his term as Flag Officer, a hat he wore in addition to that of COMSUBEAST-LANT. Rackham, a live wire, had been one of the second-generation 'bomber' COS. Polaris and Trident COS did not normally progress to the top job in the Navy, but Rackham had early been earmarked as a high flier: he might even make First Sea Lord, the appointment never yet attained by a submariner.

Farge could not understand why *Orcus* had been ordered to Vickers at Barrow. True, Faslane had been knocked about by missiles on the same day as Plymouth, but old *Orcus* was not yet due for docking or refit – admittedly, she now had minor hull damage, but her orders to proceed to Barrow had been received *before* he had sent off his damage report caused by the exploding fleet replenishment ship . . . so what was going on? Had he blotted his copybook? Was he being appointed to a nuke after all? He had, after all, done his nuke perisher – the cos' Qualifying Course – after surviving the *Icarus* incident, and FOSM's appointer had at the time hinted that if Farge succeeded in the perisher and was promoted to commander, he would, as the most experienced of the candidates, be getting one of the Swiftsures – the nuclear hunter-killers which, because of their success, were now being produced as fast as the yards could build them.

But, in the event, his appointment to *Orcus* had been wrapped up as a compliment, that Lieutenant-Commander Farge was the obvious choice. Farge had spent his service life in O-boats and was the best qualified among the four perishers to operate a boat as old as *Orcus* on wartime patrols. *Orcus*, with her mixed Mark 8 and 23 torpedo outfit was obsolescent, but would have to compete in the gaps against Soviet fleet submarines, the Charlies and Victors, and the patrol-boats, the

9

Tangos. So it was that, only two days after the hilarious end-of-perisher party, Farge had found himself taking over *Orcus*.

His cherished ambition to command a nuclear fleet submarine had been thwarted: *Safari*, the only boat with a vacancy, had gone to Janner Coombes, the second of the Navy's upper-yardmen to command a submarine. Not only was Coombes ex-lower deck, but he had not even volunteered for submarines; press-ganged as an ordinary seaman into submarines, he had worked his way up to the wardroom with meteoric speed. A commander now (he was three years older than Farge) Janner Coombes was a flambuoyant character: a showman, a type Farge instinctively disliked – and not only because of the time when their personal lives had clashed.

Coombes and Farge had shared the same conventional perisher four years ago. Over the previous three years Farge had been chasing Margot, a Wren officer from Vancouver. She was his first real love. At first, she resisted his idea of marrying but his perseverence triumphed and she half-heartedly agreed. They had thrown an engagement party in *Dolphin* at the beginning of the perisher and Farge was happy, in spite of her occasional remoteness, of her absences when she could have been with him.

Those were the days when the submarine branch was expanding so rapidly that training programmes were strained to the limit. *Dolphin* was popping at the joints. Farge and Coombes, lieutenant-commanders, were sharing a cabin in Clyde Block, overlooking the harbour entrance opposite Wylie's tower; it was during this month that Farge began to recognize the undoubted potential of the florid, red-bearded Coombes. They became friends, despite their differences. Coombes, unashamedly amoral, would regale Farge with lurid and hilarious details of Coombes' recent conquests, his *chef-d'oeuvre* being his pursuit of an insatiable contortionist. Each evening after work, Coombes would travel to Brighton, returning the next morning by milk train and *Vernon*'s liberty-boat for breakfast in *Dolphin*'s wardroom. His nightly exploits seemed to add zest to his performance in the attack-teacher, instead of, as with lesser mortals, dulling the edges of their reactions. A man of stamina was Coombes, exuberant, irrepressible and impossible to ignore: they had got on well enough, but that was before Margot . . . and Farge's mind clicked back to the present, as the tube stopped at North Harrow . . . three stations to go.

At Northwood, the staff captain came towards him.

'Morning, Farge,' he welcomed briskly. 'It pays to get the Old Man off on the right foot, otherwise we have a helluva day. Leave your grip with security.'

Farge followed the captain down into the subterranean warren which was the nation's defence headquarters. After negotiating the strict security precautions and passing through the massive access portals, they stopped outside a blue door at the end of the passage. The captain knocked and ushered Farge inside.

The room was lit by subdued lighting. Vice-Admiral Jake Rackham was striding towards the group of officers huddled over the large central table. Rackham nodded and indicated the chairs in front of his desk.

'All right, staffie,' he growled at the captain. 'Leave Farge to me. You can get on with the bumph.'

While Farge waited, he took in the details of this room, one of the vital cells in the honeycomb of Nato's defences. It was windowless and there was a steady whirr from the air-conditioning. From here, Jake Rackham could contact his submarines throughout the world. Two of the walls carried charts showing the oceans of Nato's influence. The third was devoted to the Norwegian Sea, Northern Norway, North Cape, the Barents Sea and the Kola Inlet. The adjoining wall displayed the North Polar charts, the seasonal icing limits and the disposition of all the Royal Navy's and Nato's submarine squadrons. Wren officers and ratings moved discreetly about executing the orders given to them by the duty submarine officer. Farge rose to his feet, as Rackham strode back to his desk.

'Coffee, Farge? You've had a frustrating trip, I'll bet.'

The submariners' boss deposited himself into his swivel chair, and pushed two charts across his desk – one was a small-scale admiralty chart covering the area from North Cape to the entrance to the White Sea, incuding Archangel; the other, a large-scale hydrographer's effort coloured in yellow and blue, was one with which submariners had become accustomed: Varangerfjord to the west, the Kola Inlet and Cape Teriberskiy to the east.

'Farge,' Rackham began, 'I've sent for you because I know you from our *Osiris* days. There's a job to do and it's important.' He shifted in his chair and half-turned towards the chart of the Barents Sea behind him, a chart embracing the eastern shores of Greenland to Novaya Zemlya and Franz Josef Land. 'The operation's also very secret.' He swung back and, resting his elbows on the desk, he rested his chin on his hands, his dark eyes fixed on Farge. 'For the past few days, the Soviets have been making tentative noises for a truce in the Atlantic. From the general signal we put out, you know the gist of their terms by now.'

'If we don't pack up sinking their submarine fleet in the Atlantic,' Farge said, 'they'll take out our cities with their ICBMs. Are they still refusing to withdraw from northern Norway?'

Rackham nodded. 'They're still under the delusion that their SSBN submarines, their "bombers" out there in the oceans, are inviolate because we can't find them – the Soviet case rests on this assumption. The truce depends on our disabusing them.'

'We've got to sink their SSBNs, sir?'

'Just that.' Rackham relaxed in his chair and nodded towards the staff officers crouched over the working tops of the wide tables. 'That's what we're on – and *Orcus* is vital to the operation.'

Farge met again those piercing eyes while FOSM continued:

'The Kremlin remains convinced that we can't sink their SSBNs. We insist that we can, so we have to prove our point within an unspecified time bracket. If we fail, they'll know we're bluffing.' He shrugged his shoulders in a gesture of hopelessness. 'Then they can fire their ICBMs, knowing that they have an SSBN capability still in reserve – their precious, last-resort SLBM weapon – to match our own for a second round, if we continue to reinforce Europe with our trans-Atlantic convoys. So everything depends on our sinking their "bombers", their Delta Twos and Typhoons, and proving that it is an illusion for them to think that they can really stand up against it this time round.' Rackham glared at the commanding officer in front of him:

'And that means us, you and I, all submariners and ASW forces, especially the LRMP aircraft.' Jake Rackham was warming to his task, his voice becoming hoarser as he enlarged upon his theme: 'While we're still planning frantically against time, it is vital for me to know quickly at this stage whether you, as one of my most experienced patrol submarine COs, will undertake the job I've got for you. If you decline, nothing will be held against you. We reckon *Orcus*' chances of survival are sixty-six per cent against.' He repeated his estimate emphatically. 'Against, d'you understand, Farge? In spite of the modifications which are now in hand at Vickers, your chances of *returning* from this special operation are only thirty-three per cent – which is why I've selected *Orcus* for this part of Operation Search and Destroy, West.'

'She's expendable?' Farge asked, though he knew the answer.

'Check. If you're captured the enemy can learn little from *Orcus*. We can't afford to risk one of our new boats. A U is expensive, and can do your part of the job no better than *Orcus*. If the enemy get hold of one, they'd be able to counter the whole of our ASW warfare within weeks.'

'The stakes seem pretty high, sir,' Farge said. 'If *Orcus* succeeds in her part of the operation, is there the possibility that we can destroy one of their "bombers"? *Could* it mean the truce developing into permanent peace?'

Rackham nodded. 'If we fail, God only knows where humanity will end up,' he said unemotionally. 'And I'll have lost some bloody good submariners.' He pushed back his chair. 'There it is, Farge. I'm giving you twenty-four hours to think it over. Phone me personally from leave. If you decline I must find someone else – and rapidly.'

Rackham climbed to his feet. The interview was terminated.

'You can't tell me any more, sir,' Farge asked, 'about the operation?'

'Nothing yet, except that you've to work on their doorstep.' He waved a hand to the centre of the room. 'My staff's here to help you. You see, Farge,' he said gently, 'I don't know more myself yet. If you decide to . . . volunteer, I want you back here on the twenty-ninth for final briefing, on your way back to rejoin your submarine. Remember, *Orcus* is only part of Operation SDW.' The FOSM held out his hand.

'Enjoy your four days leave,' he said, reaching for his cap. He added softly, 'I don't want to push you, Farge. But I've chosen you because I believe you're the best man for the job.' Then he called across to his staff:

'Help Lieutenant-Commander Farge all you can, gentleman. He'll be wanting to look at the charts before he leaves. Steve, look after him, will you?'

A grey-faced commander detached himself from the group: 'Certainly, sir. He's arrived at the right moment.'

Rackham raised his eyebrows.

'Washington is on the line, sir. They want to know if the First Sea Lord's special envoy has been fully briefed for the meeting on the twenty-eighth?'

3

Exmoor, 25 April. 'I'll take Meg for a walk, I think,' Julian Farge
said, after an uneasy hour at the dinner-table. 'We'll go up on
the moor.'

'Sorry about my tales of woe,' his father said, 'but it's good to
talk with someone now Barbie's gone. Don't keep Meg out too
late.'

What could have been a serene happy retreat, Newdyke, was
becoming a nagging duty. As his father had reiterated over the
port, there was considerable animosity against him. Lord
Farge was very much a political peer. He had not exactly
bought his place in the House of Lords but, as a result of vast
profits from the manufacture of plastics, his largesse had
certainly been well placed.

It was cold when Farge reached the crest of the hill where the
Roman remains still showed. The old bitch trailed behind him
for the last half-mile, her tongue lolling from her mouth, her
eyes reproachful. An old staghound which the kennels had
spared for the Farges, Meg had been Julian's since moving to
Newdyke. To his right the dark shoulder of Dunkery swept
upwards, deep purple on the skyline, fiery sepia where the last
light fell. Merging into the invisible combes and distant woods,
the great sweep of the beacon hill was silhouetted against the
darkening sky, not stark and cruel but with a warm welcome
Farge always sensed when he came to it. Exmoor was as
friendly as Dartmoor was mysterious and aloof.

Farge lay down, his back against one of the rocks on the
ancient Exmoor barrow. Meg crept into the crook of his arm,
her muzzle nuzzling against his thigh. Her grizzled face
looked up at him, her brown eyes telling him that she was glad
to have him home. She grunted with contentment as he fondled
her soft muzzle; above him a gull mewed in the darkness as it
flapped in from the sea. There would be wind tomorrow.

And tomorrow he must make his phone call to FOSM. Now, up
here, he must make the decision. It was considerate of

Rackham to allow him the choice: it would have been so easy to have assumed that his cos would automatically accept orders for even the most hazardous of patrols. This must be a very special job, for histrionics were anathema to Rackham.

Farge had left Northwood mentally and physically exhausted; his emphatic request to have Woolf-Gault replaced had left the Staff Captain unmoved. He slept for most of the journey to Taunton. After a good dinner and listening to his father's problems, he felt refreshed, better able to concentrate. He had never really known his father; his twin sister, Barbie, had been much closer, probably because she was a substitute from the earliest days for the mother whom they had never known. Barbie, born twenty minutes before Julian, had always been the bossy one. Even during those years of their childhood when a mysterious 'aunt' had been supervising the household, Barbie had been formidable. Father had not overcome his loneliness since Barbie left Newdyke on her marriage eighteen months ago. Father, a brilliant man in the industrial world, had proved incredibly insensitive among the community on Exmoor, whence he had only moved after receiving his peerage. Lord Farge was an introspective, shut-in person – and Julian realized that in some ways he must have inherited a few of his traits. This latest worry of his father's was a case in point. . . .

Yesterday, Lord Farge had run over and killed their neighbour's working dog, a black-and-white border collie. Spinneycombe was farmed by a Mrs Prynne who Lord Farge had convinced himself was behind the local animosity towards him. He was an ardent follower of the stag-hunt, but Mrs Prynne detested it and all it stood for, though she supported the foxhounds. A feud had developed when, in retaliation for some suspected slight, Lord Farge had forbidden the fox-hunt to cross his estate. There was no answer from the farmhouse when Lord Farge rang to tell Mrs Prynne about the dog, and so Julian had been persuaded by his father to go over to Spinneycombe early tomorrow with the dead dog and to tender Lord Farge's apologies.

A fine start to a leave . . . but there was nothing he would enjoy more than to get stuck in down here, if his father would allow him. Lord Farge was sixty-six but ageing rapidly and might be relieved to hand over Newdyke to his son: he might even sell up and return to his beloved Yorkshire. Farge pitched a stone at a stump sticking up from the turf. The light was almost gone. He pulled his jacket closer about him: there was a touch of northerly in the wind. He had not worried his father with his own dilemma – the old man bore enough cares without having to worry over the fate of his son. Though the family heritage had rarely been mentioned, it was obvious that Lord Farge of Newdyke was proud of his property, of the niche he was trying to carve out for himself in this part of the world.

Farge swore to himself and the old dog looked up, eager to be off. Lieutenant-Commander Julian Farge, commanding officer of HM Submarine *Orcus* . . . if he and his crew failed to return, would the incident be a shattering loss to mankind? Twelve seconds of media time: 'The Ministry of Defence regrets to announce that HM Submarine *Orcus* has failed to return from patrol. Next of kin have been informed.' And for how long would they be remembered? If there *was* to be an afterwards, how soon would they be forgotten? Perhaps a plaque in the *Dolphin* chapel?

The distant call of a curlew down on the marshy ground drifted upwards, plaintive, inexpressibly sad . . . up here in the gathering dusk, he wished with all his being that he could believe in something. He was facing the moral crisis of his life: within a few days he would, as FOSM said, probably be dead. As captain of *Orcus* he was entrusted with leading his men. But here he was on Exmoor, still wrestling with fundamentals.

The clouds were lowering over Dunkery, scudding black across the rising half-moon. A fitful light shone through the scurrying clouds. From time to time he could make out the sea to the northward, a line of silver, glistening, shivering and then merging with the night. Death. Was it the end of everything? That final patrol, which submariners knew they all had to face, was never discussed: the implosion, the split-second of recognition, the deluge – and when that was over, was life snuffed out, just like that – *kaput*?

Certainly most of his ship's company and at least two of his officers were convinced that there *was* a hereafter, but he had always declined to lead any prayer service.

He wished he could have more time – but the condemned

man always asked for that, didn't he, when facing the firing squad? His ship's company needed more training, the first lieutenant in particular. Tim Prout could only become reliable with *time* – but thank God for Bowles, the best submarine Cox'n with whom Farge had ever been shipmates. Bowles must be a Christian, though he never referred to his belief. He always accepted without rancour whatever cock-up occurred, and the hands never took liberties with him. Farge shivered. The old dog was creeping behind him for shelter, the wind fluffing up the hairs of her coat.

Farge climbed to his feet and faced the dark line of the distant coast. In his imagination he could hear the breakers, hurling themselves upon Foreland Point, curling across the out-lying rocks and spurting, like geysers, into the sky. 'Heel, Meg!' he called. She was already starting down the track for home. Farge turned his back on Dunkery and began the trek back to Newdyke House.

4

Exmoor, 26 April. It was past ten when Julian Farge finally turned to back his father's Volvo into the Spinneycombe farmyard.

'Miss Prynne's out,' the middle-aged shepherd explained in his Somerset burr. 'Er's down at the Exford lamb sales. Dunno when she'll be back,' and he accepted the sack containing the body of his dog. 'Bloody shame about Spot.' He shook his head, tilted his crumpled felt hat. 'Er's been a good dog. I'll give Miss Prynne your message,' he nodded, dismissing Farge. ''Tis a pity the mistress bain't in: Mrs Prynne be down in Plymouth.' He laid the stiff bundle in the weeds round the lambing shed. 'Oi'm danged if Oi know 'ow to tell 'er.'

Farge eased himself back into the car. It was no fault of his, but he felt acutely embarrassed. Down here at the bottom of the combe, this old farmstead had rested for centuries, as if sculpted from the gentle landscape. The stone tiles on the roofs of the farmhouse and outhouses were mossy and fern-fringed, and the beeches framing the old house were in young leaf where they leaned across the stream chuckling down to its parent, the Barle. In his rear-mirror he could see the shepherd staring after him, motionless, his arms stiffly at his sides. Farge slapped into second gear and began threading up the shale track which wound upwards to the road cresting the combe. On his right the ewes were nibbling the short grass of the spring pasture, while not far from them their lambs gambolled and skipped. He stopped at the gate to watch them: surely, the scene represented something of what he and his men were fighting for, trying to protect this England – and it seemed to him worthwhile.

He turned into the gradient to coast down the winding, high-hedged lane. He was thankful the girl had been out. He wound down the window to sniff the scents of the moor which was awakening after the long winter. He started the engine as the gradient steepened, slipped into second to brake the heavy car.

Earlier, he had phoned through to the duty officer at

Northwood without trouble. Jack Rackham had come on a moment later, keeping the conversation short and sweet: 'Thanks, Farge,' he said. 'See you on Tuesday. We're taking care of your onward transport.' End of chat.

Farge pressed back into the driver's seat, stretched his legs as the car swung into the next bend. Through the gateway he glimpsed the shining blue ribbon of the Barle – and a feeling of freedom lifted his spirits to clear the doubts from his mind: the decision was made. From now on, the action was up to him. He had always appreciated professionalism and now he could apply his years of training . . . but *what* was in the wind? The Barents? Mine-laying on the enemy's doorstep? Or. . . .

Brushing the new bracken on the far side of the hedge, the mud-spattered front of a Land-Rover was charging towards him. He wrenched at the Volvo's wheel, braked; the rear wheels skidded on the mud-smeared surface. He heard the smashing of glass, felt the jolt as the front wheel dropped into the ditch. He tried to switch off the engine, but could not reach the ignition key: he was hanging on his side, unable to free the seat-belt.

'What the bloody hell!' he yelled in exasperation. 'Can't you–'

He heard a female voice, calm, authorative. 'Don't move. I can reach the key.' A slender arm stretched through his window to reach the ignition key – and then the engine stopped.

'Take your weight while I try to open the door.'

He snapped the belt free, then found himself being dusted off by a girl in her mid-twenties. She seemed pretty cool, her hazel eyes steady beneath the woollen pom-pom hat perched on fair curls. The diesel of the Land-Rover was still chugging.

'Thanks,' he said shortly. 'You were taking up a lot of the road, weren't you?'

'You might have hooted,' she retaliated. 'It's a well-known blind corner. You were going too fast.'

'We don't *all* know the country round here as well as the locals.' He jerked his head towards the Land-Rover. 'You'd better switch off the engine.'

'I've got a rope in the back,' she said, ignoring his question. She jumped back into the Land-Rover and threw it into reverse. 'I'll back down to the bottom and return via the loop lane. I'll get you out backwards.' And the Land-Rover disappeared backwards down the hill.

'Well, I'll be. . .' He stood back, smoothing the back of his head. He inspected the canted Volvo: extricating it shouldn't be too difficult, but the inside wing was knackered. The girl might know where to find the nearest agent. He hoped his father had insured the Volvo comprehensively.

When she returned from the other direction, she permitted him to secure the rope, but insisted on driving the truck herself. She was a good-looker, her fair hair emphasizing her striking, lively eyes. Her jeans and parker jacket were mud-spattered and worn, but what little there was of her seemed to fill them very adequately. Levering and tugging, they finally extricated the heavy Volvo which, in addition to the wrecked wing, had suffered damage to the tracking. It took her half an hour to tow him to the garage at Hangstone Cross. It was clearly going to take some time to sort out the damage, and the garage owner asked if they could return after lunch.

She looked at her watch, then glanced up from beneath her curls: 'I've missed Tom by now,' she said, turning towards Farge. 'Can I drop you anywhere? There's a good pub in the village – not far for you to walk back.'

He climbed into the passenger seat of the Land-Rover and then she was off and into over-drive before he had belted himself in. He glanced across at his driver who, perched upright in the driving seat, her shapely legs stretched fully for her feet to reach the pedals, could barely see above the windscreen: she was much smaller than he had supposed. A tiny pulse was throbbing in the hollow where her neck emerged from the open shirt. The face was delicately chiselled too; a small, full-lipped mouth; weather-tanned, freckled cheeks above a determined chin. A character, this bird.

'Miss Prynne,' he shouted above the din. 'You've got to eat somewhere and I'm grateful for your help. How about a beer and sandwich with me?'

He watched the flush to her cheeks, the momentary scowl, passing like a cloud.

'Thanks, but I'll have to make a phone call first.' Then she asked, 'But how d'you know my name? I don't know yours.'

'That can wait,' he teased. 'I'm grateful, that's all.'

The sun emerged and the clouds were scurrying across the brittle blue sky when they drew up outside the pub. Over the draught bitter and ploughman's lunch, she said:

'You're Julian Farge, aren't you?'

'The car?'

'Your father's well-known round here.'

Their eyes met momentarily and he could see that she was sizing him up. 'I'm on leave,' he explained quietly. 'I was on my way back from Spinneycombe. I wanted to see your mother on my father's behalf.'

She arched her corn-coloured eyebrows. 'Oh?' she said.

He told her about her sheepdog, tried to express his father's regret. 'I'm sorry,' he ended lamely.

After a while she said: 'You're different from your father.' For the first time she smiled. Her small face seemed lit up from inside by a genuine pleasure. 'I don't mean to be unkind. You know that.' She reached across and impulsively touched the sleeve of his coat. She accepted another half-pint, and they continued to talk. She told him of her life as a sheep-farmer on the moor. 'Tell me more about yourself,' he urged. But she had to return to Spinneycombe, and could drop him off at the garage on the way.

The proprietor was waiting for them. He told Farge that the steering linkage had to be replaced, and that the nearest Volvo dealer was in Taunton.

Farge scratched his head as he surveyed the car. 'Father will be pleased,' he murmured. 'How soon can you get the parts?'

'They could send 'em up by Monday,' the garage proprietor said. 'Then I'll need half a day to fit them and to check the parallelism.'

'How long's your leave?' Lorna Prynne asked Farge.

'Monday's my last day: Taunton train, first thing Tuesday.'

'I'll take you down to Taunton today,' she said briskly after a moment's thought. She peered at her wrist-watch, a man-sized thing with a leather strap. 'We'll be back by four, William. Okay?'

The owner of the garage nodded his head slowly. 'I might even get the job finished tonight if I work on it myself.'

She had already started the Land-Rover when Julian jumped in beside her. Her small face expressionless, she swung determinedly on to the Exford Road.

5

Spinneycombe, 28 April. 'We'd better get down to the farm,' Lorna said, 'before the light goes. I've lit a fire to warm up the place.'

She was, Farge sensed, as reluctant as he was to shatter their final moment up on the hill above Spinneycombe.

'The time's passed so quickly,' she said softly. 'Like a dream – tomorrow it'll be gone.'

'It's been a leave of surprises,' he said, leaning down to brush the tip of her nose with his lips. 'You're freezing.' He felt a shiver from the north-east wind as she leaned against him. 'I'm worried about the lambing,' she said. 'My poor ewes, in this weather.'

He drew her inside the folds of his anorak. 'It'll snow again tomorrow,' he said while her arms encircled his waist. He felt the softness of her breasts while she stood there, watching the mist creeping up the combe. Snow clouds were building up, dark against the twilight sky.

'I'll come up here every day,' she said softly. 'I'll pray for you up here.'

'And for the boat,' he murmured.

'It's hard sometimes,' she said, 'the life of a sheep-farmer. Mum phoned this afternoon. She's coming back tomorrow.'

'I feel bad about my father,' Julian said after a pause. 'I've hardly seen him over these four days.'

They stumbled down the track, arms about each other until they reached the granite bridge beneath the beeches. He tried to halt her there, so that they could watch the silver stream dashing against the stones, to spot for the last time where lay the trout, but she tugged at his hand and led him back to the ancient stone farmhouse. 'Look,' she cried, when they passed the window, 'there's still an ember – get the fire going while I fetch the supper.'

They kicked off their boots, then Farge knelt to puff at the dying logs. Lorna drew the curtains, threw him some old slippers and disappeared into the kitchen. In seconds the wood crackled and then the flames were leaping. Lorna came back into the low-beamed, stone-flagged room, a tumbler in each hand. 'Mum and I like our rum when the weather's cold.' She laughed as she tossed back the spirit. 'I'm putting on something dry.' She disappeared through the door on the far side of the long room, while Farge relaxed into one of the old chairs and stretched out his legs before the blazing logs. He lay back, empty glass in his hand, as the raw spirit seeped through his system. So much had happened during these last forty-eight hours.

He was in love. Margot had been a travesty of this experience: he had lusted after her and she had enjoyed the chase. But Lorna . . . he shook his head and gazed into the fire. Their fascination with each other had sparked from the first encounter in the ditch on that first Saturday night. After the car had been fixed, they had returned to the pub. He had told her a little about himself, of his job as captain of *Orcus*, but no more. And she had poured out her life story to him.

Lorna was the daughter of her mother's second marriage. The first had been childless, but they had adopted a boy, Kevan. Her first husband then died, but two years after her widowhood she married Joshua Prynne, whose family had farmed Spinneycombe for two centuries. Lorna was seventeen when her father was killed: his tractor rolled over and crushed him as he was working the steep field at the head of the combe. Mrs Pyrnne, with the shepherd and her seventeen-year-old daughter by her side, had continued to farm Spinneycombe. Lorna's step-brother, the adopted Kevan five years older than her, had departed for the Navy to become an electrical technician. Lorna had swiftly become her mother's mainstay and companion on the isolated farm.

Farge, staring into the glowing embers, could remember every word, every moment of that first evening.

'You see,' she had said, smiling across at him from the deep armchair in the pub lounge, 'I'm firmly cast in the sheep-farmer's mould.' She'd sipped at her coffee, then added seriously, 'I can't leave mum now – and, anyway, I love the moor and enjoy the life.' She'd looked across at him as she put down her coffee cup. 'You're laughing at me.'

'No, I'm not. It's just that you're not my idea of a farmer.'

'What should I be, then? Apple-cheeked, with straw in my hair and string round my trouser-legs?' She had flushed with annoyance, while he'd tried to smother his amusement:

'No help from your stepbrother, then?'

'He used to come down regularly, but mum discouraged him,' she said, tossing her golden curls and blushing again. 'We would have married, if things had been different.' She had paused and looked away. 'He was too dynamic for Spinneycombe, too full of ideas and energy.' And then she had met his eyes. 'Problems. . . .' She jumped up from the chair, adding briskly: 'I ought to go. With mum away, I have to get up early.'

Farge had paid the bill and driven her back to the lonely farmhouse at the bottom of Spinneycombe. They kissed for the first time then; and on his way home to Newdyke, driving slowly beneath the sparkling stars across the shoulder of Dunkery, the truth had hit him: he was falling in love with this glorious girl. And Farge, alone now with her, jabbed at the logs. The sparks flew, soaring up the chimney.

Yesterday, Sunday, had been wet and windy. In the morning Julian bid adieu to his father and, borrowing his rod, drove off to Simonsbath. Lorna had fixed a sandwich lunch and, leaving the car on the far side of the bridge, they set off in the driving rain down the right bank of the Barle. They had walked down to the first bend where he tried a few casts: but the wind was blustery from the east and, as he had only his father's wet flies, casting down-stream was out of the question. To cap matters, the river was in spate and as thick as soup. So, leaving his fishing gear hidden in the heather, they had spent the rest of the morning walking in the rain and wind. They succeeded in kindling a fire to keep warm behind a wall and tried to toast their soggy sandwiches. They walked back in the afternoon, learning more about each other and revelling in their shared happiness. He had even accompanied her to evensong in the village church. And today, Monday, had been good. He had helped Lorna all day on the farm – to the mystification of the shepherd. But she had worn her heart on her sleeve and had not cared; at tea-time, he had taken her back to Newdyke to see his father. Despite his feeling towards the Prynnes, the old man had mellowed towards her and they had got on well. . . .

Then Julian heard the stairway door creaking behind him.

He rose to meet her as she walked shyly towards him, the velvet of her old dressing-gown whispering as it brushed the stone flags. Her arms reached up for him, her face glowing from the firelight as her lips sought his.

'That's better,' she murmured, gently prising his hands from her waist. 'I'm hungry.'

'So'm I.' They laughed awkwardly.

'Pull up the rug,' she said, 'while I fetch the trays.'

They sat in front of the fire, their supper on the flagstones behind them. They talked little and, if she had asked him later what they had eaten, he could not have told her. He had brought a bottle of Beaune from the pub and she had reheated some sort of spiced stew. 'It's not venison,' she laughed. 'We refuse to have it in Spinneycombe.'

He left her by the fire while he cleared away the trays and went into the kitchen. When he returned with the coffee, she was sitting as he had left her, staring into the fire, legs tucked under her, her red mules peeking from beneath the hem of her velvet dressing-gown. He stretched out beside her, while she leaned back to nestle in his arms. The light from the flames flickered in her curls, tinting them with the rich gold of a cornfield. They remained there for a long time, the glow from the embers caressing her face, like the woman in the Flemish portrait. It was she who broke the silence:

'I thought I was a sane sort of person,' she said softly. 'But things have gone so fast.'

'It's only three days,' he murmured, his chin resting on the top of her head, 'since I swore at you from the ditch.' There was a freshness, a delicious perfume about her, elusive, like the scent of new-mown fields in June.

'Julian,' she said softly, 'you've told me a bit about your submarine, but there's something worrying you, isn't there?' She half-turned, reading his face.

'I've got a lot to think about.'

'Can you tell me?'

'Very little. I don't know much myself yet.'

'About me?'

'You're involved.' His hand entered inside the collar of her gown, his fingers running lightly down her shoulder, tracing the curve of her breast. With the other hand he tilted her face up to his.

'D'you really love me as you say you do?' he asked. 'It's a silly question, I know, but take care how you answer it. D'you love me as I do you,' he repeated, 'to the end of the road?'

He was looking down at her where she had settled, half-crouched, leaning against him. For answer, she took his other hand in hers, placed his fingers on the belt of her dressing-gown. Still gazing into the fire, she drew his hand downwards. The velvet unfolded, like the petals of a flower. Looking down at her he watched the firelight flickering upon the roundness of her upturned breasts.

'You know how much I love you,' she whispered, pressing her hand against his to arrest it briefly. Farge could see the violet shadows further down, smell her delicious closeness. 'Stop there, darling,' she murmured. 'This is a wonderful moment for me.'

'I must know something, Lorna,' he said. 'Will you share your life with me? Does it mean marriage?'

She lifted a delicate gold cross which hung from a chain around her neck. She slowly nodded her head.

'I could be dead within the fortnight,' he told her brutally. 'I'm on special leave.' He felt his heart pumping as he raised his hand roughly to the other shoulder of her gown. 'We may never meet or see each other again,' he concluded. 'We're' – he could not resist the word – 'expendable.'

The lines of her face were severe in the flickering shadows. 'I'm superstitious,' she whispered.

'What d'you mean?' he asked brusquely. He could see her pink nipples brushing the inside of the soft velvet.

'If we give in now, you won't come back.' She searched his face. 'Then I'll never have you.' She spoke softly, drawing his hand inside the velvet folds. 'But we can go some of the way, can't we?'

The encircling flames about the logs flickered and died; at eleven-thirty, Julian threw more wood on the fire.

'You'd better go now.' She was on her feet, the dressing-gown fastened to her neck. Her restless eyes were shining in the firelight. He pulled her to him, stroking her hair with his hands. She strained, once more, moulding herself to him. 'Take care, my submariner,' she whispered. 'Thank you for giving me time.'

He pushed her from him. At the door he turned:

'Phone me at Barrow when you've made up your mind,' he said. 'There's still time.' The tears welled into her eyes. 'We could still be together,' he finished quickly.

The door flung back with the wind. Before he drove off, he looked back to see her tiny figure in the doorway silhouetted against the firelight from inside the house.

6

Washington, 28 April. Captain Pascoe Trevellion was thankful for the breathing-space which the hitch in the programme had produced. He sat alongside Butch Hart, the three-star admiral in the USN who was Director (Operations); he was an imperturbable southerner, resigned to the complexities of this hydra-headed organization which Trevellion was only beginning to comprehend.

'The boss has gone outside to meet the Secretary,' Hart muttered, glancing at his watch.

Trevellion extracted the file from his briefcase, sifted the papers, then leaned back to watch the scene as he filled and lit his battered pipe.

It was still less than a week since Trevellion had quit the North Sea, since nursing his sinking *Furious* into Plymouth. Two days after *Furious* docked, the First Sea Lord had summoned him to London. 'Speed', Admiral Sir Anthony Layde had said when terminating the interview, 'is the essence, Pascoe. You're flying tonight to Washington.' Trevellion had been appointed special envoy to the US Chief of Naval Operations. Layde had seemed genuine when he added, 'I'm sorry you haven't been able to get home to Rowena after what you've been through.' And that had been that.

Trevellion had spent the rest of that long day at Northwood with Jake Rackham and his staff, working on Operation SDW; and then he had been whisked off into the night. He was still having to dress the wound in his leg he'd suffered during the recent days of the battle.

Rear-Admiral Quarrie of the British Navy Staff, Washington had met Trevellion at the airport. After fixing Trevellion's accommodation, Quarrie had taken him straight to the Chairman of the Joint Command Staff, a four-star admiral on a par with the First Sea Lord. The US admiral seemed pleased at the speed with which the Brits were moving and introduced Trevellion to Vice-Admiral Butch Hart, USN. After lunch, Hart had taken Trevellion to the National Military Command Centre, heart of the American defence machine.

Today, at the crack of dawn, they had together flown to Norfolk to study the planning of Operation SDW with SACLANT and his staff who, through CINCEASTLANT and COMSUBEASTLANT, would ultimately run the operation. They seemed confident, but their optimism was restrained. SACLANT, the splendidly unconventional American admiral who was subordinate only to Nato and the US Secretary of Defense, seemed enthusiastic about the whole thing. The meeting was brisk and immediately afterwards Hart and Trevellion were flown back to Washington.

Trevellion had always been impressed by the American set-up; they were casual in so many ways, particularly in service protocol, but surprisingly hidebound in others. Their strength lay in their infectious enthusiasm and their friendliness, as exemplified by this meeting of the Joint Chiefs of Staff which Hart had asked Trevellion to attend as the British First Sea Lord's representative. Trevellion, sitting between Hart and Quarrie, found it difficult to believe that the most powerful men on earth were assembling here with such scant formality.

Admiral John Floyd, who was Chairman of the Joint Chiefs of Staff, had invited the Secretary of Defense to attend this final meeting on Operation SDW before its presentation to the President.

'The boss is arriving now,' Hart muttered. 'Better douse your pipe.'

They stood up as the grey-haired admiral entered, at his side the Secretary of Defense, a dapper little man with rimless spectacles, dressed in a light grey suit which contrasted with the green and blue uniforms around him. An aide ushered both men to their seats.

'Right, Mr Secretary,' Admiral Floyd said, 'Let's go through the plans.'

In the dim light of the air-conditioned room Trevellion listened to the terse presentation of Operation SDW. Charts were magnified, thrown up on the wall, as the most senior officers in the American fighting services made their contributions. There were no questions and the admiral, rising to his feet, turned to his civilian superior:

'Mr Secretary. We need the President's go-ahead. It should be easier, now that he's back from the hills.'

The slight man in the grey suit turned towards Trevellion:

'Would Captain Trevellion like to come along with us to the White House, Jack? Our British friends are in this as much as we are.'

It was the courteous informality which impressed Trevellion as they drove to the White House. It was open knowledge that, since the Soviets had begun making peace noises, the Commander-in-Chief of the American forces had returned from his alternative command centre to the White House, which must inevitably be the Soviets' top-priority target.

The President was waiting for them in the Situation Room. He seemed astonishingly relaxed, Trevellion thought, for a man bearing such a hideous burden. The mobile, craggy face of the politician was older than Trevellion expected. To survive, this man had to be tough: he was holding the fate of humanity in his hands at this moment.

'Well, Mr Secretary, so you've got things worked out?' the President asked, strolling towards them.

While they chatted, Admiral Floyd took Trevellion's elbow: 'Mr President, Captain Trevellion is the British First Sea Lord's special envoy.'

'Hi, Captain. I'm glad Tony Layde's sent you over. He's happy, is he, with the British part in SD?'

'Yes, sir. We're aiming to start the operation as soon as *Orcus* is ready.'

'How soon's that, Captain?'

'Our boats will be taking up their positions on the ninth of May, sir.'

The President pursed his lips, looked up from beneath his bushy eyebrows and slowly shook his head. He remained silent.

'Our end's tricky, Mr President,' Trevellion said. 'The patrol submarine has to be modified, if she's to stand a chance of success.'

The Secretary of Defense waved his hand at the empty chair. 'We'll explain our plans, Mr President, if you're ready.'

The Secretary opened the proceedings by explaining in landsman's terms the broad outline of Operation SD both East and West.

The Soviet navy was naturally exploiting its 'fortress' position, particularly in the Barents Sea. SDW would show that all this was in vain: although the geographical siting of the Barents was an undeniable advantage for the Soviets, this factor was one which the submarines of the Royal Navy also intended to exploit, as Trevellion was waiting to demonstrate.

During the current truce, it was probable that the Soviets, knowing their SSBNs were being hunted, might be sailing their Deltas, Yankees and Sierras (Typhoons) into the Arctic in order to achieve a larger arc of missile fire. To reach these diversified firing positions beneath the ice, the Soviet SSBNs would have to leave the security of their home shores. The same logic applied also to their Pacific bases. Those submarines using Vladivostok or Sovetskaya Gavan could, during these wartime conditions, be contained and trailed. The Straits of Chosen and Tsushima could be easily watched, as could also the La Pérouse Strait between Hokkaido and Sakhalin Island. It was obvious that the Soviet SSBNs could also fire from the Sea of Okhotsk, inside the protection of the Kuril Islands and the deeps of the Aleutian Basin. From their Pacific 'fortress' position, they could destroy the remainder of the world's cities – Vancouver, Winnipeg, San Francisco, Honolulu, Aukland, Sydney, Singapore, Bombay. Without even penetrating the Greenland–Faeroes Gaps, from the Barents they could take out the cities of the northern hemisphere as far south as Panama, as far west as Hawaii and the length of the North American Pacific seaboard.

'They've learned the lesson of sea power swiftly enough,' the President murmured. 'They'll be making use of the oceans, as our Trident boats do.'

The Secretary of Defense nodded his head. 'Mr President, we can take care of 'em now that our surveillance chains are established. COMSUBPAC needs only another two days for his submarines to be in position. CINCPAC's ready to go.'

'Okay,' the President said. 'What about SACLANT and Nato?'

The Secretary of Defense glanced across at Trevellion, who then rose to his feet.

'The Limeys, I regret to report, sir, need a few more days. We're waiting for completion of modifications to one of our boats.'

'Nato's got an entirely different problem to ours,' the Chairman of the Joint Chiefs of Staff explained patiently. 'Theirs is a very complex operation.' Admiral Floyd went on: 'SACLANT is convinced that SDW *can* succeed, Mr President, providing the planning and the material modifications are meticulously carried out.' He turned to Trevellion:

'When can you start?'

'Our units, backed up by the Carrier Striking Force, can be moving into position on the ninth of May, sir,' Trevellion said.

'Is that the earliest that Nato can do?' the President demanded. 'The Soviets won't hold off for long, if they suspect they're being fooled.'

'That's the earliest possible, Mr President.'

Trevellion felt acutely embarrassed during the long silence. Then the Secretary of Defense said quietly:

'Mr President, CINCPAC hasn't been involved in hot war yet, as has SACLANT. Nato's forces are only just dusting themselves off after the Atlantic battle.'

Trevellion felt irritated. He was lucky to be alive himself, having only just finished fighting through the Canadian convoy to Oslo. He had almost lost *Furious*, his old ASW carrier: thousands of brave men had perished in that particular battle. Credit was due, too, to the British and Nato planners who had anticipated so early and so accurately what the Nato submarines might be called upon to do – a planning exercise never envisaged during those peacetime war games. *Orcus* had even been recalled while the battle was still raging. Trevellion felt a smug satisfaction that the ancient submarine which had been designated to play such a vital role in SDW was commanded by one of his *Icarus* officers. Julian Farge had been his PWO (Underwater) and one of Trevellion's best officers. They had not met again since both Farge and Trevellion had been plucked from the water by the American destroyer after the sinking. Of one thing Pascoe was sure; FOSM had made a good choice when selecting this CO for *Orcus*' share in the imminent operation.

'Anything to add, Captain Trevellion?'

'Thank you, Mr Secretary,' Trevellion said, grateful for his support. He turned towards Admiral Floyd: 'The First Sea Lord asked me to emphasize several points, sir. Because of the constricted nature of Operation SDW, communication from the boats involved will be out of the question. Pre-operational training is essential, which means a day or two's delay to make certain that each submarine captain knows his job perfectly.' Trevellion strode to the chart of the Greenland and Barents Seas. He tapped the gaps between Spitzbergen, Franz Josef Land and Severnaya Zemlya. 'Our efforts might drive their SSBNS across the Pole to the Bering Strait. The First Sea Lord wants to be sure that you would be happy with this possible development, sir?'

'More than happy, Captain. CINCPAC would be delighted.'

'The First Sea Lord also asked me to tell you, sir,' Trevellion continued, 'that we are laying stress on the immediate reporting of success from our operational boats. The speed with which the kill reports are reported is crucial to the success of SDW, even at the risk of jeopardizing the submarines' safety: kills – even if doubtful – must be signalled immediately if the strategic objective is to be realized.'

The admiral nodded. 'But we'll have to accept assumptions in the classification of our results,' he said. 'It's deep under the Pole and in the Pacific: our submarine captains may be able only to guess.' He added: 'It's not that difficult, Captain Trevellion, to simulate breaking-up noises.'

Trevellion sat down. The President was staring at the global chart. Then he turned to address the Secretary of Defense:

'It's a delicate business, Mr Secretary. I speak as a politician when I tell the Navy that it must *not* overdo it. If we take out too many of their SSBNS, the Kremlin could react in desperation. I can't risk that, gentlemen. I agree with our British friends: swift communication from our SDW boats is vital.'

'What we're doing, Mr President,' the Secretary of Defense explained, 'is showing the Soviet that we have world-wide capability. CINCPAC can take care of Soviet SSBNS in the Pacific. I'm sure our British friends can do likewise in the Atlantic. We've got to clinch *deterrence* if we're to bring back peace.' The dapper little civilian removed his spectacles and huffed on the lenses.

At that instant in the White House Situation Room, a gamble was being taken with the planet's existence. The greatest monolithic system which the world has ever known was miscalculating, blundering towards catastrophe. If Nato submarines failed, the men in the Kremlin would be convinced that they had succeeded in calling our bluff. Their argument was plausible and little choice would remain to us: the West: total surrender – or the nuclear holocaust. Expressing the premise differently, humanity, a helpless bystander, had but one option: the slavery of Soviet communism was as nothing to the horrors of the nuclear holocaust and a return to the cave-man. The world was at flash-point and whether the spluttering fuse reached the powder keg depended now upon the skill and resolution of a few submariners.

The silent assembly was rising to its feet as the Secretary of Defense faced the leader of the free world:

'I need your go-ahead, Mr President.'

The big man in the casual clothes imperceptibly squared his shoulders.

'Okay, Jack,' he said brusquely. 'Tell Nato and CINCPAC I'm happy with this plan. They'd better get on with it.'

He turned and strode briskly from the Situation Room.

7

Northwood, 29 April. Farge was arranging his grip in the back of the Volvo when he heard the phone ringing from inside the hall of Newdyke House. He waited patiently for his father who was answering it: even with this early start, they would be pushed to catch the only train which could deliver Farge to London in time for his Northwood meeting.

'It's the Prynne daughter,' Lord Farge shouted through the doorway. 'She insists on speaking to you.'

Farge ran across to the doorway. 'Jump in, father. We've *got* to catch this train.' He grabbed the instrument from his father's outstretched hand.

'Julian?'

'I cant't stop, Lorna. What is it?'

Her voice was low: 'I've thought it all out. I wanted you to know before you left home.'

'*Quick*, Lorna.'

'Will you ring me from London?'

'As soon as I get the chance. Perhaps from Barrow. I *must* hang up, Lorna.'

'I'll come to you,' she said softly, difficult to hear, 'wherever you are.' A short silence then: 'D'you understand, Julian?'

He did not reply at once. He could hear her breathing at the other end.

'Yes, Lorna, I've understood.'

His father was waiting in the passenger's seat. He uttered several terse comments upon Farge's abortive leave, then remained silent for the rest of the hectic drive to Taunton. As he hustled his son into the train, his parting words cut deeply:

'There isn't much point your coming to Newdyke, if you don't give me any time, my son. You might as well join your sister in town, for all the help you are to me.'

Farge watched the lonely figure on the platform fading to a blurred speck – he, Julian, had been bloody selfish. A week ago, he would have treated with amused cynicism the notion that he could be utterly captivated by an open-air girl from the moors, a farmer's daughter. He was a professional killer, trained for the past decade to seek out and destroy his enemy: his was a mind forged for the intricacies of submarine warfare, yet here he was, succumbing to this overwhelming emotion at the critical instant when his undivided intellect should be concentrating upon the coming operation. . . .

But she loved him. Lorna loved him. In the nick of time he was experiencing the indefinable, spiritual force they loosely termed love. Like so many of his contemporaries, he had always thought 'love' was merely a respectable word for 'sex'. How else could a guy decently get the girl? That's how it had been with Margot: and once he'd had her he could never get enought of it with her . . . but Lorna, dear God, was different . . . and grinning sheepishly to himself, he opened his briefcase. A man's attitudes, even his fundamentals, were toppled remarkably swiftly, once he fell in love.

FOSM's staff were waiting for him when, half an hour late because of a suicide on the line between Edgware Road and Baker Street, Farge was finally shown into COMSUBEASTLANT's headquarters below ground at Northwood. There was a break in the hum of conversation around the planning tables when the staff captain, glancing at the clock on the wall, walked towards Farge.

'I'll fetch the admiral,' he said. 'That's your seat, Farge.'

Farge settled himself into one of the three empty chairs in the centre of the front row of the semi-circle facing the blown-up charts on the wall. He flipped his notebook from his briefcase as the assembled officers rose to their feet; FOSM entered the room, a stocky red-whiskered commander at his side. They walked briskly across to the two vacant seats.

'Farge, you remember Commander Coombes,' FOSM said. '*Safari's* new captain.'

'We've known each other a long time, sir,' Farge said.

'I hope the leave's done you good?'

'Fine, sir. I'm sorry I'm late.'

'I've been in the ops library with Coombes here.' Rackham pointed to the two empty chairs. 'We've got a lot to do,' he said, 'and precious little time.'

The lights dimmed immediately; the charts of the Norwegian and Barents Seas glowed on the wall behind Rackham as he began his briefing with a run-down of the past week's events. 'You'll have heard nothing more officially since SACLANT's general signal on the twenty-second of April.' He flicked a signal from the message clip and held it up.

PRECEDENCE: IMMEDIATE
SECURITY CLASSIFICATION: SECRET
FROM: SACLANT
TO: ALL NATO COMMAND, ALL SHIPS
DTG: 221957 (ZULU) APRIL

SOVIET GOVERNMENT IS REQUESTING CESSATION ALL NAVAL AND AIR OPERATIONS PENDING TRUCE NEGOTIATIONS. ALL SHIPS REVERT TO RULE OF ENGAGEMENT 14. ALERT STATE ONE REMAINS IN FORCE. MESSAGE ENDS.

'During this last week,' Rackham explained, ' a temporary truce has been agreed – and I emphasize temporary. Whether it develops into peace depends on the submariners of the free world.' He spoke then of the political horse-trading which had resulted in this extraordinary lull: the Soviet government had demanded cessation of hostilities because of the devastating losses to their submarine fleet during the opening phase of the Atlantic battle, the battle to decide whether trans-Atlantic convoys could reinforce Europe. The Kremlin was demanding the truce. If we refused and continued with trans-Atlantic reinforcements, the Soviets would commit their ICBMs to the battle. Their SSBNs, the vital second strike capability without which no Russian power would remain, were, the Soviets claimed, invulnerable, safe in the depths of the oceans. The West had replied that, just as it had massacred their fleet and patrol submarines in the Atlantic, it could annihilate the Soviet SSBNs, their Delta IIs and their Typhoons, wherever they tried to hide. No way could the USSR then hope to dictate terms to the world, however devastated and desolate.

'The Kremlin is sceptical,' Rackham went on 'so we have to persuade them that their second strike capability is at our mercy. The President of the United States and the Allies yesterday ordered Nato forces and the United States Navy immediately to seek out and sink a number of Soviet SSBNS. All our surface forces are remaining at Rule of Engagement 14, while Nato and American submarines and maritime air forces get on with Operation SD, an unimaginative code name for seek and destroy. The Americans, through CINCPAC in Hawaii, will execute SDE (East). Nato, through COMSUBLANT in Norfolk –and that means me, as COMSUBEASTLANT for operational purposes – will execute SDW (West).' He paused, waiting for the North Polar chart to be projected.

'The Yanks are already taking up their SDE stations,' he went on. 'We've got to get a hustle on, because the President won't be able to stay the Soviet's hand for long: if they suspect we're bluffing, their fingers will be back on the button.' He looked around at the silent officers sitting in the crescent before him: 'If we fail, gentlemen, it remains to be seen whether the policy of deterrence during our lifetime will have saved mankind from the unthinkable.' He nodded towards the land map of Europe. 'We hope that the Warsaw Pact armies will continue merely to glare at us across the Central Plain – while the West's navies get on with Operation SDW.' The admiral stabbed a finger at Coombes:

'Remember, both of you, that though you *are* key pieces in Operation SDW, you're only a small part of the whole: a calculated risk is being taken in committing our total submarine capability to this operation – both in the Atlantic and the Pacific. In deciding how many SSBNS we are to destroy, the politicians have had to weigh up the Soviet's probable reaction: if we take out too many, the Kremlin may be tempted in desperation to press every firing switch at their disposal.' He paused and glanced around at his audience before continuing:

'But we must sink enough to carry conviction, to convince them that there remains no such thing as a long-term second strike option available to them – that the rules have changed and they must reconsider. We are, therefore, to destroy a maximum of twenty. We're aiming at ten in our Atlantic patch, leaving CINCPAC to cope with the balance.' Rackham peered at the blown-up chart of the Greenland and the Barents Seas. 'SACLANT is moving his task forces into their SDW positions now. The Carrier Striking Force and Carrier Striking Group Two are already in the Greenland and Norwegian Seas, their LRMPS at immediate notice. Intelligence reports that one Typhoon is repairing at Severodvinsk and will be sailing from the White Sea within the month. The second is expected back in the Kola Inlet from patrol next week; she will be serviced with maximum priority, but she has several defects and, what with her manning difficulties, she can't be ready to sail again for her next mission before mid May. The third is in Polyarny carrying out maintenance and repairs after her shake-down patrol.

'The Director General of Intelligence confirms that the seventeenth of May is the earliest date by which any of these three Typhoons can be ready for sea.' FOSM poked a stubby finger at the dispositions on the screen:

'My submariners should all be in position by the ninth of May, well before you two are on your billets. They have orders to start the operation on the seventeenth of May, by which time *Safari* is to be in her waiting position – Zulu – here. . .' The spotlight picked out the position on the chart, two hundred miles north-east of North Cape. Rackham turned to Farge:

'And you, Farge, must be in your billet by the seventeenth, ready to mark the first of the Typhoons to leave the Kola Inlet.' Rackham paused momentarily for Farge to hoist in the significance of *Orcus*' mission. 'You are to mark and report a Typhoon for Coombes to sink. As soon as you are *certain* of the Typhoon's tasked track and speed, you are to make your flash report – two transmissions only, which CINCLANT will intercept and rebroadcast if *Safari* hasn't already picked it up. From then onwards it'll be up to *Safari* – and you can come home, Farge.'

The admiral's gaze flickered to each of the silent COs.

'Remember that your mission is complementary to many others – our fleet submarines will all be just as much involved with SDW while you are sinking your Typhoon.' He was pointing out the green-circled crosses showing the focal points on the North Polar chart: 'The difference between their missions and yours is that you are to go specifically for the Typhoons. You are to·leave the Deltas and Yankees to your chums, however tempting the target might be – and don't forget that. The Typhoons are for you two only, which is why I have cleared the area of all our boats. Any contact you make will be enemy. I repeat once again, for the benefit of you both. . .' The admiral's face was hard, implacable. 'Farge, your prime objective for this operation is to mark and report the Typhoon for *Safari* to sink. You'll probably be bottoming a lot: you may need extra buoyancy for'd in a hurry, so we've decided to fill your for'd tubes with water instead of torpedoes. Because you've got only your stern tubes, you must leave the Typhoon to *Safari*: your stern tubes are to be used in the last resort only, for self-defence. *Orcus* is not to attack *any* target, however tempting: nothing, Farge, I repeat, *nothing* is to deviate you from your prime objective. Understood?'

Farge nodded. 'Yes, sir – but how many Typhoons can I expect in the Inlet?'

'Two at the moment: one in Polyarny, the other in Severomorsk. I'm hoping they won't sail before you get there on the seventeenth.' Rackham turned abruptly to the captain of *Safari*:

'Coombes, it's vital for you to be in your Zulu position by the seventeenth.'

'Roger, sir,' Coombes said. 'Have I plenty of time in hand?'

'Not much, because of our deception plans: the staff captain will give you details. You too, Coombes, have one objective only: nothing, I repeat, *nothing* is to deviate you from your target, the Typhoon. Understood?'

Coombes' massive head inclined slowly. 'Yes, sir. Understood.'

'That's all from me. It's all yours, George.' The admiral glanced at his staff captain, then walked across the room towards the two COs who, with the remainder of the company, had risen to their feet. He shook Coombes and Farge by the hand.

'Good luck.'

The silence was complete while FOSM strode from the room.

The lounge bar of the large pub was packed with Northwood personnel. Uniforms of the three services were preponderant and Farge was lucky to snaffle the last of the circular tables.

'I'll get the beer,' Coombes said, 'Ploughman's?'

'Fine.' Farge took Coombes' cap and set it on the seat of the other vacant chair. He sat down and watched while Coombes joined the queue at the long bar.

An incredible morning! Farge found it hard to believe that

during these past few hours Coombes and he were part of reality. It was barely a week since *Orcus* had been limping home north of Shetland with her damaged casing. And for the first few minutes at Northwood this morning, Farge could not accept that he, captain of HM Submarine *Orcus*, was to play a vital role in this gigantic and complex Operation SDW. After FOSM had left, when the tactical side of *Orcus*' mission was being explained in detail by the staff captain, Farge's mind at last began to grapple with the practical minutiae. He would remember for a long time the silence in the room while everyone stared again at the blow-up photographs of the Typhoons, the blurred pictures hastily snapped by brave Nato agents: twice the size of the Americans' Ohios, these titanium Typhoons were monstrous engines of destruction.

Farge began to relax. He doubted whether Coombes and he could talk here about SDW: secrecy was such that they had been forbidden even to take notes during the staff captain's briefing. They had much to discuss and to co-ordinate together, particularly in the realm of deception, but that would have to wait until they met again next week in Scotland. Secrecy had produced one bonus: both submariners were not to deviate from normal 'between-patrol' routine. While in Loch Alsh and the Inner Sound of Raasay, on the nights of 6 and 7 May, normal leave was to be given. Coaches to Glasgow were out of the question, but a night to each watch in the Kyle of Loch Alsh and Kyleakin was permissable: the wartime attractions of Wester Ross and the Island of Skye resorts were unlikely to tempt jack to break ship. No mention of the impending operation was to be made to any officer or member of the ships' companies until after *Orcus* sailed during the night of 8 May. *Safari* and *Orcus*' sailing orders would be delivered by hand during the forenoon of that Thursday, when the submarines were to be in all respects ready for sea – ostensibly for their next, normal wartime patrols. By then, all routine ranging and noise-trials should have been completed in the Inner Sound.

Watching Coombes giving his order at the bar, Farge sensed that there was an indefinable change in the chap. Since Coombes had won his brass hat, some of the old bull seemed to have gone – perhaps he was feeling sensitive about the past and Margot – but the first awkwardness was rapidly evaporating under the immediacy of the mission they were now sharing. A visit to the library and that had been that: the two COs were lucky to catch the pub before closing time.

'Cheers, Julian.'

'Cheers. Don't wait, Janner, but I must spring a leak.'

Careless talk costs lives – the posters were everywhere, even in the lavatories. On his return across the hall, Farge saw the phone booth. Shutting the door behind him, he fished out the coins, then dialled Lorna's number. He waited, and then:

'Just a minute.' Lorna, out of breath: 'Just a minute, please.' He could imagine her, in her old jacket and blue pom-pom, kicking off the mud-splattered wellies and tip-toeing in her socks to the phone near the fireplace.

'Hullo? Who's that?'

'Lorna.'

He could see her, even from here, the colour mounting in her cheeks. A brief silence, then:

'Tom's in the yard,' she spoke softly. 'What is it, Julian?'

'Can you be with me up in Scotland next week at the beginning of May? The sixth and seventh, Wednesday and Thursday? I'll book rooms somewhere.'

'Yes . . . *oh, yes.*'

'I'll ring from Barrow. Good-bye,' and he lowered his voice, 'dearest Lorna.'

'Julian! Are you there?' She was difficult to hear. 'But where . . . *where?*'

'I'll tell you later. Be ready to travel, that's all – from the Tuesday onwards.'

'What shall I bring?'

'You won't need much: outdoor things. I must go now.'

She was whispering something when he hung up. He felt the ridiculous thumping of his heart as he handed over the booth to the waiting woman. The meter had not even gobbled all his money. The woman pushed past, glancing at him. 'Worth it, wasn't it?' she laughed. 'Wish mine could be as good.' The door slammed in his face and he threaded his way back to the table in the lounge.

'Can't see what you've got to grin about,' Coombes told him. 'Personally, I'm doubling the value of my life insurance.'

'Cheers again.' Farge peered at the flaming beard across the table. 'It's a long time, Janner,' he gulped. 'Six years, isn't it, since we shared that cabin in Clyde Block?'

'Ah . . .' Coombes brooded. 'Footloose and all that, in those days.'

Farge did not intend to open old wounds. Margot belonged to another world, and he didn't care now, hadn't for a long time.

'When did they call you in for this lot?' Farge asked.

'When I got in from patrol. I left the boat with Number One,' Coombes murmured, glancing over Farge's shoulder. 'Rum coincidence, ain't it?'

'What d'you mean?'

'That it should be us – you and me – for Jake's little jaunt. Does it make any difference to you, the past?' Coombes asked.

Farge stared into those blue eyes, sensed the concern behind the banter.

'I forgot Margot long ago,' he replied. 'I've no hard feelings. She wasn't worth it, was she?'

'Thanks, Julian,' Coombes murmured. 'I married Trix in the end. Two marvellous kids.'

Farge drained his beer. 'Happy?' he asked, watching Coombes across the rim of his mug.

The leonine head was in profile, the red moustachios twirled to a point, like a sergeant-major's in the Guards. Coombes did not answer directly.

'Trix may have cancer,' he said. 'They did a biopsy just before I left for patrol.' He downed his pint to the dregs and slammed the empty glass on the table. 'How's that for you, mate? I haven't even had leave to see her.' He hurried on, adding, 'You're a West Countryman, aren't you?'

Farge covered up too: 'I was born in West Yorkshire. My father moved down to Exmoor when he retired three years ago.'

'He's a noble lord now, isn't he?'

'He's a lord,' Farge said. 'It doesn't make much difference but he finds it difficult to get used to. But aren't you from the West Country, too – I remember at *Dolphin*. . .'

'Yeah. Wurzels, mud on me boots and straw in me beard,' Coombes was laughing and it was good to hear his Devon burr. 'I've hardly been back since I was a sprog.' He was staring across the lounge, his thoughts miles away. 'Drink up. I could

44

do with another.'

'I'll get it.' Farge pushed his way through to the bar. From here he could watch the man who first had nicked his girl, then the nuke upon which he had set his heart. Curiously, no resentment lingered: they were in at the deep end together now.

'Same again?' the barman asked.

Rough luck for Coombes - off on SDW, with the burden of his personal tragedy to bear. He had certainly changed from the man Farge had known during that March perisher.

'Thanks.' Farge handed over the money. He began slopping his way back to the table when Coombes was threading through the throng to help.

'Get round this, Janner.'

They spent the last minutes of time swapping phone numbers at Barrow and Faslane.

'I've got Trix at Lochgoilhead,' Coombes said. 'Bloody awkward to get to. Luke and Sarah come home next week, but Trix isn't feeling too well at the moment, with the treatment they're giving her. I won't get her up to Loch Alsh. She has enough to worry about at the moment.' He gave a wry grin. 'What about you, Julian? How's about your love-life? You were always a crafty one.'

Farge took a long swig at his beer, 'I've escaped so far,' he said, changing the subject. 'But I've got one worry. How the hell do you, Janner, get rid of an officer in whom you've no confidence?'

'That's a tricky one,' Coombes said. 'With the officer shortage, unless he's buggered the cook or run off with the funds, he's unsackable.'

'Even in submarines?'

'Even in submarines.' Coombes was looking directly at Farge, those steady blue eyes weighing him up. 'What's your trouble?'

'Remember Woolf-Gault?'

'The spare Jimmy?'

Farge nodded. 'He needs operational experience before they can recommend him for perisher; he's been sent to me to understudy Tim Prout for a couple of patrols,' and Farge briefly recounted Woolf-Gault's failure.

'Your troops must have seen it all,' Coombes said. 'He ought to be shot straight back to "gens".'

'That's what I asked for. Not a hope. There aren't enough officers to go round, anyway. The usual story. Peacetime politics. No money.'

'You've got to lump it?'

'Yeah. You can imagine the effect on my wardroom.'

'Rough on you, mate. War's a tough taskmaster: decisions inconceivable in peacetime are forced upon us in wartime.' Coombes stared pensively towards the doorway through which the last of the customers were disappearing.

'I'd like to hope that Woolf-Gault might turn out differently: but that's not likely, as you know.'

'We'd better go,' Coombes said, 'or I'll miss my shuttle to Glasgow.' He pushed back his chair. 'Share my taxi to Heathrow. You can take the tube into London for Euston.'

8

Skye, 6 May. The flashes from the lighthouse of the Point of Sleat were already tinged yellow with the advent of morning twilight. *Orcus*, having rounded Ardnamurchan at first light, was now ploughing up the Sound of Sleat to catch high water in Kyle Rhea. Farge felt relaxed: with the last of the flood under him and only two days after full moon, he could guarantee fifteen feet under her keel. The quick-flashing green light of Mallaig harbour faded on *Orcus'* starboard quarter and an hour later the submarine was entering the approaches to the bottleneck of Rhea.

'I have the ship,' Farge muttered to the officer of the watch at his side on the diminutive bridge. Alastair Murray, the navigating officer, was bent over the bearing ring of the compass repeater as he checked his last fix.

'You have the ship, sir.' Chris Sims, sonar officer and the Third Hand, stepped back from the voice-pipe as his captain took over the conning. Above them, the radar mast twisted in its rings as the officer on the plot in the control-room confirmed Murray's visual bearings.

'Control – bridge,' Farge called a few minutes later over the intercom, 'plot: are you happy with your position?'

'Bridge – control: yes, sir. On track, in the middle of the channel. We're up to time. You should sight the buoy any time now.'

Farge lowered his binoculars and spoke into the mike. 'We've got it. Cable party up top: prepare the anchor ready for letting go.'

The passage was narrowing as the submarine nosed into Kyle Rhea. It was dark here, cold and inhospitable, where the hills dropped into the dark, steely sea. High above the submarine, the tops of the larger hills scraped the base of the mist which was swirling up, towards the peaks where the rising sun was touching the mountains. The black water hissed down her sides as *Orcus* forged through the kyle which had been gouged from the rock by the eternal rhythm of the tides.

'Nothing to port, cox'n.'

'Nothing to port, sir.'

The passage was less than half a mile wide here: shags were perched on their favourite rocks; a seal stared in curiosity at its giant cousin, the gleaming, black submarine. As *Orcus* swung into the final bend of the kyle, Farge glimpsed the blue water of Loch Alsh sparkling ahead. Ten minutes later he brought his submarine round to the north-west: the rays of the sun were suffusing the hills and the loch with that magical, fragile luminosity which only Wester Ross and the Western Isles can produce. Below the fields, carved from the heather, the northern shore was sprinkled by a patchwork of white-washed cottages and crofts. Their slate roofs, still wet with dew, were glistening in the freshness of the new day. `

'Steer 280°, cox'n.'

Farge again lifted his binoculars. There was the Balmacara hotel and to the west of it the inlet in which he would anchor tonight. He could see the road now, skirting the water's edge –and he grinned secretly to himself. If all had gone as planned, she would have travelled along it yesterday evening, on her way to the Kyleakin ferry. Then *Orcus* was through the worst of the Rhea narrows; there remained only the Kyle of Akin, the bottle-neck debouching into the open water leading to the Inner Sound. He was lucky to have CPO Bowles. He was as competent a helmsman as he was a cox'n, that key man in a submarine who was responsible for the well-being and routine of the ship's company. Yes, he was fortunate to have Bowles, particularly as *Orcus*' first lieutenant, Tim Prout, still lacked experience.

'Steady, sir. Course 280°.'

The fishing haven of Kyle of Lochalsh was coming rapidly into view: the brightly coloured trawlers and purse-net boats were nestled about the quays and he could distinguish the yellow upperworks of the fleet tenders huddled on the nearest jetties.

'Nothing to port.'

'Nothing to port, sir.'

There was no more than a cable between the rocky shore and *Orcus* as she slid through the Kyle of Akin. Farge glimpsed the red-painted ferry and its sleepy crew preparing for the first trip of the day. Behind the houses huddled about the hard, he spotted the hotel where Lorna should be sleeping.

'Fourteen metres, sir . . . fourteen, fourteen, fourteen and a half . . .' Murray was reporting as he monitored the depths.

Then the submarine was through and into the open water where lay the channel to the Inner Sound. The panorama opened before him: to the north-east, the distant mainland sprawled, mauve and silvery-blue with mist where it merged with the far mountains. He lined up *Orcus* between the Crowlin Isles and the islet of Longay, which passage was the final gateway to the Inner Sound, North Minch and the Arctic oceans beyond.

Again Farge felt the twinge of apprehension, once more the weight of the secret he was carrying. He could tell them all on Friday off Loch Cairnbawn; he would drill them silly there, the last opportunity before the real thing. Today, the vital trials lay before them: the deep dive to check that the leak round the after hatch was cured, during the forenoon; in the afternoon, bottoming drills, then back to the anchorage in Loch Alsh, to give night leave.

'Open up for diving,' he passed down over the mike. 'Diving stations in three-quarters of an hour's time. Secure the anchor for sea.'

He watched the cable party, Woolf-Gault supervising, while Parry, the lanky, black-bearded second cox'n and the hands secured the anchor. The precocious sub-lieutenant, Halby, had fallen sick at the wrong moment, and Farge had to accept that Woolf-Gault was the obvious replacement.

Orcus was steadying nicely between the islands: up ahead lay the long whale-shaped island of Raasay, sloping towards its northern tip. To the westward behind the island, the Cuillin Hills of Skye formed a breath-taking backdrop, powder-blue with distance in the purity of this soft, clear air from the Atlantic. Scalpay lay close to port; and due south the islet of Pabay where, north of the wreck of the World War II ammunition ship, *Safari* would anchor tomorrow at the end of the day. She too, as part of the deception plan, would give normal leave. Woolf-Gault was standing beneath the fin and yelling upwards:

'Anchor and casing secured for sea, sir.'

'Fall out specials.' Farge nodded at the lookout, 'Go below.' He picked up the mike:

'Diving stations in ten minutes' time. Navigating officer, report when I'm in my diving position.'

The last man of the special sea-dutymen was disappearing through the fin door. 'Carry on below, Sims,' Farge ordered his officer of the watch.

'Bridge – control: boat opened up for diving, sir,' the MEO reported. 'Boat shut off for going deep. Q tank empty.'

Up ahead were the fleet tenders, waiting in position to keep the exercise area clear. The crofts were distinguishable, huddling along the shore at the northern end of Raasay. When the cottages were abeam, he would dive. He would take her down slowly to the deepest patch off the kyle between Rona and Raasay. He could dive to a thousand feet there, but he'd have to watch his navigation. Vickers had carried out a pressure test on the hatch, but there was nothing like the real thing to create confidence.

'In diving position, sir,' Murray called. 'Good fix.'

It was peaceful without the coughing of the diesels, while the submarine glided ahead on her electric motors. A pair of gulls dived angrily upon the periscope rearing behind him; he watched them peeling off, screeching furiously towards Raasay. He glanced round the horizon, yanked out the mike and leaned over the voice-pipe:

'Group up, half ahead together. Open main vents.'

The boat trembled to the added power as the screws threshed at her stern. Plumes of spray spouted upwards as the vents opened. Her stern came up; the bows dipped. He crossed to the upper lid, the soles of his boots feeling for the rungs of the ladder. This was to be a deep diving test, but it was the final trial for Woolf-Gault. If he cracked, Farge would put him ashore before *Orcus* sailed in two days' time – whatever officialdom decreed, and by force if it had to be. He pulled the hatch shut over his head and slammed on the long-handled clip.

'First clip on!' he shouted. 'Take her down, periscope depth.'

Lorna thought he raised his hand to her, when the submarine

slid past the slipway of the Kyleakin ferry. The black fin looked so close, the men on the bridge recognizable, as they concentrated on guiding their sinister submarine through this narrow channel. Her white ensign fluttered proudly, and at the front end of the boat, sailors and an officer were standing by the anchor. The submarine made no noise: just the hissing of the water along her waterline and the bubbling of her wake. And then she was moving away up Loch Alsh to anchor.

One of the ferry crew pushed past her to throw the mooring rope. The engines rumbled and the ferry was off, ploughing across the kyle to the mainland. She'd wait for Julian at the top of the hard where she couldn't miss him.

Lorna Prynne tried to suppress her excitement: since her mother had seen her off at Taunton and throughout the long journey and its wartime frustrations the tension inside her had mounted. And she had just seen him: tall, lean, cap slightly askew, standing apart on the bridge as he conned his submarine.

Kyle of Lockalsh, the bustling little port facing Kyleakin, grew larger with every second and then the ramp of the ferry was grinding across the concrete hard. Lorna had plenty of time, so waited for the cars to roll ashore. She strolled towards the road and found a corner in the sun by the wall where she could see up the loch: *Orcus* had turned and was pointing towards her. She watched the anchor splashing into the dark water, saw the Union Jack fluttering from the staff at her bows. Minutes later men were emerging from her hull and mustering on deck.

Lorna recognized the emotion of belonging to this mysterious, lone submarine. Those men, from the youngest to the captain, lived and worked inside that black hull: they all had their fears, their loves, their hates; many must have families to care for, wives and children; perhaps there were some like Julian and her, cherishing a secret love; most still had parents, while some, she feared, would be enduring their own private despairs. But each one of them shared the common denominator: *Orcus*, their submarine. And any one of them, through carelessness, idleness, cussedness or fear could, in a brief moment, put at risk the lives of all the others. Submariners, like flyers, *were* different: each man depended entirely on his neighbour – one day, perhaps, she would understand them better, their independent, forceful decisiveness.

A black-hulled boat with yellow upper-works, a blue ensign at her mast, was nosing alongside the submarine's port side. Ropes were flung across and then ant-like figures were swarming into the liberty boat. But why didn't the tender leave the submarine? Why did she stick there, rolling gently alongside *Orcus*? Lorna took off the blue suede jacket she had thrown across her shoulders on leaving the hotel. It was hot here, out of the wind in the setting sunlight, even at six o'clock on this beautiful May evening.

'Oh – come on . . .' she whispered impatiently – and then she saw an officer saluting on the deck as the last, tall figure jumped across the gap. She caught her breath as she recognized Julian. He entered the boat's wheelhouse and she lost sight of him. The bows of the tender were slowly separating from the submarine; the gap widened; and then the liberty boat was forging towards her, its bow-wave frothing white on the placid surface of the loch.

It was ten minutes past six when Julian, the first to leave the tender, clambered up the ladder to the quay. She watched him as he casually surveyed the scene while two officers and the libertymen swarmed ashore. All were in uniform, neat and tidy, an animated, jolly lot. How young they looked! An older man with frizzled hair, a chief petty officer, stopped to chat with his captain. Julian returned the salute and then the Chief was off with several of his friends, striding towards the little town.

Gulls screamed about the quays; a fishing-boat was chugging in through the kyle, rusty red gear and a glistening, emerald hull. Fishermen were laying out their nets to dry on the quay; the Kyleakin ferry was tooting, announcing its imminent departure. Julian straightened his tie, picked up his grip and hurried along the quay for the ferry.

She had to run to catch up with him. They were closing the ferry gates as she jumped on to the ramp, already scraping from the hard. She could see him threading his way through the cars to reach the far end of the double-ended ferry. He had plonked down his grip; he was leaning on the rail and gazing towards the village on the opposite side of the kyle. She was still out of breath when she crept up behind him. People were glancing at her, amused, but she did not care. She edged to the rail, close to his side.

'Looking for someone?'

He did not speak as a slow grin creased his pale face. The hard lines vanished as he greeted her formally with the traditional salute of the sailor, but his eyes were telling her all she wanted to know.

'I was afraid you couldn't make it,' he said quietly, glancing over her head at the interested onlookers. 'Have a good trip?'

She nodded, pulling at her jacket when the breeze slapped the ferry's prow. She moved closer to him, her heart still racing, as in silence they watched the Kyleakin shore approaching fast. He gave a final glance up the loch towards his submarine and then they were hurrying up the hard while the cars groaned past them.

She pointed to the white-washed hotel sprawling across the neck of the little peninsular. 'They've got our rooms,' she said shyly. 'They're nice people.'

She ran up the few steps and he pushed open the door for her. He dumped his bag on the plum-coloured carpet.

'Lieutenant-Commander Farge?' the proprietress asked, sliding a registration form and the visitors' book towards him. 'Wartime regulations, I'm afraid, sir. Your room's ready for you in the annexe,' she added, glancing at Lorna.

Lorna stood behind him, watching his hesitation. 'Supper's at seven,' the woman said as he scribbled in the details. 'I've reserved a table by the window.' She was smiling at them both, 'I hope you'll enjoy your stay.'

'Thanks. I'll get cleaned up for supper.'

'I'll show you to your room.' The kindly Scottish woman glanced across at Lorna.

'Don't bother, I'll take him across to the annexe.' Julian picked up his bag and Lorna led the way to the door opening on to the small courtyard at the rear.

'Number eight,' she said quietly as Julian unlocked his door. 'Mine's in the main building: room five.'

He dumped his bag on the chair and, taking her hands, drew her into the room. He shut the door and encircled her in his arms. He kissed her then gently pushed her from him. 'Let's eat,' he said. 'Then we can talk.'

Later, while the sun crept downwards across the Cuillins, they took the shore road out of the village. When they were clear of the houses, he took her hand. They strode along and for a while he spoke of mundane things: his trip up north, the difficulties of trying to find accommodation at Kyleakin. 'So I left it to you in the end,' he said, smiling down at her. There was a constraint between them which she did not understand.

The deserted road was evidence of the recent petrol-rationing. On their right, the Sound opened up to the northward, the last rays of the sun for a brief moment brushing rose-pink the slopes of the islands. The valleys running down from the northern slopes of the Cuillins were turning blue, deep mauve across the lower slopes where the shore tumbled into the narrows which separated Skye from Scalpay. The granite boulders scattered along the roadside were fringed with gorse, the trembling, golden spikes stilled now that the breeze was falling away. The sea was very blue and white cotton-wool clouds drifted high in the evening sky.

Farge led her by the hand, as they scrambled across the rocks which sprinkled the turf running down to the sea. The heather scratched her bare legs as they strode onwards and she was thankful her coat was long enough to protect her tweed skirt from the worst. At the shore-line he stopped, outlined against the brittle light of sunset, tall and lean in his old grey trousers and blue sweater.

'There,' he said. 'The little bay, out of the wind.'

They spread her coat on a spur of turf and leaned against the rock edging the sand. He drew her into his shoulder and began stroking her hair, pressing her head against his chest. She could feel the beating of his heart and, encircling him with her arms, she turned her face up to him. His brown eyes were flickering with darts of light as he stared down at her, but then his face blurred as he bent to brush her forehead with his mouth. She closed her eyes, felt his lips touching her lids. She reached up and entwining her hands about his head, pulled him down to her. She sealed her mouth to his and, slowly parting her lips for his probing tongue, felt the lick of desire reaching to the very depths of her body. The world dissolved and she was lost, overwhelmed by the frenzy of his loving. She drew back and watched his eyes opening.

'My Lorna,' he whispered. 'I've been searching for you for so long.' He kissed her again, then suddenly pushed her from him. 'I love you so much.'

'Why d'you think I've come up to Scotland?' she whispered.

'We've such a short time.' He traced the outline of her face with his strong fingers.

'Tonight – and tomorrow,' she said.

Neither spoke then, as they leaned back against the rock, her hand on his chest, his hand on her thigh. He began flipping the shale pebbles towards the wavelets lapping the beach.

'Stop,' she said, 'or you'll frighten that lovely bird.'

'Oyster-catcher: look, there's his mate.'

The beautiful sea-birds, resplendent in their spring plumage, with their red eyes and legs, and their long, orange beaks, had alighted on a tide-washed rock, barely ten yards away.

'They must have a nest nearby,' he said. 'Look how contented the hen looks.'

She caught his answering smile as she whispered:

'It's not only the birds who have maternal instincts.' She took his hand and slid it beneath her heavy sweater. She did not know how long she lay there, eyes closed, savouring the delicious seduction of his hands. From somewhere far away she heard his voice:

'Will you marry me if . . . *when* I get back?' A small, golden cross hung from a fine chain between her breasts. She lifted it and held it up to his lips. He kissed it and enfolded her hand in his.

'I'm yours totally and for ever,' she replied softly as, gently separating her breasts, he replaced the emblem. Above the lapping of the wavelets, she could hear the oyster-catchers calling to each other on the shore.

'You're cold,' he said, pulling down the sweater. 'I'll find somewhere out of the breeze.' He climbed to his feet and scrambled down to the tide-line fringing the cove. She watched him scouting round the rocks and then, when he was out of sight behind the promonotory, swiftly climbed to her feet. Sweeping her sweater over her head, she slipped into her gaberdine raincoat; unzipping her skirt, she watched it tumble to the turf. She stepped from it and folded it inside the sweater. Placing the makeshift cushion on the turf, she buttoned her raincoat and sat down, her hands behind her, waiting for him.

The last rays of the sun were streaming across the wild countryside behind her, deliciously warm, heightening every glorious colour, the vivid greens, the blues, the shining golds. . . . 'Dear God,' she cried out, 'please, oh please, don't take him from me.' She turned abruptly as she heard Julian scrunching on the shale from somewhere between the rocks.

'There's nowhere better,' he called to her.

She smiled, holding a hand out towards him. 'It's lovely here,' she cried. 'Warm, now, in the sun.' She lay back. 'Come,' she called softly.

Kneeling beside her, he took her face between his hands. Then, without a word, opening the collar of the coat, he began to caress her body.

'My God – you're beautiful.'

She felt his fingers at the buttons, undoing them one by one. She watched his dark eyes lingering over her, saw the gleam in them as he folded back her coat. Her arms went around him, pulling him down roughly, taking him to her:

'I want our child, now, *now*,' she whispered fiercely. 'Then I'll have you for ever. Whatever happens . . .'

The peaks of the Cuillins, tipped crimson and orange by the afterglow of sunset, cotton grass whispering in the moorland behind them, and the call of a curlew floating plaintively in the silence of the gathering dusk . . . she would cherish this instant when time stood still, this moment when finally she opened her eyes, until the end of her mortal days.

9

HMS Submarine Safari, 7 May. 'Is that our last run, Number One?' asked Coombes.

'Yes, sir. Noise trial completed.'

Commander Coombes glanced at the clock above the submarine's chart table. 'Time to go home,' he said. After surfacing, you can send your libertymen to clean. I'll take her on the watch to Pabay Island.'

'Thanks, sir.'

'What time's the liberty-boat?'

'1615, sir.'

'ETA Pabay, pilot?' Coombes asked his navigating officer, Lieutenant Everard Farquharson, who was crouched over his chart table in the starboard for'd corner of the control-room.

'1605, sir.'

Coombes glanced at the men around him: Fleet Chief Petty Officer 'Bull' Clint, his extrovert cox'n on the planes was keeping the ordered depth of two hundred feet. Standing alongside the cox'n in the port for'd corner of the cramped control-room was the 'outside wrecker', MEA/Mech 1 Hank Botham, who was supervising the newly-joined PO MEM watchkeeper on the SCC. Between the two athwartship periscopes stood the WEO, Lieutenant-Commander Simon Grenville. The first lieutenant, the senior two-and-a-half on board, Stuart Hamilton, hovered on the port side of the masts from where he kept an eye on his AI team.

'No other contacts, sir: only *Orcus* bearing 015°.'

'*Cabot's* keeping the area clear: I won't stop on the way up today, Number One,' Coombes said. 'Stop engine. Periscope depth.' He nodded at the ship control officer of the watch, 'Six up.'

The captain stood between the periscopes, watching as the incredible machine responded to the sensitive controls, all 4,500 tons of her. He could feel her under his feet, the angle coming on as she adopted her six-degree bow-up angle.

'No contacts,' the sound-room reported. In the hands of a

good operator, the 2001 sonar was a magnificent set.

'No contacts, watcher,' again from the sound-room.

Coombes was happier now, after the hard time he'd had licking his ship's company into shape before his first wartime patrol off the Faeroes.

'Seventy-two, seventy feet.'

'Up search,' Coombes snapped, taking his hands from his pockets. This was the tricky bit, blind still, unpleasantly vulnerable to deep-draught ship tankers – vLccs now drew ninety feet. To be safe these days, *Safari* had to be at 190 feet.

'Sixty-four . . .'

He opened the periscope handles. The light from the surface was percolating downwards . . . and then suddenly came the bubbles and the frothing.

'Breaking.'

'Sixty-two . . .'

'No contacts, watcher.'

'Sixty feet.'

As the glass cleared Coombes could see Raasay, bare, fresh green at this time of the year – and he swept round in low power: Scalpay, Pabay, Longay and the Crowlins between which *Safari* would be slipping, the rounded cliffs of the Ross-shire coast: then, back to the north, towards the top of the Sound and Rona – there was *Orcus* . . .

'Nothing close,' he snapped. '*Orcus* bearing *that*, six thousand yards.'

'Red 147°, sir,' the bearing-ring reader reported.

'Sonar standard. Fall out, 2001,' Coombes could dispense with sonar now.

'Sector contact: *John Cabot* ten thousand yards.'

'Roger.' There she was, a speck on the edge of the area, keeping guard.

'Officer of the Watch on the search periscope.'

'Officer of the Watch, sir.' Grenville stepped forward to replace Coombes at the handles.

'Up attack,' Coombes ordered. The thin tube slid upwards and he jammed his face into its eyepieces, carried out a careful all-round look and then, relieved to see no ships dangerously close, gave the order. 'Stand by to surface.'

The scc watchkeeper repeated the order and the crew began its drill of opening up valves on the ventilation exhaust and draining the low pressure blower system. When he was satisfied, Coombes barked the orders which had now become part of his existence. He heard the bolts being knocked off the lower lid as the drill continued:

'Mast draining down ... shut the inter-space drain. Inter-space drain shut. Roger. Ready to surface, sir.'

'Down attack,' Coombes snapped. He briefed the officer of the watch on the surface situation, then slammed shut the handles of the periscope. He stood back to glance at the gauges.

'Pipe, "Surfacing now". *Surface*! Blow all main ballast tanks.'

The scc repeated the order, then began counting, '... Four, five, six. Stop blowing.' High pressure air was precious: there was not much of it.

'Open the upper lid. Start the blower,' Coombes ordered. 'Raise the radar mast.' He turned over the submarine to the officer of the watch on the bridge, then glanced at the first lieutenant: 'Patrol routine. Specials in a quarter of an hour's time, Number One. I'm going up top.'

As Coombes began climbing up the ladders in the tower, he heard the intercom piping the Red Watch to Patrol Routine and for the White and Blue Watch libertymen to clean. Emerging through the upper lid to the daylight of the overcast May afternoon, the thought crossed his mind that this would be his last ascent for some time. He tucked himself into his corner of the bridge and picked up the mike: 'Control – bridge: bring the plant to three-quarter power state. Revs for ten knots.'

He opened and shut four main vent, to expel the air in four main ballast tank. This would bring her stern down so that the propeller could bite deeper and he could ring on a few more revs.

'Six-nine revolutions set, sir,' the control reported. The bridge watch was now complete: the oow, Lieutenant Geoff Punt, the boat's TASO and the weak link in Coombes' officers; Midshipman Basil Spurle, still wet behind the ears; and the lookout, a sonar plotter, Able Seaman Joe Robinson; he was a West Indian from Tobago, a popular, cheerful man. The search periscope revolved above their heads as the navigating officer fixed her position, below in the control room. Coombes pulled the collar of his jacket closer about his neck as a rain squall swept down upon them.

'Take her between the islands, Lieutenant Punt. Leave

Longay half a mile to starboard.' Coombes leaned over the lip of his bridge; he sniffed the humid air, pulled down the peak of his cap on which the commander's oak-leaves still gleamed with pristine newness. Beneath his anorak, he had shifted into his number ones, so that he would not hold up the liberty-boat. The weather was notoriously unpredictable in this dreary neck of the woods: he certainly understood Trix for not wanting to settle up here. She longed to be in her native Surrey again, particularly since the biopsy. He picked up the mike. 'Give the Signals Communication Officer my compliments and ask him to speak to me.'

Orcus was still visible, her fin showing to the northward where she was finishing off her calibration and de-gaussing runs. She was completing her noise trials this morning when *Safari* arrived at midday, entering the Sound from the north.

'Signals Officer, sir.' Wesley was a good officer, a bright lad, the sort of bloke Coombes liked: robust, plain-spoken, he would stand up to his captain if necessary.

'Have you got *Orcus* on VHF?'

'Yes, sir. No problem.'

'Make to her, "CO to CO – RPC 1830 Carnburn for a quickie. I have to return on board by 1900 boat".'

'Roger, sir.' Farge would understand and in half an hour they could fix tomorrow's arrangements.

Safari was through the narrows five minutes later and lining up for her anchorage off Pabay.

'Specials in five minutes time,' Coombes said into the intercom. 'Tell the first lieutenant that the liberty-boat is lying off waiting for us. He can pipe libertymen.'

'Aye, aye, sir. Message to *Orcus* passed, sir.'

'Very good.'

Ten minutes later Coombes had anchored *Safari* in twenty-one fathoms, half a mile to the east of Pabay. After checking his anchor bearings, he went below. He could hear the after hatch opening, the hands in good spirits as they hustled up the vertical ladder. When he reached the after casing himself, Punt was already supervising the coming alongside of the tender, abreast the fairing of the exhaust discharge. The skipper of the drifter was having difficulty as he nudged his boat against *Safari*'s pressure hull. The bowman was working closely with his skipper and biding his time for the right moment to catch a turn with the headrope. Twice Punt yelled at the older man, finally:

'Hurry up, for'd. Turn up the rope round your cleat.'

The grey-haired man in the eyes of the drifter glanced up in disbelief.

'Hurry up, there,' Punt shouted excitedly. 'Secure at that.'

The deckie glared at the impatient young officer. 'See here, laddie,' he complained resignedly, 'look after your boat, mister, and I'll look after mine.'

In the amused silence, Coombes glanced from the corner of his eye at his senior ratings mustering on the after casing. They had heard the exchange too, but were staring nonchalantly towards the far horizons.

'Carry on,' Punt told the duty PO.

The libertymen started to nip across into the pitching drifter. The transfer took five minutes and then Coombes followed his only two officers to be going ashore, the midshipman and the instructor lieutenant who was still borne on *Safari*'s books. Coombes joined the skipper in the wheelhouse and then the tender was wallowing towards the Kyle of Lochalsh. Through the window, Coombes watched his submarine growing smaller, her black, whale-like shape silhouetted against the rounded island.

'This fair weather's breaking up, skipper,' Coombes said.

'Aye, 'tis that, captain.'

'Are you running the 1900 trip back?'

'Aye.'

'Hold on for me, will you? I may be a few minutes late.'

'Sure, captain. That's what we're here for. Your lads could do with a run ashore.'

The boat chugged towards the Kyles, the shore road to Kyleakin now in sight, an occasional car moving ant-like along it.

Coombes watched his men, huddled on the lee side. They were in good cheer and he hoped that there would be no leave-breakers. Number One had piped that the ship was under sailing orders and that they must keep their mouths shut when approached by talkative strangers. And as for himself? He was nipping ashore early, but not solely to take advantage of the liberty-boat; an intriguing hour lay ahead of him, if what he had learned was correct.

10

Skye, 7 May. 'Yes, Commander?' asked the kilted, grizzled Scot, from behind the reception desk of the Carnburn Hotel. 'What can I do for you?'

'I'm meeting a friend here at six-thirty,' Coombes said. 'Lieutenant-Commander Farge.'

'Ah, yes, they checked in early this morning. I think Mrs Farge is in her room, sir.'

Coombes smiled from the depths of his beard: 'That's fine. She's my sister. Could you tell her I'm here?'

The hotelier's experienced eyes flickered momentarily, giving nothing away:

'Whom shall I say, sir?'

'Commander Coombes.'

'Very good, sir.'

Coombes ensconced himself in one of the chintz-covered chairs behind the door of the airy lounge. The old-fashioned windows, high and narrow, gave a magnificent view towards the Cuillins. So mum *had* been right.

Then Lorna was tripping down the stairway and across the hall. She stood in the doorway for a second, strained and nervous, before spotting him.

'How's my kid sister? Mystery girl, aren't you?' Coombes smiled at her. 'Tell me what's up, while we have tea.'

He watched her, the stepsister he had once loved and always adored, but whom he had not spoken to for so long. She was tense, up-tight at first, giving nothing away.

'What are you doing here, Kevan? I thought you were on patrol in the Atlantic somewhere. Mum was terribly worried until this truce thing came along.'

He was non-committal. 'Exercising with another submarine.' He sensed her awareness of his connection with the ssk exercising up here. '*Orcus* is here too: she's coming into the loch this evening.'

'Is she?' She looked down, fiddled with her handbag. 'How long are you staying, Kevan?'

'Only a short time,' He tried to suppress a smile: beards sometimes had their uses. 'I'm meeting *Orcus*' captain here at half-past six.'

He sensed her anxiety while she poured the tea.

'I'll introduce you,' he said. 'Julian Farge. You'll like him.'

He reached across and took her hand when the little cry escaped her lips.

He told her how he had rung up home to see how his stepmother was.

'You know how mysterious mum can be,' he said. 'She said you'd gone up to Scotland. She asked me not to let on, like she always does. You were in love, she told me, with a submariner called Farge.'

A smile twitched at the corners of her mouth. 'I'm happy, Kevan,' she said softly. 'We want to marry.'

He looked into her eyes, trying to gauge the depths of her feelings. 'I'm glad you've told me,' he said. 'He'll make you happy, Lorna.'

'Don't tell him, will you, that you know about us? He knows I have a half-brother but he doesn't realize it's you. I'd like to tell him myself.'

'He's a funny chap, is Julian. Keeps things to himself.'

'It's all been so sudden. No one knows yet. He's told his first lieutenant that he's got friends here, that's all.'

He could see the desperation there, deep in her eyes. 'You can never know what it's like to love someone in submarines,' she whispered. 'Especially . . .'

'Especially what?'

She shook her head, close to tears. 'I'm going to blub, if you go on.'

'He and I are meeting here for a tot together,' he said. 'I won't give your secret away. I'm glad for you, that's all. You love him very much, don't you?'

Those amber-flecked, hazel eyes were staring straight at him. 'Yes, Kevan. I do.'

They talked a little of their affection for each other in earlier days, of his wife, Trix. 'I would have married you myself, you've always known that, haven't you?'

She touched his hand. 'Mum never wanted it.' She lowered her head and stared at her sensible brogues. 'But whatever happens,' she said, 'I know I can always turn to you if I need help.' Glancing at the clock, she rose from the sofa and kissed him. 'I'll go now. I'll be waiting at the ferry for Julian, so don't keep him too long . . . take care, brother-mine.' He wiped away her tears and walked with her into the hall.

11

Skye, 8 May. The dappled moonlight on the ceiling, criss-crossed by the shadows of the window-bars, awakened Farge. Lorna must have felt him stirring because she called to him from her dreams as she wrapped her arm about his chest. He tightened his hold of her and, crooking his free arm behind his head, watched first light stealing upon the distant, shadowy hills of Skye.

So it had arrived, this Thursday, this moment which for the past week he had hoped would never come. The same moon was hanging now, like a golden dish over the Cuillins, as it must have over Golgotha and that God revered by Lorna. A silvery pathway was shimmering across the dark surface of the sea, a bejewelled motorway leading to the mysterious, magical island of Skye. When the sun set on this day, he, Farge would be driving *Orcus* out of the loch, through the Sound, to the north and the unknown. The danger wasn't bothering him much, nor his possible death. What troubled him was the pain he would inflict upon this woman lying by his side if *Orcus* did not return.

Lorna was turning towards him, suddenly stiffening, half-awake. She crooked her arm round him, moulding him to her, then sighed with reassurance. She was breathing deeply again, heavily asleep, but he remained awake, his mind too full of confused emotions: his world had been turned upside down during these past twenty-four hours.

He'd considered himself a normal product of his generation: realistic, ostensibly detesting humbug and hypocrisy, frank to the point of brutality when it came to things spiritual. He knew he was moderately intelligent but, as was the fashion, he used his intellect to deride with cynicism anything smacking of tenderness, with snide contempt any suggestion of that elusive, spiritual world for which he unconsciously hungered. But cynicism, that so-called champion of truth, bred its own falsehood, corroding like acid at the roots of contentment, serenity, happiness. . . . On Wednesday night, when finally they returned to their Kyleakin hotel, they had slept in their own rooms. He had slipped at dawn to catch the first ferry. The day's trials in the Sound had gone well but, for him, the return to Loch Alsh for the last night's libertymen could not come quickly enough.

And then there had been that strange meeting with Janner Coombes in this Carnburn bar. They had downed a couple of whiskies while they arranged for today's meeting on board *Safari*. The deception ploys could not be more normal: the submarines were acting habitually, each independent of the other. Wherever the Soviet agents lurked, perhaps even amongst the bureaucracy of the scientific teams ashore, no one would remark any abnormality from an operational submarine's usual routine. Coombes' and Farge's meeting in the Carnburn merely cemented the normality, but Farge had sensed a strangeness in Coombes' bearing towards him. Those blue eyes flashed, not with their customary amusement, but with a curious sympathy, and he had left promptly for his return boat to *Safari*.

Lorna had been waiting for Julian at the ferry and they had returned immediately to the Carnburn Hotel.

'Lieutenant-Commander and Mrs Farge : yes, sir, room nine,' and the porter had handed Farge the key. After supper they went straight up to their room.

And with Lorna beside him, as the memory of these last, precious hours flooded back into his mind, he knew that never again in this life would he reach such heights of intense happiness. Together they had watched in silence the sun dipping below the hills of Skye, sharing the magic of that luminosity which characterized the atmosphere of the Western Isles.

Some people, he supposed, prolonged their honeymoons, taking time leisurely to explore the delights of love-making, leading each other from one experience to the next. But theirs, begun so short a time ago, had swept onwards with the fury of a tempest. Last night, as the shadows lengthened across the hills, there had been her trembling anticipation when he had undressed her, then that fragile moment when she stood before him in her nakedness, proud and unashamed. He had lifted her in his arms, carrying her to the bed, and she slipped the chain from about her neck and laid the little cross on the bedside table.

He had thought her shy and reserved, but little did he know woman. At first he had been impatient and demanding, too swift for her. What was it she had whispered? 'Don't be silly, my own beloved: I can never be the same woman again, not now. You're part of me, for ever, whatever happens – don't you know that?' Afterwards, lying across him in the delicious aftermath, she had whispered into his ear: 'It's your turn now. No, don't talk. I want to make you happy.' And, gently, at first, not sure of herself, she began to rouse him. But this time, unhurriedly, deliberately, aflame herself with desire, she led him on, giving herself totally to him. And in the tranquillity of the awakening dawn, he groaned softly to himself: he could not allow these last hours together to slip away. He enfolded her roughly against him.

'What's the matter, darling?' She was awake, reaching for him. 'Oh, Julian, what's the time?'

His hands were caressing her, gently at first. 'It's nearly dawn,' he said. 'Look, the sun'll soon be on the Cuillins.'

'When d'you have to go?' she murmured sleepily.

'The boat's at seven-thirty. We've got two hours.'

She did not reply. Lying passively in his arms, she was awakening again to his loving, while they talked softly. He spoke of his submarine, of his men, of his officers. 'I'm worried about one of them,' he ended. 'But I've got to take him with me, even on this trip.'

He hesitated, then told her briefly of Woolf-Gault's failure. 'He knew we were watching him yesterday forenoon, during our deep-dive,' he said. 'He was okay – almost too much so. He's a cocky bastard.'

'There's so much I want to ask you,' she said.

'Go on, then, ask me. I shan't answer if it's *verboten*.'

'Julian, you're working on something with Kevan, Commander Coombes, aren't you?' Her hands were responding now, rhythmically, with his.

'Why d'you ask that one?'

She rolled on top of him, her face above his. 'Open your eyes,' she whispered. 'I love looking at them.' She was staring down at him, her eyes flickering.

66

'Kevan is my half-brother, Julian,' she said softly, 'Kevan Coombes.'

'Janner?'

She nodded. 'I didn't know you called him that.'

'Why didn't you tell me?'

'I didn't realize. Down at Spinneycombe, I told you about my half-brother: how he joined the Navy.'

He took her head between his hands, the better to watch her face:

'You were in love with him? Might have married?'

'He loved me very much,' she whispered. 'I was seventeen, infatuated: it was a long time ago.'

'I knew him way back. We shared a cabin during our first perisher.'

'I didn't know. But now . . .'

'Now?' he queried softly.

'Kevan came here last evening, before *Orcus* anchored. We had tea together.'

'He was looking for you?'

'He'd rung mum to say goodbye. She told him I was up here.'

He did not answer. So, during their brief meeting last evening, Coombes had known that Farge was up here secretly, chasing his stepsister.

'What a turn-up for the books,' he chuckled. 'What was Janner's reaction?'

'I told him everything, that I loved you,' she said simply. 'That we'll marry when you get back from patrol. Kevan was pleased, Julian, happy it was you.' Her eyes were alight with mischief. 'He said he didn't think I had it in me.'

'What d'you mean?'

'Coming up here to you – like this.'

'The old devil . . .' and then for a brief hour, the frenzy of their love claimed every precious minute. Wordlessly, rejecting the complications of the world, they loved again until they heard the clock downstairs chiming six-thirty. She clung to him then, for the first time overwhelmed by tears. He tried to soothe her, and as the shuddering of her body eased, he gently slid from her arms.

'Stay there,' he said, 'while I get ready.'

He shaved in the bathroom and when he returned, she was in

her dressing-gown, packing his grip. He dressed in silence while she stood at the window, staring across the shimmering sea.

'Don't come down,' he said. 'When I get back this afternoon from *Safari*, I'll go straight alongside *Orcus*.'

'When are you sailing?' she whispered.

'Dusk. Don't hang around: it's better for you to go quickly. Your mother'll be worrying.'

She did not answer, but shook her head.

His voice hoarse, he asked: 'If it's a son, you'll call him Julian?'

As she turned, tears streaming down her cheeks, he brushed her golden hair with his lips. He picked up his bag and swiftly left the room.

By the evening of Thursday, 8 May, the weather in the Hebrides had worsened to half a gale. Blustery and bleak, the wind was gusting through the Kyle of Lochalsh and whipping the running tideway into flecks of white. The fishing-boats, lungeing against each other along the quays of the little harbour, were pitching in the scend.

The harbour master was worried as he leaned against the gale, on his final rounds to check the warps. When he reached the harbour light, he found a solitary woman sheltering in the lee of the boat which was shored up on the extremity of the outer jetty.

'Dirty night,' he remarked, darting her a glance: not a local girl, she was in her mid-twenties; her face beneath the scarf about her head was pale and drawn. 'You all right, miss?' he asked kindly.

She nodded, but he could not catch her reply as she stared up the loch, her back to the wind. From the darkness three pin-points of light were emerging, growing rapidly in brilliance: one white, above the other two, green and red. The harbour master stood back, watching the sleek, black submarine as she swept towards them. Her bows showed now, a bulbous dome on her stemhead; she rounded up for the narrows, then slid abeam of the two lone observers, her long fore-casing glistening from the light cast by the harbour lights. She was abreast of the jetty, a flurry of spray dashing against her fin as her bows clove the confused waters of the kyle.

The men on her bridge were mostly indistinguishable, hooded in their heavy-weather gear as they peered into the night. The only exception must be her captain who was still wearing his cap. He stood apart from the others, leaning over the lip of the bridge as he conned his boat through the narrows.

The girl standing beside the harbour-master had dragged off her scarf. Holding it above her head, she let it stream in the wind while the submarine slid past. The submarine captain was peering toward the Carnburn Hotel, when he seemed to spot the two figures under the light at the end of the jetty. As he raised his binoculars, the woman started brandishing her scarf back and forth. The captain lowered his glasses; he raised his arm and waved towards the jetty. Swivelling round to cope with the rapid change of bearing, he stood momentarily rigid, his hand at the salute. A final wave and he was lost among the huddle of figures on the bridge, as the boat swept onwards through the kyle.

The girl's arm fell listlessly. The harbour-master could not see her face while, facing the wind, she stared after the submarine until the stern light vanished into the filthy night.

'They're brave men,' the man shouted. 'You'd best go home, miss. This is no sort of night for the likes of you to be out in.'

A smothered cry broke from her, and the harbour-master could see the shaking of her body, wracked by dry sobbing. He watched her stumbling blindly along the jetty, until she was lost to sight.

12

HM Submarine Orcus, 9 May. 'Stand by to surface!'

The cox'n of HM Submarine *Orcus*, Bill Bowles, shifted his buttocks in the planesman's seat. Grasping the control column lightly between his hands, his eyes on the depth gauge, he was thankful that at last things were under way. Today, Friday, had been a long day.

'Open two, four, six and seven LP master blows,' ordered Lieutenant-Commander Foggon, the MEO trimming officer, who was standing behind him and watching points. Eddie Foggon was good at his job, a sound engineer officer who allowed the cox'n to use his own judgement. *Orcus* was a responsive old lady and Bill Bowles had the measure of her, providing the trimming officer kept the trim right: only when things became tricky did Foggon take firm charge of his cox'n. The main vents were being cycled and soon she'd be on the surface. They could all do with a bit of fresh air after today's exercises – and before the long patrol lying ahead of them.

'Permission to open the lower lid,' Lieutenant Sims, the bridge officer of the watch, asked after the captain had finished briefing him. He and the lookouts were already dressed for the weather.

'Open the lower lid,' Farge ordered, swinging round on the search periscope for the last time. The clips of the lid clunked free.

'Permission to man the tower?'

'Man the tower.'

'Ready to surface sir,' the control-room OOW reported.

Farge snapped shut the handles and the periscope hissed downwards into the well.

'Surface,' he ordered brusquely. 'Blow two, four, six and seven main ballast.'

Bowles dragged gently back on his column, watched the bubble gliding for'd, felt the bow-up angle coming on the boat. He had done this so many times in his life, but this was to be the last surfacing until they returned from the patrol. The Old Man looked drawn, seemed edgier than usual: it had been a long day for him especially. Farge must have been carrying the secret in his mind for a while now. Perhaps, like Bowles, he was thankful that action was at last beginning.

'Stop blowing seven, six, four and two main ballast.'

Farge, happy with *Orcus*' stability on the surface, called from his periscope:

'On the surface! Open up.'

Bowles heard the far-away shout from the oow at the top of the tower:

'Upper lid open.' Seconds later the voice-pipe cocks were opened and the bridge-intercom snicked when it was plugged in.

'Start the blower,' Farge ordered. He picked up the mike and turned over the state of the submarine to the bridge.

'I'm happy to take the submarine,' the oow reported.

'You have the submarine,' Farge snapped.

'Aye, aye, sir. I have the submarine.'

Farge zipped up his anorak, slung his binoculars about his neck and disappeared into the tower. Bowles relaxed in his planeman's chair, waiting for the pipe, 'Red watch patrol routine'.

'Flood Q,' the MEO ordered. At war now, they were becoming used to flooding the emergency diving tank when on the surface.

'Start generating port side,' Farge yelled from the bridge.

The chuntering of the diesel sounded from aft and then the fresh, cold air was streaming through the boat. Bowles glanced up at the first lieutenant who was relaxing beside the passenger, Lieutenant Woolf-Gault, against the safety grilles surrounding the masts.

'It's been a full day. No leave-breakers, no drunks: reckon we deserve it, sir,' Bowles answered, extricating his tobacco pouch.

The cox'n enjoyed this moment, snug in the red lighting of the control-room. Supper had been up to scratch: the first days of patrol were always all right, while the fresh veg. lasted. The cox'n lit his old pipe; he stretched his legs, oblivious to the subdued chatter around him. Murray, the navigating officer, was at the search periscope taking his last fix before the light of Ru Stoer faded below the horizon.

The cox'n felt a certain smugness, an emotion which he suspected Jimmy shared with him. Though Prout was twenty-six and fifteen years younger than his cox'n, Bowles respected him, particularly as Prout was losing his forced abruptness. This was his first Jimmy's job, which probably explained their initial strained relationship. And, since that bloody Woolf-Gault episode Prout and Bowles had drawn closer to each other, both relieved by the philosophical reaction of the ship's company. *Orcus* was welding into a taut ship under their new skipper.

The captain had dived the boat in Eddrachillis Bay during the early hours of that morning. He had kept them busy all day: bottoming, shutting-off for going deep, shutting-off for counter-attack, assuming the Ultra Quiet State – he had repeated the drills over and over again until he was satisfied. Emergency breakdowns in the engine-room and the spaces; escape drills – the whole shooting-match, until the hands were muttering. Even Jimmy got the sharp edge of Farge's tongue when he failed to settle at periscope depth when coming up from deep. Prout had been made to repeat the evolution five times before the Old Man would let him off the hook. Breakdowns, breakdowns, breakdowns; main vents in hand, plane failures, hydraulic failures, until everyone was fed up. Bowles too had become chokka: he'd begun to suspect that something special was up, forebodings which were confirmed later when the captain asked him along to his cabin before speaking to the rest of the ship's company.

Farge had bottomed the boat in three-hundred feet – and during that final drill, they would not have cracked a watch-glass. Bowles mustered in the fore-ends all the hands who could be spared from their duties. The chief radio supervisor rigged a mike to the tube space and from there with eighty per cent of his company around him, the captain talked over the broadcast. Bowles would never forget that scene: the tight-lipped, determined Farge, standing on the rungs of the fore-hatch ladder, the packed compartment jammed solid by his silent men.

The captain spoke quietly: no histrionics, for as the details of their mission unfolded, even the dimmest amongst them latched on that this was going to be an unusual patrol. Until that moment, from Barrow onwards, various incidents had started the buzzes flying around the messdecks: the landing of the torpedoes and the empty for'd tubes were for the mines which *Orcus* would be loading in Faslane. Obvious, wasn't it? There had been many wild guesses to explain the alterations and additions which Vickers had carried out at such speed: extra H/F sonar transducers fitted, the existing sets serviced again and checked; doubling-up the supplies of absorbent for the CO_2 scrubbers, and the oxygen candles; renewal of the main W/T aerial; checking the insulations and the transmitters, and a complete overhaul of the EW aerials; special wire-cutting tools (nets?); the wardroom pistol locker topped up – and several other mods which had been outstanding. But it was the personnel changes which were the most difficult to explain.

By chance *Orcus* already bore an able seaman diver, yet a Leading Seaman Diver, Malcolm Robertson, had joined at Kyle of Lochalsh. The unannounced arrival in Barrow of Surgeon-Lieutenant Tomkins had posed an accommodation problem for the officers, but to the pleasure of the junior rates, Sub-Lieutenant Halby had been rushed ashore with suspected meningitis and was now languishing in Barrow hospital: an unlucky turn of the wheel for the captain, because his argument for replacing Lieutenant Woolf-Gault had been demolished. 'Windy-Gault' was officially appointed as Halby's relief and was now the boat's TASO – but at least the wardroom would not now have to sleep 'hot bunks', the doc taking the spare bunk. As a wag in the senior rates mess had put it: 'At least Windy-Gault can't foul things up in the tube space: we've got no fish.' Joker Paine, the sonar chief, had added: 'Jimmy's no fool either: he's got Windy-Gault as far from the control-room as he can get him.'

Bowles leaned back, puffing at his pipe. There was no doubt that everyone felt better, now they knew what they were up against. After talking to his company, Farge had gathered the senior rates and the officers in the wardroom, where he explained his plans more fully: he and his officers would be studying the secret sailing orders while the boat was on passage to North Cape, which they should reach at dawn on the twelfth.

Farge was turning out a better CO than they had expected; he was a reserved bloke, difficult to know – but, as much as he could, he kept everyone informed of what was going on. With luck and God's help, the war might finish soon: whether it did depended, it seemed, very much upon two submarines . . .

'*Safari*'s calling us.' The signalman at the after-end of the bridge was shouting above the wind buffeting the fin. 'Red 120, sir.'

Farge turned and saw the light winking on the port quarter: through his binoculars he could make out the blur of the nuke's silhouette.

'Take her on the lamp,' he said. 'For once, we want to announce our presence.'

Twilight was nearly gone and the north-easter was cutting through them. *Safari* was on time, exactly as Coombes and he had planned yesterday. *Safari* sailed this afternoon, deliberately trundling on the surface up the Sound, for prying eyes to see. After this brief rendezvous, she would alter south-west for the Little Minch. With her nav. lights burning, she would bumble southwards to be off Bara Head tomorrow morning where, hopefully, the habitual prowling Russian submarine would report *Safari* heading west into the Atlantic. The deception ploys were being carried out to the letter, while other Nato submarines were taking up their billets encircling the Barents.

'From *Safari*, sir,' the signalman called. ' "Interrogative?" '

'Make to her, "A.O.K." ' Julian glanced at his watch: 'Date time group 092151 Zulu May.'

The lamp began clacking, the pencil beam cleaving the dusk. The umbilical cord was severed: no further contact with anyone until *Orcus* returned home . . . but Coombes knew now that *Orcus*' final bottoming drills were satisfactory; that she could dive immediately and be on her way. The success of Operation SDW depended upon both submarines being scrupulously punctual and exact in the execution of their allotted commitments. The MOD's deception plans were thorough – and not only were the diversionary ploys taking place at sea. Labelled crates of white tropical clothing had been dispatched to *Orcus* in Barrow; chart folios of the Indian Ocean had arrived, and curiously coded mail-bags had been delivered via British Rail and the Fleet Mail Office – this unnecessary junk, taken on board unopened, was taking up every inch of space; Farge's orders authorized him to ditch the weighted stuff as soon as *Orcus* was north of Rona. A variation of the same theme had been adopted for *Safari*, as Farge had learned from Coombes yesterday, when together they sifted through their secret sailing orders. Corrupt signals had even been dispatched – there was no end to the DGI's skulduggery.

'Message passed, sir.'

In spite of modern electronics, signals were still being passed by eyeball methods. This paradox of modern warfare had developed because of the ability of both sides to pick up through their EW apparatus the faintest transmission pushed out over the ether. The satellite had transformed communications, and the Soviet navy, with its centralized Moscow control, was more vulnerable than Nato's. This weakness had been recently demonstrated when Rosy Boyd, at the critical moment, forced the Soviet Northern Fleet to break off action when it had the Canadian convoy, HX-OS 1, at its mercy: Boyd had knocked out their command ship – and from that instant the enemy's thrust had disintegrated.

The sailing orders, waiting below for Farge to digest, emphasized, as FOSM had done, the vital importance of *Safari*'s and *Orcus*' communications. *Safari* would be counting upon *Orcus*' enemy report on the Typhoon: the MOD (and the Prime Minister and the President of the United States) would be waiting for *Safari*'s signal of her Typhoon sinking, the signal upon which, exclusive of other kills the West might score, so much depended. . . . *Safari* was merging into the gloom, vanishing. Farge picked up the mike:

'Steer 230°. Diving in five minutes' time. Clear the bridge.'

He glanced at the silent, broad-shouldered figure standing behind him. Woolf-Gault, remarkably, had said nothing since surfacing. He now leaned across and yanked out the mike connection. He waited for the lookout and signalman to disappear through the upper lid before following them himself.

Farge peered carefully around the horizon: vis. was two miles but he could see only the lights of a couple of fishing-boats to the westward. With his nav. lights showing, he had been deliberately pointing in their direction, for almost an hour, hoping that *Orcus*' course might be registered.

'Switch off navigation lights,' he ordered. 'Diving stations.'

Only the search periscope was raised, the control oow and the navigating officer being down below and sharing it for their final fix. Farge felt the knotting in his guts, the instinctive urge to prolong these last few minutes on the surface. He shoved back the hood of his anorak in order to feel the breeze.

Yesterday's meeting with Coombes in *Safari* had been invaluable. Farge had gone straight to the point, so that they could then concentrate for the rest of the day upon their sailing orders – and Coombes had been as frank about his stepsister as Farge was of the woman he intended to marry. The latent jealousy which Farge harboured against Coombes evaporated as they talked of Lorna. Coombes apologized for his secrecy in the affair. It was evident to Farge that Janner and Lorna had always been very fond of one another; and this made Janner's approval of his future brother-in-law all the more satisfying – Farge even felt able to ask Janner to give Lorna the note he had hurriedly scrawled, should anything go wrong.

The remainder of the day, until Farge had to return to *Orcus*, had been spent wrapping up the operation. Each now understood to the smallest detail the other's intentions. . . . Drawing in to the depths of his lungs a last draught of this clean, soft air of the Hebrides, Farge crossed to the voice-pipe: he was tired, not only because of a leave spent with Lorna but also, since his second Northwood meeting, he had not wasted a second in briefing himself, and in planning how he was to achieve the objective expected of him. He'd dive *Orcus* now, turn to the north, ditch the weighted gear off Sule, then spend the next four days on passage to North Cape resting and planning for every eventuality.

Farge relished those final moments alone on the bridge. However often he had dived a submarine, there was always this kick of excitement, this realization that the lives of the men below lay in his hands. But today's dive was especially significant, a dive which could be their last. He sniffed the air, for an instant peering up at the darkening clouds sweeping above him. He leaned over the voice-pipe:

'Group up, half ahead together,' he ordered. 'Open main

vents.'

He watched the flying plumes of spray as the vents opened. He crossed to the upper lid and dropped through the dark hole, firmly grasping the longer handle and pulling the hatch shut over his head.

'First clip on!' He smacked on the second. 'Second clip on. Take her down, Number One,' he shouted down into the tower. 'Two hundred feet.'

He began descending the clammy, slippery rungs of the ladder. In the gloom and chill of the tower, a momentary shiver passed through him leaving an unease he could not explain. 'This is it,' he muttered to himself. 'Next stop, Kola.'

13

HM Submarine Orcus, 13 May, 'That's Vardø, all right,' Farge murmured. 'Store Ekkerøy beacon, pilot, bearing *that*. Down search periscope. The radar dome on the shoreline is a monstrous, great thing.' Farge stood back as the stick slid downwards, the palm of his hand slicking back his thinning black hair in that mannerism which showed when he was under stress. 'Got your D/F bearing yet?'

'Green 92,' the periscope reader called, his eyes glued to the bearing-ring which encircled the steel tube hissing downwards into the well.

'Vardø radio beacon 265°, sir,' Murray called. 'Good fix: we're nine decimal six from the nearest point of land.'

'Down EW mast. Take her down, Number One,' Farge ordered. Three hundred feet. Don't speed up. We'll remain at the Quiet State.'

'Three hundred feet. Six down.' Prout ordered, glancing at the cox'n.

Then *Orcus* was sinking again into the depths, invisible, silent. Seeing the low-lying island of Vardø, black against the flat hinterland, hostile since the Soviets had invaded northern Norway, had jolted Farge and his whole crew into the reality of war. Forty miles to the westward of Vardø, in the Varanger uplands, survivors from 42 Royal Marine Commando Brigade were still holding out. Organizing Norwegian guerrilla resistance, the gallant Booties continued to harass the Russian convoys streaming southwards to Narvik along the E6 highway.

'One hundred feet, sir.'

The MEO stood silently watching Bowles while he delicately took the boat down at a six-degree bow-down angle. After five days on passage, Foggon had mastered the trim with a competence which Farge had not previously experienced. They had snorted most of the way, the EW mast giving them ample warning of prowling aircraft. But, apart from three distant warnings, *Orcus* had uneventfully reached her planned position forty miles to seaward of North Cape at 0730.

After the radio bearing from Slettnes – the Russians had re-instituted the international beacons after the truce talks had begun – Farge altered course at 1100 to 156° for the final run-in to his landfall off Vardø. He had decided to take this risk, because an exact position was vital for his final approach into the Kola Inlet – Murray had not been entirely happy about his SINS position: although that box of tricks rarely let them down, there was nothing like an eyeball sighting to give Farge the confidence he needed when bearding the lion in his den. The bad weather had helped all the way and snorting had kept the box right up, until going deep when approaching the 200-metre line off Syltefjord. He had managed to average twelve knots but at 2000 hours he would reduce to ten on main motors until he could snort again: it was vital to have his batteries fully charged before his final approach to the eastern tip of Poluostrov Rybachiy, the thirty-mile long peninsular guarding the western entrance of the channel into Murmansk.

'Three hundred feet, sir.'

'Very good,' Farge acknowledged. 'Happy, Number One?'

'Trim's fine, sir.' The sound-room was cutting in on the intercom:

'Bearing 096°, distant, group of fishing trawlers, sir.' Chris Sims, the sonar officer, stuck his head around the door: 'They seem to be moving fairly slowly, sir. Range about sixteen miles.'

'Nothing else?'

'All-round sweep completed, sir. Nothing else.'

'Go to watch-diving, Number One. Ten knots. The Quiet State is to continue from now on. I'll try to stick to the deep water: we don't know how far out they've got their hydrophones.' Farge glanced at the clock. 'Everyone is to get his head down: this is our last chance to get in some zeds before we reach the tricky bit. What's our ETA Cape Nemetskiy, pilot?'

'2200, sir. If you could come up for a D/F from the radio beacon, it would help.'

Farge checked the log: *Orcus* was settling nicely to her ten knots. 'If the fishing-boats are still around, I'll come up,' he told Tim Prout, as the watch took over. 'I'll be in my cabin.'

'Right, sir.'

'Who's the control officer of the watch?'

'WEO, sir.'

Farge nodded at David Powys. 'Have you been able to solve the problem with SINS?'

'Fixed, sir. One of the few spares we carry did the trick.'

'Good. Call me at once if you pick up anything on sonar – and watch the trim as we near the coast. There are several river estuaries on the north side of Rybachiy.' If the oow wasn't on his toes, the crossing of a freshwater estuary could upset the trim: if the insidious change in water densities went unnoticed, the boat could in seconds become tons heavy – with devastating results.

'Aye, aye, sir.'

Julian Farge drew the curtain across his doorway and lay on his bunk. This was his last chance to relax for he knew not how long. If he could sleep for a few hours, it would help during the crucial days ahead. He had done all he could, read up all the bumph, all the physical conditions: in the Barents in summer, fog could clamp down in seconds. This year's pack-ice limits, upon which everything depended if Coombes was to intercept the Typhoon before she reached comparative safety, was reported to be normal for May, extending as far south as the seventy-sixth parallel. The unnavigable polar ice was just clear of Spitzbergen and Franz Josef Land. That gave *Safari* a leeway of five hundred miles from her position Zulu in which to track down her Typhoon before she reached the polar ice.

Sleep eluded Farge, though with the trial of his life imminent he felt amazingly serene. He knew he was not alone; for the first time, someone was remembering him in her prayers, including them all. . . . Almost a third of his men had in peacetime carried out a patrol in these waters. Farge had noted the steadying effect their apparent nonchalence was having upon the younger element. His ship's company seemed to be itching for the chance of getting their own back, to bloodying the enemy's nose after the raids on Plymouth, Faslane and the Clyde.

The early w/T routine this morning brought for the first time something tangible: intelligence reports that two Typhoons were in all respects ready for sea. Typhoon Kilo was expected to sail 17–18 May; Typhoon Lima, 20–21 May. Northwood's forward planning had been accurate. There was also the good news that the Americans had reported their first kills in the Pacific: a Delta II off Hawaii, a Yankee on her way home from Seattle; and an Oscar, one of the enemy's 24,000-ton jobs, sortieing from Petropavlosk in the Kamchatka peninsular. The routine also confirmed that in Nato's neck of the woods things were also hotting up: *Carl Vinson*, with her Striking Force, was in the Greenland Sea, and Nato submarine forces were in position at the ice edges. The Barents Sea was effectively surrounded.

There was a tap on his doorway and David Powys poked his head through the curtain:

'187 confirms the fishing-boats, sir: quite a fleet, the nearest, six thousand yards, stretching to nine thousand. We'll soon be abeam of them.'

'How long do you need to get the box right up?'

'About an hour, sir.'

'Anything else on 187?'

'No, sir. Clear on all sectors, except for the fishing-boats.'

'Start bringing her up on the watch to fifty-eight feet. Stand by to snort, both sides. Tell the Chief.'

'Right, sir.'

Powys pulled the curtain across: he was efficient, the most highly qualified officer on board, with a London honours degree in physics. He was intelligent all right, but he lacked the quality of confidence – perhaps this trip would remedy that deficiency. . . .

The fishing-boats provided the chance Farge needed to get the batteries fully charged. Inside the Kola Inlet, the detection of his snort mast would be suicidal: to the hazard of certain discovery by radar would be added the risk of sighting from the shore, because *Orcus* would be working in close if she succeeded in negotiating the minefields. Farge slipped from his bunk and walked into the control-room.

'Anything on 187?' he asked.

'Contacts bearing 085°, sir,' the oow reported. 'The fishing fleet: nothing else, sir.'

Orcus was sliding nicely up to periscope depth.

'Seventy feet, sir.'

'Up search periscope.' Farge stood astride, waiting for the steel tube.

'Sixty-five feet.'

'Watch the bubble,' Powys said, correcting the planesman. 'More dive on the after planes. That's better. Keep her there.'

'Put me on the bearing,' Farge ordered.

'Red 118, sir. You're on.'

The periscope was breaking through the grey film that was the surface; the lens blurred, cleared suddenly – and there were the fishing-boats – just right, about six thousand yards.

'Raise EW mast.' He heard it hissing behind him while he swung round the horizon, searching for the enemy – the air menace was priority, and he continued to flick the lens from the surface to the band of sky above the horizon.

'Clear all round,' he reported, 'except for the fishing-boats bearing *that*.'

'Red 95.'

He slapped shut the handles of the periscope and the tube slithered downwards. 'Anything on EW?'

'Radio beacons, sir,' the Chief RS called out. 'Vardø bearing 294°, Cape Nemetskiy 177°. No other contacts.'

'Very good,' Farge acknowledged. 'Stand by to snort, generating both sides. Up search.'

Powys repeated the order and the pipe echoed through the boat:

'Red watch, watch snorting, both sides. Shut the intermediate flood and drain valves. Open the tundish valve.'

Farge was staring again through the search periscope. The pale sun was sinking below the olive-green sliver of land on their starboard quarter. Several of the fishing-boats were visible, bucking on the horizon-line.

'Raise the snort induction mast three feet . . . open snort drain one . . . open the outer tube vent,' and the drill continued until at last they were ready.

'Start generating both sides,' Farge ordered. He heard the diesels firing, waited an instant for the slight vacuum to clear the stale air. 'Raise the induction mast fully.' He could see it now, the ugly bulb of the snort, clear of the crests. He turned to the OOW, who was manning the attack periscope. 'You have the induction mast.'

'I have the induction mast, sir,' Powys acknowledged.

Farge took another swift all-round search, then lowered the periscope. 'Keep a good lookout and report when the box is up,' he said. 'I'll be in my cabin.'

It was still daylight up top: there was no need to shift to red lighting because it was twilight all night up here, never dark. There was little chance of detection from the enemy with *Orcus* close to and in line with the fishing-boats, and an hour's charge on both generators should bring the box right up. The massive batteries should give him all the amps he would be needing.

In his cabin again, he tried to put his mind at rest, but sleep still evaded him. Murray had worked out the tidal streams off the inlet: always northerly in the upper reach. He had jotted down the times of the easterly and westerly sets which ran parallel to the coast. Farge decided to ignore the current, which was never more than a knot, though if this north-easterly persisted the currents would become a factor in their calculations.

The unknowns were the whereabouts of the enemy's hydrophones and minefields, though Northwood had given him the suspected positions of these dangers. His only course was to ignore them and trust to luck. The Soviets were known to have stocks of moored mines in addition to their intricate, accoustic, magnetic and pressure jobs – but at least the moored mines were likely to be sited only in depths of over five-hundred feet. Murray had marked these areas with hatched red lines on the charts.

A further problem was bothering Farge: the cox'n had reported to Tim Prout that several cases of flu – or what resembled it – had broken out, and the doc had confirmed the diagnosis. In this rarefied, oxygenated atmosphere bugs had a habit of raging through the boat. Apart from warning the hands of the obvious, there was nothing Farge could do. So long as he could keep clear of flu himself . . . at last, he drifted into uneasy sleep.

'Captain, sir. The box is up. EW reports enemy maritime aircraft search frequencies in northern sector.' Powys was in the doorway.

Farge was immediately awake. 'What's the time?'

'2117, sir.'

'Stop snorting. We're getting close to land anyway.'

And so, the batteries charged, their position fixed from the radio beacons of Cape Nemetskiy and Tsyp Navolokskiy at the tip of the Rybachiy peninsular, *Orcus* lowered her masts to glide down again into the depths. She was ten miles from the Rybachiy coast and Farge made a mental note not to overrun his reckoning, a common error, apparently, due to the easterly current. At 2326 the 187 sonar picked up a motor ship to the nor'-nor'-west, range twenty miles.

14

HM Submarine Orcus, 14 May. At 0015 Farge altered course parallel to the southern boundary of the former mined area. He reduced to six knots and, after an all-round sonar search, brought her up to periscope depth. The red-tinged grey of the arctic night pervaded the surface world. On his second sweep he picked up a pin-point of light from the masthead of the merchant ship. Seven minutes later the plot, using sonar references, had produced her course and speed; by her signature she was evidently an Altay support tanker escorted by a turbine ship and probably homeward from a Narvik run.

'She's steering for the entry into the inward traffic lane, sir. She'll be at the outer end at 0215 if she maintains her speed,' Murray reported. Farge moved across to the chart table where Murray was pricking off the distances:

'Course for an interception, pilot?'

'You're about right, as you are, sir: you'll be two miles from her at two o'clock.'

'Diving stations.' Farge grinned. 'We'll refine and wait for her at the entry point. She can take us right into the inlet, bless her little socks. Three hundred feet, Officer of the Watch.'

There was a ripple of excitement, an intangible expectancy in the control-room. Farge was stretching out his hand for the mike to inform his company of his intention when the sound-room cut in:

'Contact dead ahead, sir, range four miles, classified Natya.'

'How many?'

'Can't be sure yet – possibly five.'

Murray was turning up the identification manual. His finger underscored the minesweepers' potential.

'Damn. They've got MBUS,' Farge added. 'They're on their passive sonar.' He turned to the oow:

'450 feet. Shut off for going deep. Assume the Ultra Quiet State.'

Their optimism had been short-lived, Farge mused, as he

watched the bubble sliding aft. A spanner dropped now and it would spoil their whole day. Working on the assumption that what the approaching merchant ship and escort could do, *Orcus* could do better, Farge altered course to the north-east in order to ease round the minesweepers. *Orcus* would scrape the southern boundary of the prohibited area, but if the Altay tanker and her frigate (both now confirmed by sonar from their characteristics) could steam safely across the area, there was little risk to *Orcus*.

The sweepers passed a mile to the south of the submarine which, with only sufficient speed to retain depth-keeping and steerageway, remained undetected at 450 feet, with a further 200 feet of water beneath her keel. At 0120 Farge went to action stations. He then talked to his men over the intercom:

'Captain speaking,' he began. 'I want a word with you, while I still have the chance. We're going to be busy and I rely upon you all to be at your most vigilant, however tired you may become. Get in as much rest as you can, even at action stations. We are now on the enemy's doorstep and are about to go in through his front door, probably the best protected door in the world. Everything depends upon your efficiency, upon your ability to maintain the Ultra Quiet State for hours on end. Move about slowly, thinking about what you are doing: one mistake and they might pick us up, so watch it.' He paused. 'Because I can't read the crystal ball, we *must* conserve our battery power and our air, both high pressure and life-support, to the utmost, in case we run into trouble. Talk and eat as little as possible. If we want to get home, it's up to each one of us to carry out his job to the best of his ability. *Orcus* may be an old lady, but she's manned by a good team. That's why we've been chosen for this job.' He glanced at the officers in the control-room then continued:

'We're on the edge of the main shipping channel into the Kola Inlet. I'm coming up now for a quick look: an Altay fleet support tanker, probably in ballast after supplying Narvik with oil, is four miles to the north of us. A modified Kashin, I think, is weaving ahead of her. She's armed with two twelve-barrelled MBUS, VDS and a helicopter. Once she's past us, I'll get in under the tanker and follow her in.

'Remember, conserve your energy and remain silent. Some

of you, notably the torpedo crews, won't have much to do, but the sonar team will need all the help it can get, so share the work as much as you can. From one point of view we're in luck, because there's a north-easterly gale blowing up top. There's bound to be a sea running: that can't help their sonar, but can hide our periscope. I'm coming up for a look now.' He cleared his throat and ended: 'That's all.' He replaced the mike and faced his first lieutenant who was standing by the TCC and keeping an eye on the plots.

'Any other contacts on 187?' Farge asked.

'No other contacts, sir. Just the two bearings, 355°.'

'Ten up,' Farge snapped. 'Periscope depth.' He crossed his arms behind his back, glanced at the log. On slow one and at minimum revs *Orcus* was creeping inaudibly through the depths. He felt her bows slanting upwards. Bowles had her firmly under control.

'380 feet, sir,' the scow, Woolf-Gault, reported. '370 . . . 360 . . .'

At two hundred feet Farge held her while he made a sonar check of her stern arcs and a final all-round search. 'Periscope depth,' he ordered.

The whine of a motor somewhere, that was all, the subdued commands, the murmured acknowledgements. Thank God, Farge thought, the destroyer is remaining passive on her sonar. He could hear her propeller beats echoing softly from the sound-room.

'Ninety feet, sir, eighty . . .'

'Up attack.' Farge straddled his legs. 'Put me on the bearing.' As the head swept upwards from the well, he snatched at the handles. He glued his eyes into the rubber eye-guard: the suffused greyness of the surface was already showing.

'Sixty-five feet, sir.' The MEO had taken over. 'Sixty-two . . . fifty-nine . . . *Breaking*.'

The dullness of the lens persisted, smeared by the draining water. For God's sake, *clear*, you bastard. . . . Farge could her the MEO flooding, trying to keep her down.

'Fifty-seven feet . . . fifty-six . . .'

Farge was crouching on his knees. Hadn't he drilled them enough, damn and blast them? A break-surface now, dead ahead of the escort . . .

'Fifty-seven . . . fifty-eight . . .'

The glass was clear: the modified Kashin's dark silhouette was unmistakable, with the unbroken sweep of her upper deck, the exaggerated rake of her bows and her two widely-spaced, squat twin funnels. Her helicopter platform was visible, her chopper on it, presumably secured for entering harbour. He swung on his heel, sweeping round the horizon.

'Bearing *that*. I'm 70° on the escort's starboard bow. No aircraft.' He shut the handles. The tube hissed downwards.

'Red 110,' from the bearing-ring reader. The drill was running smoothly.

'Happy with the trim?' Farge asked, an edge to his voice.

'Got her now, sir,' Foggon said.

'Stand-by for a range of the Kashin. Up attack.'

'Bearing of target should be red 98,' the TCC called.

Farge was peering again at the enemy: he could see the two ss–N–2 missile launchers aft on her starboard side.

'Range *that*,' he snapped, adjusting the range-finder vernier. 'Masthead.'

'Twenty minutes,' the reader called.

Farge snapped the handles shut, waited for the tube to slide downwards. 'What masthead height are you using?'

'Mainmast ninety feet, sir – range is eighteen hundred yards.'

'What should my relative bearing be of the tanker?'

'Red 105.'

'Put me on.' He snapped his fingers. The periscope operator flicked the control. Farge grabbed the handles. It was difficult to see with the flying spray. Hell, where was the Altay?

'Bearing's *that*. I'm 70° on the tanker's bow. Range of the funnel, *that*.'

'Fourteen minutes.'

'Down periscope,' Farge said quietly. 'Take her down, Number One: two hundred feet. Course for a 120° track?'

He waited, watching the bubble sliding aft.

'145°, sir,' the TCC called.

'Starboard ten, steer 145°,' Farge ordered. 'I'll come in under her stern, round up and follow her in.' He glanced at

Prout who was watching the operator on the TCC. 'What's my distance off track?'

'Six hundred yards, sir.'

'Let me know, sonar, ten degrees before I should alter course. I want to get right under her – a cable astern at the most.' Farge watched the gauge as *Orcus* sank to her ordered depth.

'May I pump, sir?' Foggon asked. 'We're a bit heavy.'

Farge shook his head. 'Wait until I'm under the tanker.'

Orcus levelled off nicely, dropping only a couple of feet below two hundred.

'Course, sir, 145°,' the helmsman reported.

At 0216 they heard the tanker rumbling overhead, the noise of her diesels and propellers resonating throughout the boat.

'Alter now, sir,' Prout reported.

'Enemy's course 180°, sir,' the LOP operator called. 'Speed twelve knots.'

'Sonar: track and report,' Farge said. 'Tell me at once if she slows down.'

Farge watched Chris Sims, half in half out of the sound-room. Their lives depended on his sonar team and their efficiency.

'You're to port of her track, sir. She bears 186° now.'

'Starboard fifteen. Group up and speed up,' Farge snapped, taking advantage of the tanker's racket as she trundled overhead. 'Steer 210°.'

Three minutes later, they were tracking in astern and following in her wake. 'Eighteen knots,' Farge commanded. 'And watch your steering: I want to keep right under her.' He glanced at Sims. 'Tell me immediately of any alteration in her course or speed.'

'Aye, aye, sir. Range four hundred yards.'

The tension in the boat was tangible as at two hundred feet they blindly overhauled the tanker above them. Gradually the company realized that this was the safest fashion of penetrating the enemy's defences; whispered conversations were starting up, and soon they were relaxing, leaving the tricky stuff to those on the controls: Bowles, the cox'n on the planes, Foggon, the MEO in his white overalls, behind him; the second cox'n, Ronald Parry, tall and black-bearded, tensed over the wheel as he steered the boat, meeting each sheer before it began; and the outside wrecker, Chief MEM Tom Grady, at the panel, waiting upon the trimming officer's orders. Taking advantage of the noise, Foggon had pumped and her trim should be about right: guesswork, but with plenty of experience behind him. As the pressure increased with depth, the submarine was squeezed; as she displaced less she became effectively heavier.

'Watch leader, you have the control. Twelve knots.'

David Powys stepped from between the periscopes.

'I have the control, sir.'

Farge moved across to the chart table. 'Pilot, this alters things. Where are we?'

'Coming abeam of Tsyp Navolokskiy. Here, sir, in the inward shipping lane.' Murray's finger traced the dotted line on the chart, a track skirting the mined area two miles to the eastward. 'I've checked with SINS, sir. The tanker's heading straight into the inlet.'

'This is throwing my original plan out of gear,' Farge murmured as they crouched over the chart table. 'But it's a chance too good to miss. Scrub my intention of bottoming in Ura Bay. We'll follow her in.'

'How far, sir?' Murray asked softly. 'Right in?'

Farge was poring over the chart. He traced the track until he reached Set' Navolok, the headland at the north-western tip of the inlet, where the main enemy radar dish was sited and off which a wreck was marked. The inshore traffic lane led close in, a mile off the beach. It was a tight squeeze.

Murray extracted the larger scale chart upon which he had marked off their furthest-on positions. At this speed, *Orcus* would be abreast Set' Navolok by 0400. By 0430 she would be at the focal point, where the western and eastern traffic lanes converged. A black and red conical whistle buoy marked the centre of this maritime roundabout which the shipping circled anticlockwise. Farge glanced at the small brass clock above the table: 0250 already.

'Sunrise is at 0315, sir,' the navigating officer said, reading his captain's thoughts.

Farge's finger was stubbing the narrow bay which ran north-east/south-west between Set' Navolok and the next headland. 'There,' he said. 'I'll break off above this bay –

Lodeynaya Bay. I'll bottom there. Bags of water.'

'The sailing directions say it's too deep for local shipping to anchor there,' Murray said.

'Look, pilot,' Farge said. 'If we bottom *here* we'll be wooded by the foreshore from the radar dish. The shipping junction will be visible to us – if we can use the periscope.' Farge turned, slicking back his hair. 'Get me to that position. I'll break off when you tell me.'

Murray wasn't looking happy. 'What can I use to get a clearing bearing into the bay?' he asked. 'You'll be coming up for a look?' he pursued, glancing at his captain.

'Not bloody likely. The 100-metre and 50-metre sounding lines can take us into the entrance of the bay.'

'I can use the sounder?'

Farge nodded. 'They'll have a job picking that up, with all this clutter around the place.'

Sims was standing by Farge's side. 'Three fast power-boats are moving up the port side, sir. At speed, outward bound in the far lane.'

Farge grinned. 'See what I mean, pilot. There's a lot of stuff about. We'll run in on soundings.'

Farge left Murray at the chart table. Up top, the murky twilight would be merging into dawn. The beat of the tanker's propellers was still audible, a reassuring sound. The first lieutenant had pushed the old canvas chair forwards and Farge slumped into it as the RS approached:

'Bad news from our midnight routine, sir,' he said. 'The satellites are on the blink. We won't be able to receive COMSUBEASTLANT via the satellites.'

'Any reason given?'

'Interspace war perhaps,' and he twitched a bleak smile. 'I can't receive, sir, here in the inlet. The signal is too weak.'

'Okay. You can still transmit? That's what matters.'

'No problem yet.'

'Thanks, chief.'

The watch leader had things in hand. The boat was steady, following nicely at between one and two hundred yards. Farge began to feel drowsy, lulled by the murmurs around him. At 0355 he was aroused from his half-sleep by the watch leader.

'Tanker's slowing down, sir. Sonar's on to a lesser contact, closing on a steady bearing: probably taking a pilot on board, Number One reckons. We're three miles from the cape, sir.'

Farge climbed to his feet: 'Group down. Stop port. Try and hold her, cox'n, until we see what the tanker's doing.'

The enemy had reduced speed and tension heightened again in the stopped submarine as Bowles tried to hold her depth. The tanker then went ahead at eight knots, *Orcus* following in her wake.

At 0405 Murray asked if he could use the sounders. *Orcus* was about to cross the two-hundred-metre line. The transducer was directional, its frequency almost impossible to detect amidst the clutter around them. *Orcus* crossed the line at 0420.

'Four decimal two miles to go, sir.'

Farge nodded. The ship overhead was still ploughing on steadily.

'Time to the hundred-metre line, pilot?'

'At eight knots, sir, in twenty-eight minutes.'

'I'll hold on while she's still blanketting us.'

During the next half-hour the minute hand of the clock seemed stationary. While the tanker remained directly ahead *Orcus* was safe, but the radar dish on the cliff at Set' Navolok must be only a mile distant. On the 187 sonar, they could already hear the seas pounding on the shore.

'One hundred feet, Number One. Six up.'

In the tanker's wake, with the destroyer lost up ahead, *Orcus* glided up to a less dangerous depth for her entry into Lodeynaya Bay where, in forty-eight metres, Farge hoped to bottom her. At 0445 she crossed the hundred-metre line, three minutes earlier than calculated.

'Alter to 263°,' Murray called. 'One mile to go.'

'Starboard ten,' Farge said brusquely. 'Steer 263.' He watched while the ship's head began to swing, saw the cox'n compensating with more rise on his planes.

'Stop starboard.' Farge waited for the way to come off, then nudged her ahead again.

Six minutes later, Murray switched on the sounder. They scraped the edge of the fifty-metre line at 0453, the log showing two knots.

'Difficult to hold her, sir,' Foggon reported.

'How far to go, pilot?'

'Four cables.'

'I'll give her a kick ahead, chief,' Farge told Foggon. 'Port 15 – and try to hold her, cox'n. I'll turn while there's still sea room, so that we're heading out of the bay.' He caught Prout's eye. Ten minutes later, *Orcus* had turned and steadied on 070°, the way coming off her.

'Depth under the keel?' Farge asked.

'Forty-seven feet.'

'Stop port. Bottoming.' He glanced at Foggon. 'Carry on, chief.'

The MEO reached up and flicked the pump order instrument to 'flood for'd', the command being relayed to the ballast pump watchkeeper in the engine-room.

'Ballast pump, flood two hundred gallons into Ms,' Foggon ordered over the intercom. He nodded at Grady on the panel, 'Pump three hundred gallons from aft to for'd.'

And so, slightly negatively buoyant and with a bow-down trim to keep her shafts and propellers clear of the bottom, *Orcus*' forefoot scraped gently on the gravelly bottom of Lodeynaya Bay.

'Open Q tank main line suction and inboard vent,' Farge ordered. 'Flood into Q tank.'

There was a hiss as the foul air from the emergency diving tank vented into the submarine.

'Stop flooding Q.'

With Q half filled *Orcus* was now anchored for'd by the weight of three tons of seawater.

It was 0459: five hours of battery power consumed since *Orcus* had stopped the charge.

The chiefs' mess was above the coxswain's store and next to the wardroom bulkhead. For *Orcus*' cox'n, sitting at the table with his messing accounts spread before him, this was the longest day he had ever endured during fifteen years' service in submarines. He shared the mess with his three companions, the Chief MEA; Joker Paine, who was the Sonar Chief PO and known as 'Chief Ops'; and the Chief RS. They had been cooped in there since bottoming at 0500. Bill Bowles had just returned from accompanying the First Lieutenant on a tour of the boat.

Morale was good, the nonchalence of those who had

been this way before having a steadying effect upon the remainder. It was the doc who was causing despondency; he had pronounced Adams, Pinkney and Robertson sick: flu and high temperatures.

The boat had been at watch-diving since bottoming, but the sound-room had been watch-on stop-on, listening to the traffic up top. Sonar conditions were difficult because the beach was so close: rumbling and squelching background noises were intermittent and irregular between the steady crashes of the swell on the shoreline.

Lodeynaya Bay was open to the north-east; with the wind from that direction the scend lumped into caves at the foot of the cliffs of Pushka Point, half a mile north of *Orcus*. The boat was rocking on the gravel, and the scraping against the hull was getting on their nerves – both M tanks had been flooded to make the boat bodily heavy, in the hope that this would anchor her. At the back of everyone's mind was the unpleasant feeling that she was being remorselessly swept by the swell on to the beach only four cables under their lee. The navigator was running the depth recorder every fifteen minutes, beaming it to the surface: during the last half-hour, *Orcus* had crept towards the twenty-metre line – and, according to the chart, the beach shelved steeply. During the last few minutes, Bowles was sure that the unnatural movement had increased. The captain had been huddled over the chart with the navigator during the past hour, and looked strained when Bowles had a word with him on passing through the control-room.

Bill Bowles began to sort out the bumph in front of him as his mess-mates, disturbed by the change in the rhythm of the boat's movement, began stirring in their shallow slumbers.

'What's the time, Bill?' croaked the Chief MEA, his grizzled head appearing from behind his bunk curtain. 'I could do with some scran.'

'1745. Supper's in a quarter of an hour.'

The air in the compartment was becoming stale: to conserve amps the captain had shut down the life-support system at 1000. For Bill, the ability of modern submarines to provide breathable air was as big a miracle as the provision of nuclear power in the SSNs and SSBNs: *Orcus* could survive for several days on her own air supply, but the cold and the consequent

94

condensation was becoming unpleasant.

There was a tap on the door frame and Able Seaman Riley, their messman, entered with the tea, cold spam and bread.

'Big eats, 'swain,' Riley said, his thin face expressionless. 'Hope it don't choke yer.' He nipped out again before Joker Paine could reply. Riley lacked the social graces but was a good messman.

The three senior ratings talked quietly, feeling the food doing its stuff. They were all now thoroughly sick of the continuing topic of Windy-Gault; even if Bowles and his messmates deliberately avoided talking about it, the worry persisted.

Woolf-Gault had shaken the morale of the boat more than the cox'n had at first realized. Turle, the disrated leading hand in the JRs' mess was stirring it in the fore-ends. Bowles had even been to see Jimmy about the trouble, but Prout was as powerless as the captain. 'Windy-Gault', as the ship's company referred to him, now talked in monosyllables and only when addressed. It was that hunted look in the poor sod's eyes which pricked Bill Bowles' conscience. Windy-Gault must be going through hell, unable to escape the contemptuous glances of everyone on board, including the snide, just-audible comments from the JRs. Once a sailor had lost trust in someone he could be brutal without saying much – what the army called 'dumb insolence'. The officer was rapidly developing into a pathetic wreck: he should never have been allowed to come on this trip. Fear is only the unknown; it can strike anyone, and when you can't control it, trouble begins. With the appalling manning situation during the recession, the service couldn't be blamed for officers like Windy-Gault, but it's tough, Bill Bowles thought, when your life is the price.

It was 1530 when Farge began to worry seriously about stranding on the lee shore: by SINS, *Orcus'* position had shifted imperceptibly to the westward and, judging by the external wave noises and the reverberations from the seas walloping into the Pushka cliffs, the gale was continuing to rage up top – as the met. had forecast.

The sonar team had been closed up since dawn listening to the inward and outward traffic trundling overhead. It was paradoxical, but *Orcus* was too close to the roundabout for

Joker Paine, the sonar chief, and his boys to sort out the constant stream of traffic. Analysing the mass of data was proving too much, even for the whole attack team. Of one thing Farge was certain: the sonar picture indicated clearly that the submarines of the enemy's Northern Fleet were using the easterly lane, both inward and outward. This discovery, and the knowledge that *Orcus* was being shifted bodily towards the rocks in spite of the total flooding of Q, prompted Farge to have another scrutiny of the chart. By being driven inshore *Orcus* was wooded by the cliffs from the radar dish on Set' Navolok. The sailing directions also warned that a north-easterly caused an onshore set of the tidal stream. The sooner he was out of the bay the better. Trim would be the hazard, after flooding Ms and Q. But, even if he was forced to speed up to prevent a suicidal break-surface, his periscope was unlikely to be spotted in the windswept seas. He could risk waiting until 1945 and could begin coming up at 1930.

At 1830 he summoned Murray from the fitful sleep he was snatching between depth recordings. 'Let's move, pilot, to our second waiting position, WP2, three miles from the roundabout. Work out a course, but get your sums right, because we'll be creeping across at four knots. We're on neaps but, with this north-easterly, the westerly tidal stream is bound to be running faster.'

Murray nodded. 'The set's always northerly out of the northern reach of the inlet, sir. That can help us too, quite a bit.'

'It's in the right direction – away from this rotten hole. But apart from our own safety, in WP2 we should be able to monitor where the action apparently is.' Farge paused, watching the navigating officer drawing out his course, as a loud rumble from the caves reverberated through the submarine. 'And there's one other thing . . .'

'Sir?'

'I've a nasty feeling we've been detected.'

Murray turned his grey face to meet his captain's eyes:

'Can't have been.'

'Just a hunch. Sonar insists there's distant, active pinging north of Set' Navolok.'

'Those sweepers?'

'Could be . . . but keep it to yourself. Let me know when you're ready and I'll talk to the troops. You can brief me at supper in the wardroom.'

Farge made his broadcast, concealing nothing except his suspicions of detection:

'We'll be coming to periscope depth soon after supper. Enjoy your meal because it could be our last peaceful one for some time.' He paused, then added, 'We may be able to snort for a bit, if the cliffs screen us from the radar station. We're doing all right, so far: at least we know that their warships are using the other lane. Don't forget, we've got a date for midnight, the sixteenth. That's all. We'll shift to red lighting now. An extra can of beer all round, please, cox'n.'

He registered the murmur behind him, then moved into the wardroom where the officers were changing the light bulbs. The place was always snug, almost homely, in red lighting.

'Sherry, Number One? Reckon we've earned it.'

The exception to his drinking rule added a warmth to the gathering, a comradeship which even Woolf-Gault, sitting apart at the end, could not lessen. Riley entered with the supper. With the aplomb of a head waiter, he placed the dish in the centre of the table cloth.

'What's that revolting looking mess, Riley?' Tim Prout asked, pointing at the grey sausages, sweating in their wrinkled skins under the red lighting.

'Bangers, sir,'

'*Bangers?*'

'Yes, sir.' Riley shifted his feet. He adjusted the stained cloth which, affectedly, hung from his hairy fore-arm. 'Yesterday's left-overs, sir.'

'Disgusting,' David Powys screwed up his nose. 'Definitely not up to your cordon bleu standard.'

Riley glanced at his captain. 'I've warmed 'em up, sir.'

'*Warmed* them?' Prout asked in astonishment. He probed one of the obscene things with a finger. 'There's a ban on all cooking.'

'On top of an over-'eated motor casing, sir,' Riley explained, regaining confidence.

'Not the defective motor?' Powys interrupted, 'in the – ?'

'Yes, sir,' Riley said, edging towards the door. 'In the JRs' 'eads.'

'What you laughing at?' Murray said, pushing his way into the wardroom as Riley went out. He halted, staring at the table. 'God, what's *that*?' He swung round, but Able Seaman Riley was hurriedly disappearing down the passageway.

'Have you laid off your course yet, Alastair?' Farge asked his navigating officer.

'051°, sir,' Murray said, sitting down alongside Woolf-Gault. 'The easterly tidal stream starts running at 2025.'

Farge looked up at the clock. 'Luck's on our side. By the time we've come up and fixed our position . . .'

'And caught a trim, sir,' Foggon chipped in.

'Tricky,' Farge acknowledged, 'after this lot. By the time you've got your trim, Eddie, it'll be time to cross the western lane.'

'A bit of activity'll do you good,' Chris Sims grinned, glancing at the MEO. 'Some of us have been working.'

'Hanging around like this gets under my tits,' David Powys murmured.

'That's not the medical term,' Tomkins said. A newcomer to the wardroom, the surgeon lieutenant was emerging from his shell.

Powys glanced at Farge. 'You know what I mean, sir.'

They laughed, forcing themselves to eat, but Farge's eyes were constantly drawn towards the clock. He finished hurriedly, pushed away his plate, then sliced himself a slab of cheddar.

'Action stations in ten minutes' time, Number One. The party's over.'

They rose to their feet as the captain threaded past them to the doorway.

'Or just beginning,' Farge heard someone murmuring as he crossed to his cabin.

'Don't over-pump, chief,' the captain told his trimming officer. 'I'd rather speed up to keep her down, than risk a break-surface.'

Farge realized only too well that catching a fresh trim would be tricky after fifteen hours of scraping about the bottom: but all the transducers and sonars seemed to have been unaffected, thanks to the keel block. He felt the slight tremble as, going slow astern on both screws, *Orcus* unstuck herself.

'135 feet, sir . . . 130,' the oow sung out.

'Course, sir, 080°,' the helmsman reported.

Foggon turned to Grady on the panel: 'Pump three hundred gallons from for'd to aft.'

The bubble crept slowly back on the inclinometer, slid past the central graticule and, as Farge went ahead slowly on his port propeller, settled on four degrees up.

'Hundred feet, Number One.'

'Hundred feet, sir.'

'*Don't* overpump on Ms,' Farge insisted, as Foggon tried to help the cox'n lift her upwards.

They stopped at a hundred feet to catch a trim. It was 1945 when the sound-room finally cleared the sectors.

'Periscope depth,' Farge snapped. 'Sixty feet. I'll use the attack periscope.' At eighty feet, *Orcus* began to feel the motion of the restless sea.

'Seventy feet .'

'Up attack.'

Farge crouched by the well from which the slender steel tube was sliding upwards. He snatched at the handles as the head came level with his chest. He knew that the next few seconds were crucial: whether the fin broke surface at forty-eight feet remained in the hands of Foggon and the cox'n. If a bad sea was running, they might not be able to keep her down – suicidal here, five cables from the shore and a mile and a half from the radar dish – and then the pale light was glimmering from the surface.

'Sixty feet. *Breaking* . . .'

The smeared lens cleared and Farge was seeing the world above again. He spun round on his heels. 'Nothing close.'

'Fifty-five feet, sir.'

Farge inverted the thumb of his right hand. The stick responded, descended until he was forced to crouch. He could still feel the bow-up angle beneath his feet.

'Fifty-one feet, sir,' Powys called out. 'Still coming up, sir, Forty-nine . . .'

'For God's sake, chief. *Keep her down*. Speed up.' But in those few seconds, Farge had checked once again that there was nothing close – only a mast. 'Bearing *that*,' he snapped. 'Masthead.'

'Red 14.'

'Flood Q', he heard Foggon shouting. 'Vent Q inboard.'

'Down periscope,' Farge rapped. 'Group up, half ahead together.'

He watched in desperation as they struggled for control: a couple more feet and the fin would slice through the surface to throw up plumes of spray.

'Get the trim under control,' Farge shouted, above the roar of Q venting inboard. 'There's a bad sea running.' But he knew the worst was over: the nearest ship was a couple of miles to the southward. Gathering way, the planes began to bite; the bubble slid aft; the depth began to increase. The cox'n was silent, wrestling with his planes as he tried to prevent her porpoising.

'Forty-nine, fifty-one feet . . .'

'Blow Q,' Foggon ordered.

'Stop both,' Farge commanded. 'Group down.' He waited for the log to fall back. 'Up attack.'

'Fifty-eight feet, sir.' An audible sigh whispered through the sombre control room.

'Have you control?' Farge asked brusquely. 'Up periscope.'

'I've got her, sir,' the cox'n said quietly. 'Fifty-nine feet.'

They dipped him, the lens going dark again, but then she settled. The trimming crisis seemed to have ended, judging by the calm reigning behind him. Working fast, lowering and raising his attack persicope, taking swift, short looks, Farge registered the surface scene. Rapping out the bearings of his sightings, he gave the LOP and CEP enough data with which to build up their pictures.

To the south-east he could see the flashing light of the roundabout whistle buoy, a warship (a frigate?) on the far side of it. Coming abeam, on his port side, was the sloping outline of Set' Navolok. The yellow light-tower, atop its single-storied building, was perched upon the sepia-tinged granite cliff, the giant cupola of the radar dish rearing behind it. The coast running down to the Pushka caves was devoid of vegetation, the bleak cliffs plunging sheer into the sea. He could see the gulls wheeling in the wind above Lodeynaya Bay, the breakers leaping in curtains of spray where they battered Pushka Point; and the dark tower, astern now, which perched on the point guarding the southern entrance to *Orcus*' recent refuge. Though the submarine must be a mile off now, he could distinguish the white band of the horizontal markings on the tower. He could just make out the eastern tip of the entrance to the inlet, the coast a dull green above the shoreline where the granite showed. In spite of the scrub in the breaks of the cliffs, the eastern side was as desolate and dreary as the western shore, now slowly drawing astern. The mast was enlarging to a bridge and funnel: 'Bearing *that*, and two more masts.' Farge slammed the handles shut and turned to Murray:

'Got your fix?'

'Okay, sir. We're entering the western limit of the inward lane now.'

'Happy?'

The navigating officer nodded. 'Everything checks, sir. Plenty of water now.'

'150 feet. Assume the Ultra Quiet State. I'll keep her slow together.'

Orcus slipped down to her depth, her company remaining at action stations. Except for the reports of sonar contacts from the sound-room, no one spoke; each man listening, nerves taut. *Orcus* was crossing what must be the most heavily defended, monitored and mined entrance to a naval port in the world. The old submarine had penetrated the first stockade. If she could reach WP2, between the diverging lanes, Operation SDW was going to plan – provided *Safari* was in Position Zulu on time.

15

HM Submarine Safari, 15 May. It was unusual for *Safari*'s senior rates' mess to be empty at this hour, and CPO Derek Scanes was savouring his few minutes of peace before going on watch. Privacy was at a premium in *Safari*, though at 4,500 tons she was vast compared to the conventionals he had left long ago, or so it seemed. The most striking difference, and one which was still foreign to him even after his time in *Valiant*, was the fashion in which the nuke was a 'split' submarine, the seamen and weaponry up for'd, the propulsion department to which he belonged, back aft.

The split was natural, inflicted upon them by the reactor which divided the boat geographically and practically into two. The outside wrecker and his for'd staff took care of the engineering for'd of the reactor, but to pass from up for'd to back aft required passing through the huge doors of the tunnel over the reactor. People could not wander throughout the boat as in conventionals, and the ship's company, however hard the officers tried to break down the division, lived two existences. Scanes did not like the system, but they had to live with it.

Scanes was one of the minority who had decided to look after his health, to arrest the inevitable deterioration caused by no physical exercise and plentiful food. He conscientiously did his daily pedalling on the cycle, but the struggle to keep down his weight was hard, now that he'd packed in the cigarettes. Beryl didn't like fat men.

Scanes glanced around the mess, the compartment which the senior rates had tried to make homely. The two royal portraits hung above the bar; and on the bulkheads, the mess committee had hung prints of country scenes given to them by Vickers. Messes were usually adorned with toothy, busty nudes, but the President of the Mess, the Fleet Chief MEM, an old-timer and a stickler for standards, was right: the mess was pleasantly dignified and peaceful, except when the mess idiot and his buddy, Bull Clint were around.

Bull, the cox'n, tried over-hard to project his image as a character, brandishing that ridiculous fly-whisk he had picked up in Beira, he was, to Scanes, a trifle pathetic. Scanes felt embarrassed when sometimes intercepting JRS' glances behind Clint's back.

Scanes glanced at the clock: he was the MEAOW for C watch, a watchkeeping roster of one in four which this section of the propulsion department kept. The propulsion department ran the 'Augment' or five watch system, even in wartime, with a fifth watch, and those under training, always on leave. This was the only practical way to run the one department in the nuclear submarine which could never shut down; the kettle was a demanding mistress. Scanes remembered those hard days when he had started in *Valiant*, and the fifth watch system had not been devised: the incessant work for the senior rates was hellish. Things were better now, but trickle drafting still threw too much weight on the senior rates: no sooner had a youngster been trained to be useful, than he shoved off to another boat. But what else *could* the Navy do? If it had not been for Beryl he would have quit long ago. She had been right to persuade him during those hard years to stay in the service – and Scanes leaned back, shutting his eyes to retrieve in his imagination those last days they had shared before the Soviets took out Faslane. Beryl had travelled down to Meavy near Yelverton to see her mum, when *Safari* had put in for five days before her first wartime patrol. It was a lucky escape for her, because their married quarters in Faslane had been one of the houses destroyed. And what was more, in Devonport, she'd had her hopes for a child confirmed by their doctor: after six years of marriage, they were having their first in November – and they had begun to swap possible names for it in their letters.

Safari and *Orcus* had picked up their bags of mail in Lochalsh. Scanes had a good run ashore with Tom Grady, Scane's oppo from training course days. Grady was enjoying being *Orcus'* outside wrecker; he liked his new skipper, an unusual, solitary sort of bloke, apparently, but efficient and fair. Grady had received some good news in his mail: a cousin of his in the Fleet Air Arm called Osgood, who had been reported missing from *Furious*, had been picked up and was recovering in hospital. Grady had insisted on celebrating that evening and he and

Scanes had drunk too much of the local fire-water.

They were lucky, too, in *Safari* to have a good skipper, but Commander Coombes could not be a more contrasting character than *Orcus*' CO, judging from Grady's remarks. Coombes was flambuoyant, irrespressible, an extrovert. The troops loved him, and not only because he'd been in the boat longer than most. He knew every inch of the boat and exuded confidence: not a bad quality when belting along at thirty knots at five hundred feet, outward bound on a special mission. He'd told them all about SDW after they'd finished mucking about south of Ireland, frigging around with other SSNs and exposing themselves deliberately on ECM as part of the deception plan. It wasn't until 1100 on 14 May that they had started north from the Flannan Isles; *Safari* had been steaming at thirty knots ever since. Being in the propulsion department was bloody hard work.

Scanes enjoyed his duties, liking the freedom and the edge given to the job by the continuous search for trouble. Scanes had a roving commission: the MEAOW was a trouble-shooter, monitoring the remoter machinery, searching for faults before they occurred, checking the junior stokers isolated as watch keepers on the remoter auxiliaries. These young men kept their four-hour watches on the machinery until they could barely stand in the overwhelming noise and heat. The poor sod, the lower watchkeeper, always emerged pale and grey at the end of his watch. His one craving was for sleep, but six hours was the maximum time off-watch he could get, six hours in which to eat, wash and sleep before his treadmill duty began again. The lives of everyone hung upon these lads: if the vital distiller went duff – it could happen in seconds – the boat would come to a grinding halt. How many lads in civvy street, Scanes thought, of the same age as these junior MEMS bore such responsibility? Scanes got up, stretched himself. He'd take over his watch, then start his rounds.

He walked aft along the middle deck, climbed up the ladder to the top deck and negotiated the tunnel to enter the world he knew and understood. The screaming of the turbo generators permeated this gleaming space of white paint, twisting pipes and shining, steel gratings. Scanes reported to the manoeuvring-room, took over from his predecessor, then started his tour.

The PO on his electrical panel seemed happy enough and so did the watchkeeper on the throttle control panel. The chief on the reactor panel nodded his greetings and Scanes moved out into the less rarified world outside.

He paused on the manoeuvring platform, fascinated however often he saw it, by the vastness of the open space that was the main engine-room. Over thirty feet from deckhead to bilges, it gleamed in its white paint even after months of running. Here were the bits and pieces which, apart from the boilers, turbines and gearboxes driving the huge propeller, were vital to the functioning of the submarine: the turbo and motor generators provided the electrical energy and charged the small battery which was so vital if the reactor was scrammed.

Scanes moved down to 2 deck and had a word with the upper-level watchkeeper: the air compressors of the freon plant, dangerous if it leaked its gas, were giving no trouble for once. He walked into the switchboard room and had a word with the watchkeeper: *Safari* was, in reality, an electrical ship; though the back-up procedures were plentiful, all hydraulics and controls were actuated electrically. Down on 3 deck, Scanes checked the diesel and motor generator compartment, with its ear-splitting noise level. The watchkeeper grinned and held up his thumb. In the adjoining compartment, he found the eighteen-year-old junior MEM writing up his readings. Atkins had joined the Navy only four months ago, but here he was, enduring the long watches in this isolated, sweltering steel box, monitoring the distiller and its tanks as if he had been accustomed to the job all his life. His pale, serious face split into a nervous grin:

'Yeah – everything's okay, chief,' he yelled into Scanes' ear.

Scanes systematically read the gauges, checked the lad's entries. There was little room to move and the air was foul. He was about to sign the log when from somewhere above there was a roaring noise. He heard the shouts, recorded in his minds the emergency commands.

'God!' he yelled, shoving his way past the stoker. 'A steam leak – *can't be anything else!*'

16

HM Submarine Orcus, 15 May. 'Happy with the trim?' Farge asked.

Eddie Foggon was watching the depth gauge and the bubble. 'She's settled nicely,' the MEO said. 'Qs half full.'

Lieutenant Woolf-Gault stood silently at the after end of the control-room: the boat was bottomed at 632 feet with a four-degree bow-down angle, in her second waiting position, three miles from the V-junction of the main shipping lanes. The roundabout buoy was six and a half miles to the south-south-west: from this new position *Orcus* should be able to monitor both lanes more satisfactorily.

'Who's the officer of the watch, Number One?'

'TASO, sir,' Tim Prout said. 'He's willing to keep the watch until 0300.'

Woolf-Gault sensed the hesitation, felt awkward at the first lieutenant's announcement; he intercepted the glances passing between the plotting team but registered the flash of understanding in the cox'n's kindly eye.

'Right, then,' the captain said. 'You have the submarine, officer of the watch.'

Woolf-Gault stepped forward, between the periscopes. 'I have the submarine, sir.'

'Call me at once if you're bothered or if the sound-room picks up any major war vessels,' Farge said, firmly. 'There could be a lot more activity at dawn. Shake me at 0400.'

'Aye, aye, sir.' The captain crossed to the chart table, had a word with Murray, then disappeared into his cabin.

Three minutes later, the control-room had emptied. The boat had adopted a modified action state, with a reduced attack team closed up on the sonar, the LOP and the CEP. Farge was remaining in WP2 until the sound-room had built up a comprehensive sonar state.

Woolf-Gault moved over to the chart table. Four hours ago, the captain had crossed the western lane by running deep and taking advantage of the overhead traffic. When he came up for a quick look, he found good vis. and the wind moderated to five or six. He did not hang around, having sighted a group of choppers to the west. Their active pinging shortly afterwards dispelled the hope that *Orcus* had penetrated the Kola Inlet undetected. The captain bottomed her half an hour before the westerly tidal stream began to run and reinstated the Ultra Quiet State.

Woolf-Gault straightened his back, glimpsed the reflection of his hollow-cheeked, grey face in one of the dials of the control-room. His adorable Eve wouldn't recognize those haunted eyes staring from their sunken sockets. He compressed his lips and crossed to the doorway of the sound-room. The operators took no notice of him as they concentrated on their displays, monitoring, counting the revs, analysing the shaft and blade signatures. Chris Sims, the jovial, fair-haired sonar officer with the freckled face, was leaning over one of the operator's shoulders, helping to analyse a contact in the eastern lane, when from the corner of his eye, he glimpsed Windy-Gault's arrival. Pointedly, Sims bade his team good-night and, easing past Woolf-Gault, made his way for'd to his bunk. The operators continued making their reports to the anonymous oow in the control-room, where only the relief panel watchkeeper was half asleep at his panel. The lieutenant sat down in the captain's canvas stool and began his long vigil

The life-support system was the only machinery still running: the boat had not snorted since after Vardø. The weo had reported that the battery was down to sixty per cent: nothing to worry about yet, but a lot might happen before they could get in another charge. Denzil Woolf-Gault shivered in the silent control-room. The clammy cold? Or was this tingling at the nape of his neck the onset of flu? The doc, Bob Tomkins, the only man in the wardroom to remain tolerably friendly, was worried by the epidemic: three men were running high temperatures, all three, Bob said, would be virus-pneumonia cases, if the drugs didn't take hold.

Without the doc's unspoken sympathy, Woolf-Gault might have been tempted to put an end to this misery – and he thrust away that moment when he'd considered the revolver cupboard above the wardroom table. Messy for everyone – and the act would only compound his cowardice. And how could Eve live with the shame for the rest of her life? Jeremy, their four-year old: would he inherit his father's trait? It was going to be difficult enough explaining to Eve that moment of panic which had overwhelmed him on the bridge, that split-second of derangement which had wrecked his service career. His future depended upon Eve's reaction. She'd married a man with feet of clay, not a knight in shining armour. In the prison of his personal world, alone in the control-room with the petty officer at the panel intent on his girlie magazine, Woolf-Gault began to sense again the advent of black depression.

How could anyone begin to know what ostracism by one's peers was like? He realized how insufferable he must have been, lording his seniority and experience over Prout. But, virtually sent to Coventry, he wasn't going to crawl to them – bloody hell, no. He'd been top of his term on passing out from the college, had a successful career ahead of him. He knew he wasn't as calm, sometimes, under stress, as some of the others, but he'd managed to keep the knowledge to himself. To compensate he'd gone flat out as soon as he joined the fleet, throwing himself into any extra activity he could: the cross-channel races in the yacht; the sub-aqua clubs which led to his qualifying as a ship's diver, a skill he had conscientiously kept up to date, never missing his routine proficiency tests; and his standard A1 as a Russian interpreter. He had more to offer than most . . . and he felt again the stab of remorse as his eyes wandered round the control-room: depth 634 feet; bubble three degrees bow-down; ship's head steady on 039°. The hum of the ventilation was making him drowsy.

The hands of the clock moved imperceptibly. The reports from the 187 sonar were all that kept him awake: the initial contact, the classifying, the refining, ship after ship, but mostly in the eastern lane. When at 0105 the operator came up with a contact on 030°, it dawned in Woolf-Gault's half-consciousness that the bearing was odd. He ordered a check: the bearing was confirmed, with an estimated range of six miles. He dragged himself from his chair and walked quietly to the captain's cabin. He tapped on the door frame and drew back the curtain half-way.

The dark head on the pillow turned, the dark eyes meeting

his suspiciously.

'187 reckons she's a diesel, sir, medium-sized. They can't identify her.'

'030°?' the captain asked. 'That's between the lanes.'

'Yes, sir,' Woolf-Gault said. 'About six miles from us.'

Farge propped himself on his elbow. He slowly smoothed back his thinning hair.

'Sure you're not giving me the reciprocal?'

'Certain, sir. I've had a recheck: confirmed 030°.'

The captain slumped on his bunk. 'Let me know if she comes any closer or if the active transmissions to the west start again.' Glancing at the clock at the foot of his bunk, he added, 'I'll sleep better now. Don't forget to shake me at 0400.'

'Right, sir.' And as Woolf-Gault slid the curtain across, he heard Farge murmuring: 'We must be clear of the minefields then, if there's a ship tooling about ahead of us.'

Woolf-Gault's long watch crept to its close. At 0217 he noted from the navigator's notebook that the sun up top was setting. The hour and three-quarters of dreary twilight would be casting its weird, red-tinged gloom upon the surface, 630 feet above the submarine. At 0255 Woolf-Gault shook the first lieutenant. Prout, bleary-eyed, took over the watch; Woolf-Gault left the control-room to crawl into his bunk where merciful sleep eased his misery.

'Captain in the control-room!'

Farge shoved back his chair and left his officers at the wardroom table, finishing their cold lunch. The officer of the afternoon watch, Sims, was standing at the entrance to the sound-room.

'I wasn't sure,' Farge said, 'but I thought I heard it on the hull . . . active pinging?'

'Affirmative, sir. 290°. They're hunting off Set' Navolok.'

'The same choppers?'

'Same frequencies, sir. Getting closer.'

Farge paced his control-room: it was 1324, the day already half-spent. He crossed to the chart table to think things out.

He had suspected for some time that the enemy's ASW forces were on to *Orcus*' penetration. Loops off Set' Navolok? Hydrophones on the shallow spur at the eastern end of the

Rybachiy peninsular, when *Orcus* entered beneath the tanker? Towed Surface Arrays? Or sheer bad luck from routine ASW helicopter sweeps? At least the second chopper group was to the north-eastward, and moving northward up the eastern shipping channel away from *Orcus*. He pricked off the distance to the declared danger area to the north – if he continued on a course of 038°, the southern limit of what must presumably be a moored minefield (the soundings were over two hundred metres) was 10·2 miles off. Though he had succeeded in insinuating *Orcus* as far as this, he still needed luck: the state report was taking an eternity to build up, and *Orcus* could not wait here for ever.

The constant irritant in any conventional CO's mind was his remaining battery power. The boat had been dived for forty-one hours since her last charge off Vardø: the air was tolerable, but the life support system and lighting were using up the amps. As David Powys had reported quietly in the captain's cabin, thirty-six per cent had already been expended.

The forenoon's sonar classifications confirmed the suspicion which first entered Farge's mind while *Orcus* was lying in Lodeynaya Bay. The Northern Fleet's outward submarines and heavier units seemed to be routed to the eastern shipping lane, which was three miles wide. The outward traffic must be using the starboard side of this swept channel and the submarine targets for which he was searching should be in that farther lane. Opening his dividers, he pricked off the distance: four miles. He'd take *Orcus* further north to a position, 2·6 miles south of the declared minefield and within three miles of the western edge of the inward shipping lane; she'd be ideally placed – and clear of those chivvying choppers off Set' Navolok. Though the 187 sonar had classified a Delta II and a Yankee outward at dawn this morning, it had pin-pointed only one other, an Oscar at 1151. There was such activity that even Joker Paine, the sonar chief, had had difficulty in sorting out the grain from the chaff. Farge decided to move immediately to this third waiting position, WP3.

Making use of the tidal stream which started setting easterly at 1642, Farge went to full action stations at 1600: twelve minutes earlier, the sound-room reported active pinging approaching on a steady bearing from the west-north-west.

Unsticking herself without trouble from the mud, *Orcus* rose silently to four hundred feet, Foggon and the cox'n having her under firm control this time. With infrequent kicks ahead on slow one for his northing, Farge virtually drifted on the easterly set for his easting to WP3. Averaging four knots and with minimal active use of his mine detecting sonar, at 1810 he put her down again in 650 feet on to mud, sand and shingle.

He relaxed action stations to a modified attack team as the long vigil began again. The sonar department were bearing up, but the strain was beginning to show; and at this discharge rate, it was not difficult to calculate when the battery would become dangerously low. If something didn't turn up soon, Farge would have to make for the deep field in order to charge.

'Have *you* got the watch, Number One?' Farge asked.

'Yes, sir, until 2000.'

'I'd like to go through the boat with the cox'n,' Farge said. 'It's time I saw for myself how everyone is.'

'I'll send for him, sir.'

Farge shook his head. 'I'll pick him up on my way for'd. Shout for me on the broadcast if you need me.'

17

HM Submarine Orcus, 16 May. Fitful though his sleep had been, Farge felt less ill when at 0300 on Friday morning he slumped into his chair in the control-room. He'd got in five hours' sleep after supper and the sonar room's reports did not start in earnest until 0230, when intense activity began developing at the exit to the inlet: first a group of sweepers, then two Krivaks. He had started his own vigil in the control-room then, sorting in his mind the picture which must be developing up top. Was this present flurry up top the prelude to the Typhoon's sailing? Or was the crescendo of activity a blind?

Although Chris Sims had logged several major Soviet warships the sound-room had been unable to keep track of the smaller, escorting units. But the crucial information was confirmed: the enemy's submarines, the Northern Fleet's nukes and SSBNs, were using the eastern route. If Farge could now position *Orcus* closer, to pin-point their driving positions, he was three-quarters of the way to success. Farge rose from his chair and joined Murray at the chart table.

'I'm going to move nearer, pilot,' Farge murmured. 'I'd like an accurate position, after all this time. You should be able to identify Kildin Island, Set' Navolok and the right-hand edge of the Rybachiy peninsular. To give you better visibility, I'll wait till 0730 before coming up for your fix: with luck there'll still be a sea running. Sonar *must* have more time to refine, so I want to stand off a bit.'

Farge did not disturb the troops, letting them sleep while he tried to ignore the hands of the clock above the panel crawling around its dial. During his rounds with Bowles he found the sailors subdued but still smiling, as bored as he was tensed. The fore-ends were cold and running with condensation, but it was always clammy there, with the grease and the sweating, shiny white paint. Those with flu were turned in, some of them on the makeshift beds above the reloading racks. The SRs and the chiefs were fine, as confident as ever, but were beginning to show strain. The engine-room was empty, its diesel fumes rank in the silent, deserted space, but in the after-ends the MEMs and stokers were cheerfully playing uckers. Farge was glad he'd seen them all: he sensed that the crisis was near, the climax of their mission. If he didn't have a grain of luck soon, he'd be forced by lack of amps to make for the open sea again, just when his quarry was booked to sail.

Farge had been furnished with every known detail of the enemy's monstrous weapon, his Typhoon, the secret plans of which must have already been decided upon when the Kremlin attached its signature to the Helsinki agreement. During the early eighties the Soviets had built two classes of boats, the Typhoon and the Alfa. The Alfa was constructed of titanium alloy, instead of steel, to give immense strength. Because of difficulties in welding techniques, the Alfa was originally plagued by leaks, but the difficulties were rapidly overcome: Nato deep-field SSNs lost the Alfas when they increased to forty-two knots and went deep. Armed with MRV nuclear missiles, Nato assumed that their function was to escort and cover the Soviets' cruise missile attack SSNs, their Charlies and Echos. The second class was the Typhoon. Even now, the West could not satisfactorily explain the enemy's strategic thinking behind this incredibly expensive weapons system: size was not always beautiful in submarine warfare.

The Typhoon was gigantic: only a cricket pitch shorter, but twice the displacement size of the British CAHs *Invincible*, *Illustrious* and *Ark Royal*, and as Julian's father had remarked, the Typhoon was identical in size to Cunningham's famous flagship, *Warspite*. The monster submarine carried twenty ballistic missiles for'd of its fin, weapons with a range of over four thousand miles. But the Delta IIs, with their SS–N–X–18 ballistic missiles, could already cover half the world from the Barents citadel, so why the Typhoon?

Its immense size suggested that it carried stocks or reloads and the complicated machinery for the tricky reloading operations, and several reactors to drive the underwater monster at speed. Intelligence guessed that they also were built of titanium: if so, the Typhoon could dive to perhaps four thousand feet and lie on the bottom for months, impossible to detect in the shallower wildernesses of the polar seas, such as the Lomonosov Ridge. Once concealed there, she would only have to lift from the bottom to find a *polynya*, a window in the ice, through which to launch her deadly ICBMs.

How many in the ship's company? Farge mused. An admiral commanding? And discipline for months on end? Hundreds of bored men without women, though Russian women were known to be at sea, some even in command. He smiled to himself. I must be going down with flu, he thought, as at last he watched the hands of the clock creeping up to the hour.

'Action stations,' he ordered, nodding at the outside wrecker. 'Time to have a look.'

It was good to see daylight filtering through the lens of the attack periscope as the submarine crept up to the undulating, grey surface. The glass broke through, cleared. Farge spun on his heel – no aircraft, nothing close.

'Down attack. Up search.'

More leisurely this time, flicking to high power, as he picked up a masthead to the eastward.

'Bearing *that* . . . looks like a destroyer's mast. I've got Cape Sunduki, pilot . . . bearing *that*.'

Swift five-second looks to fox the enemy radar; rapid identification of the land points – and Murray had his bearings for a three-point fix. 'Down search.'

Farge smoothed his black hair, watched the wider steel tube disappearing into its well: 'Great day up top. Bright and blustery. Force five, from the east; good vis.' The trimming was going famously: up from deep without a hitch, settling bang on fifty-eight feet. The team's spirits rose with his own optimism.

'0752 fix, sir,' Murray called out. 'Puts us three-quarters of a mile to the east of our EP.'

'Roger.' Farge grabbed the handles as they swept upwards again. He'd take another bearing of the destroyer while Murray, allowing for the easterly stream which began at 0506, worked out his revised course to WP4 on the easterly edge of the easterly and outward lane. Ah, there was the destroyer: no nearer, but her bearing was drawing seawards, up to the north-east. Odd that she should be on her own – and he flicked to high power. That was better . . . He could distinguish her aerial, but could not identify her bridge. He swung slowly to the southward.

'Bearing *that*,' he rapped, trying to smother the excitement in his voice. He slammed shut the handles, turned and grinned at Prout. 'A Delta II, I'm pretty certain . . .'

'Green 112, sir.'

At 0755 he swung round for a last look to confirm his Delta sighting before taking *Orcus* deep to the shipping lane. The sea was sparkling on this fresh morning, the waves curling rhythmically, lazily, the crests tumbling merrily: ideal conditions for the judicious use of his periscope. There she was: her ugly, protruding missile housing, with its down-turn abaft the black match-box fin, confirmed his indentification.

'Bearing of the Delta II is *that*.'

His periscope had been up for only a few seconds. He was in the act of shutting the handles when something strange caught his eye – a white mist clouded her bow: must be the bow-wave she was pushing ahead of her as she worked up speed . . . but the white plumes were spouting high, abaft her fin.

'Down periscope,' he blurted. 'She's diving!' The 187 sonar had got her too: Farge heard the murmuring behind him as the stick streaked downwards – here was the evidence for which they had been seeking for so long.

'Assume she's in the centre of the far lane, pilot. Give me a course to the eastern edge, four miles north of her diving position.' Farge caught Number One's eye, grinned in return. 'Starboard ten. Six down, two hundred feet.'

'Course 098°,' Murray called.

'Steer 098°.'

'Steer 098°, sir,' the second cox'n reported from the wheel. 'Ten of starboard wheel on.'

'Pilot, how far to –'

But Farge stopped midway in his sentence, canted his head, listening . . . then he heard it, as they all did: standing, or crouching, suddenly rigid, like the Pompeii victims sculpted in lava for eternity, listening to the scraping noise from the eyes of the boat. At first, it was a barely audible ticking, then as the mooring-wire of the mine scraped across the hull the scrabbling along the casing rose to a screeching crescendo – then stopped, to continue with a low-pitched, rhythmic creaking.

'Loud banging noises on the sonar,' the sound-room called.

Farge could hear his own breathing. He glimpsed Woolf-Gault, propped in the corner, his eyes fixed on the deckhead, his jaw clamped, the muscles twitching in his cheek. The way was coming off the submarine, and to the ominous creaks was added a low thrumming noise which, the hull being like a sounding board, was reverberating throughout the boat.

'Stop both,' Farge rapped, shattering the silence. 'Half astern together. Shut off for depth-charging.' He raised his voice. 'Quiet with the doors.' In seconds, each compartment was an isolated world cut off from its neighbour.

'Fore-planes jammed at twelve degrees of dive,' the cox'n reported, as if he was on exercise in West Bay. 'Can't hold her, sir. After planes at hard-a-rise.'

Farge was watching the log-pointer walking back in its dial down to one knot.

The bight of the mooring-wire must have snagged in the fore-planes. Turning at four knots under rudder, *Orcus* was dragging the infernal mine down upon herself. It had only to kiss the fin . . .

One of the plotters at the scc was crossing himself, his eyes shut, his lips moving. Farge registered the depth: ninety-eight feet. He raised his hand, touched Lorna's cross beneath his shirt and momentarily closed his eyes.

18

HM Submarine Safari, 16 May. Commander Coombes slung the sheaf of orders on to his bunk, leaned back in his chair and closed his eyes. The steam leak had blown at 2135 yesterday and, in spite of the efforts of his MEO, Malcolm Gunn, and his team, *Safari* remained at two hundred feet, under way at snail's pace on her noisy egg-beater and battery. Coombes could not resist sneaking glances at the clock above his desk: it was already 1505, seventeen and a half hours since the breakdown.

'Hell's bloody bells,' he exploded, crashing his fist on to his desk. He resisted sending for the chief again: he'd wait another half-hour before going to find him himself. SDW was a ghastly fiasco: *Orcus*, at appalling risk to herself, was at this moment creeping about the enemy's backyard. If her luck held, she could be transmitting her enemy report at any time after midnight: that last 'immediate' which *Safari* had received before the satellite went on the blink late on the fourteenth had indicated that the Typhoon (and a suspected Alfa II) could be capable of sailing from 0001 17 May onwards. COMSUBEAST-LANT was presuming that she would sail either on the 17 or 18 May, or on the 20 or 21 May, so it was essential for *Safari* to be at Zulu by midnight of the sixteenth.

The breakdown in satellite communications was a further aggravation: he wondered whether the Russians had started the space war. Presumably their manned vehicle launches in the early eighties had been to learn how to destroy the West's vital communication satellites. *Safari* had been ordered to listen to hourly W/T routines from midday of the sixteenth onwards.

When *Safari* had sailed, Coombes knew that Nato's surface forces were unobtrusively streaming for the Greenland and Norwegian seas. *Carl Vinson*'s Striking Force was to bottle up the western exits from the Barents Sea and, apart from her maritime air patrols, she was leaving the Barents clear for Operation SDW. *Safari* need have no worries about friendly boats until north of the seventy-sixth parallel, when she would be informed of the positions of friendly units. Nato's intention was to seal off the enemy submarines' escape routes to the North Polar Basin: for too long the Northern Fleet and the Kremlin had presumed that the Barents was their citadel. For SDW to succeed Nato had to achieve a fine balance; by constricting the net too tightly, the Striking Force might dissuade the Soviet off-patrol SSBNs from putting to sea.

There was some consolation in the fact that, while trying to curb his frustration during this breakdown, Coombes had time to memorize the ice conditions. The polar ice was average for April and May: the gales had broken it up a bit faster, that was all; Franz Josef Land should be free by the end of May; the pack limit was average too, and expected to be latitude 77° north for June. *Safari* needed every hour she could gain in order to overtake her target before it reached the shelter of the ice, where sonar conditions could be much more difficult, especially in bad weather. *Orcus* also needed time for her breakaway, once she'd made her enemy report. *Safari*'s Position Zulu was the best compromise which the computers could predict.

Coombes swore softly: he had for the umpteenth time checked with his navigating officer the latest time for *Safari* to be under way again in order to reach Zulu by midnight on the seventeenth – only nine hours' time – but the deadline had already passed. If *Safari* could get going at once, she would still be five hours adrift, even assuming that she could maintain thirty knots. Coombes regretted having lost his temper with his MEO. Malcolm Gunn was long-suffering, having to cope with the problems not of his making in addition to having to put up with a bad-tempered captain. And he had insisted that the repair *must* be one hundred per cent – no bodging.

The navigating officer had worked out *Safari*'s furthest-on positions for every hour which passed – and for each hour which slipped by *Safari* would have to make her intercept further south. Coombes opened his eyes as he heard his curtain swishing open.

Malcolm Gunn stood in the doorway in his streaked, white overalls, his hard hat black with grease, his face grey.

'Ready to try her now, sir. Permission to change the reactor state?'

Coombes nodded and jumped to his feet. 'Well done, Malcolm. Every second counts. Give me thirty knots as soon as you bloody well can.'

'I'll have to work up slowly, sir.'

Coombes nodded as together they hurried into the control-room. 'Diving stations,' he ordered brusquely. 'Let's get this ruddy thing going.'

By 1540 the chief was satisfied. The steam joint held as *Safari* worked up slowly to full power. By 1602 she was steaming at thirty knots on a course of 081° to cut the corner. Coombes had decided to risk passing closer to North Cape but, even so, *Safari* would be seven hours adrift and eighty miles further south of Zulu than she should be.

Janner Coombes paced his constricted control-room, hearing only the subdued commands, the acknowledgement of orders. The hands were keeping well out of his way: they did not realize that *Orcus*, because of *Safari*'s let-down, could be sacrificing herself needlessly. He, Coombes, was failing them, that bloody fine team headed by the man whom his stepsister loved, the Lorna whom Janner had loved once himself.

19

HM Submarine Orcus, 16 May. Farge tried to guess how long they had listened to the unforgettable scraping sound of the moored mine: the ordeal seemed interminable, but could not have been more than thirty seconds. The wry grin spreading over Bill Bowles' face told Julian that the worst bit of the emergency could be over. Surprisingly, *Orcus* managed to hold her trim, with judicious kicks ahead on slow one and with fifteen degrees of rise on the after-planes.

The tidal stream was setting easterly until 1121, so the mine, which must be floating within feet of the fin, might be being held more vertically by the tidal stream. Who the hell knew? They were alive, creeping along at two knots, at a nine degree bow-up angle. Farge wiped the top of his head with his palm while he waited for the reports to come in.

Tim Prout elbowed his way through the bulkhead doorway. He stood, out of breath, at the for'd end of the control-room, all eyes upon him:

'We can't shift the fore-planes, sir – even in hand. Depth gauge in the fore-ends shows seventy-six feet.'

'124 feet aft,' Farge said. 'We're nine degrees bows-up and holding her.'

'I'm bodily heavy, sir,' Foggon, the MEO interrupted. 'Permission to pump on Ms?' His matter-of-fact question, spoken with his calm North Riding accent, was a reassurance to all who heard him.

'Yes, chief – but don't overdo it. I'll turn to the southward to clear the bastards.' The mine detecting sonar was pinging, but had picked up only one more contact, fine on the port bow. 'Starboard ten, officer of the watch. Steer 160°.'

'Spoils your whole day, doesn't it, sir?' Chris Sims murmured from his sound-room.

The chuckles in the control-room relaxed the tension as the boat slowly made her wide turn. She was now steering south-south-east, away from the minefield.

'Can you hear anything in the fore-ends, Number One?'

'A very faint sort of scrabbling, sir. Nothing else.'

'We can't tool around with a bloody great lethal bollock suspended over us,' Farge said. 'It must be hovering over the fin – or even further aft.'

'The fin can't be much more than sixty feet below the surface,' Foggon said.

Farge was hoping someone might come forward with what he knew they had to do.

'If we don't clear it, we've had it,' Murray said softly.

'And so's SDW,' David Powys added.

And then Farge saw the moonlike face of Able Seaman Hicks, who had joined at Barrow. He was edging his way through the press at the bulkhead doorway.

'Leading Seaman Robertson and me will go outside, sir, to cut the bastard.'

Farge met the man's steady gaze (never volunteer, they always said, didn't they?). 'Have you worked at this depth?' he asked. 'Seventy-five feet?'

'Course, sir.' Hicks' glance was scornful, his reputation at stake. 'We'll get togged up, sir.' He was turning when Farge saw them making way for the slight figure of the surgeon lieutenant.

'Leading Seaman Robertson's very ill, sir,' Bob Tomkins said.

'He's the only man, doctor, who can work with Hicks,' Farge said curtly.

'With respect, sir, Robertson can't do the job, however much he wants to.'

'He'll have to try,' Farge said. 'Tell him to dress.'

'You'll kill him, sir. He can't possibly do it.'

'That's enough, doctor. Robertson . . .' Farge, annoyance surging within him, turned as he felt a slight tap on his shoulder. Woolf-Gault, strained and pale, met Farge's angry eyes.

'I'll go with Hicks, sir. I'm as highly qualified as he is.'

Farge heard the ticking of the clock, the shuffling of feet. He turned back to the burly Hicks in the doorway:

'Are you happy, Hicks, for Lieutenant Woolf-Gault to help you?'

The able seaman did not know how to put it. Facing the lieutenant, he asked haltingly, 'Do you know your stuff, sir? I mean . . .'

Woolf-Gault nodded. 'I'm a qualified ship's diver,' he said softly.

The able seaman beckoned with his hand. 'C'mon sir. Better get our gear.' He stood back for the lieutenant to proceed him, as the press about the doorway parted for Woolf-Gault to make his way for'd.

It was 0910 before Able Seaman Hicks and Lieutenant Woolf-Gault were finally ready to dress into their suits. Sorting out the gear under Leading Seaman Robertson's glazed supervision had taken time: the weights, knives and lamps; fitting the primers to the explosive cutting charges; the long handled cutting tool; they all had to be checked and their lanyards adjusted. The noise risk when using the charges would have to be accepted. The submarine was still creeping southwards and was barely making enough way over the ground to prevent the mine's sinker from snagging on the bottom.

The conference in the control-room took longer than Woolf-Gault expected, Hicks taking charge of the diving side, while Number One went through the escape chamber drill. The captain re-emphasized the signals: two knocks, *Orcus* to go ahead; three, astern; four, stop. Then, surprisingly for Farge, he shook Hicks and Woolf-Gault by the hand.

The first lieutenant moved for'd down the passage-way, Hicks behind him, Woolf-Gault last. As Woolf-Gault passed the messes, faces peered outwards, wishing him luck. Hicks and he dressed in the cold of the tube-space, each checking the other's bottles. Hicks had the line, the charges and the saw; Woolf-Gault, double-checking the lanyard which secured the long-handled cutter to his hip, took the mini-grapnel. They switched on each other's headlamps and closed their masks. They opened the valves of their breathing-mixture, blew through and checked the depth rate on their dials. Hicks gave the thumbs-up, grasped Woolf-Gault's forearm and began climbing the ladder into the escape-chamber, his flippers clumsily feeling for the spaces between the rungs.

Woolf-Gault glanced about him, met Prout's anxious gaze, then followed Hicks into the chamber. The lower hatch shut beneath them. Woolf-Gault saw Hicks mouthing the orders they knew by heart:

'Open the flood . . . open the vent.'

In that instant, as the icy water began swirling beneath his feet, Woolf-Gault again felt that terrible uncontrollable panic tugging at him. Trapped in here, the water rushing up to his knees now, the pressure mounting on his ears – it was all he could do not to wrench off his head-set and get out. But his terror evaporated as he remembered his drill: he wouldn't survive if he did not balance the pressures, keep his head, adjust the air-flow. He cleared his ears again, was jabbed in the stomach by Hicks' elbow. The level was up to his mouth, swirling over his visor. He was underwater, the noise of the deluge decreasing as the pressure eased. A tap on his shoulder and the body next to him was reaching up for the releasing wheel.

Drill, drill, drill. The hatch was springing open. Hicks was moving upwards, as agile as an otter. Woolf-Gault, the moment of agony past, floated up after him, his mind calm, concentrating upon the job lying ahead of him.

Even at seventy-five feet it was as black as pitch: Woolf-Gault felt the steel of the casing beneath his hands as, pushing against the upturned hatch, he swam steadily forwards, inches above the casing, keeping pace with the creeping submarine. In the beam of his headlamp, he could see Hicks to his right, his arms encircled about the wire glinting in the beam of his diver's lamp. Hicks' beam swung upwards, following the thrumming wire which curved like a bow into the blackness.

They saw it together, a ghostly cylinder swaying slowly across the casing. Whorls of bubbles glinted in its stream as it was hauled through the sea by the submarine twelve feet below it.

Peering downwards, below where the wire was scraping the side of the casing, Woolf-Gault saw the shadowy outline of the starboard fore-plane. On the for'd side of its inboard edge, by the axis-trunnions, the wire was nipped hard against the curve of the pressure hull – or so it seemed. He glanced at his luminous watch: four minutes under pressure already. Hicks decided to use the charge. Even if their special saw and cutter *could* scythe through this case-hardened, cable-laid steel wire, how were they to maintain a foothold in this stream?

Woolf-Gault laid the edge of his hand across the wire at a height level with his face. Hicks, with his free hand, unsnapped a charge from his waist and slapped it on the wire. The charge clamped on hard by its own magnetism. Hicks hung on, his finger poised over the time-switch, while he waited for his partner to return to the escape chamber.

Woolf-Gault let go the wire, faced the bows and, still swimming steadily, judged his re-entry better than he had hoped. A minute later he saw Hicks' flippers probing around the lid – and then he was dropping downwards into the chamber. Woolf-Gault reached up and pulled the hatch shut above their heads.

They waited, tense, trying to regain a rhythmic breathing after their exertions. A few feet below the soles of their feet their shipmates must be standing, Numbr One peering through the spy-hole. In those few seconds Woolf-Gault knew that he had compensated for his failure: he felt a sudden lifting of his spirit, knew that soon this cold fear would be over, his terror conquered. . . .

Clang! That was all – Hicks was flailing with the palm of his hand at the hatch release – and floated again into the blackness. Woolf-Gault followed, chasing the flippers, beating steadily in front of him. Hicks continued swimming, judging his relative movement with the shadowy casing scraping beneath them, like a trout nosing into the weeds. With a swift movement Hicks slid to port, pointing with his hand. Woolf-Gault saw the needle-sharp splinters from the cable, splayed outwards like an old shaving brush. Even from where he was he could see that the wire was only three-quarters severed where it quivered two feet above the casing.

Reeving the bight of the line around the wire, below the cut, Woolf-Gault lashed Hicks loosely against the wire; then he took a leg-purchase round the wire from where it extruded from the trunnion joints of the hydroplane.

Hicks, bracing himself against Woolf-Gault, began methodically to saw. Eleven minutes had already slipped away. Although he had not been working as hard as Hicks,

Woolf-Gault was already feeling weary, unable to relax for an instant against the remoreseless pressure of water.

Hicks' saw-strokes were becoming feebler and more spasmodic as exhaustion overtook him. He and Woolf-Gault had found the knack of bracing against the wire, and Hicks was not going to relinquish his part of the job, unless he was forced to: precious minutes would be spent in relashing each other if they exchanged roles. The strands were flicking apart more easily now – only one to free. Hicks' eyes behind his mask had that dazed, fixed look of frenzied concentration while his weary arm barely moved. If the wire parted uncontrollably, they would both fall backwards as the mine above them sprung free and the weight came off the lower section. Woolf-Gault had to use force to stop Hicks, whose eyes slowly registered understanding: Hicks must hold on to the hatch lid to recover his strength, while Woolf-Gault finished off the strand with his long-handled cutter.

Slipping the bight of the line, Woolf-Gault kept hold of the exhausted man until he was safely at the hatch. He swam back to the wire and, after immense difficulty, succeeded in fixing the cutter in place. Swimming steadily, just clear to port of the wire, he cut through the final strand. It parted with a slick of streaming phosphorescence and, as his head jerked upwards, he glimpsed the hideous cylinder spiralling above him, gliding upwards and aft into the blackness. He tried to continue with his regular breathing, his eyes rivetted on the dark void as he waited for the cataclysmic explosion . . . but nothing, only the sibilant hiss of the sea against the hull, while Hicks trod water, keeping one thumb pointing upwards from the rim of the upturned hatch to show that he was okay.

Woolf-Gault canted his head to throw the light beam upon the starboard plane. The bare end of the wire had whipped backwards to ensnarl its frayed strands inside the upper end of the mooring-wire from which the sinker must be dangling two hundred metres below. He yelled in jubilation inside his headset: they had won the main battle – now they couldn't all be blown to bits.

Slipping the lanyard of the long-handled cutter around his wrist and swimming with slow leg strokes above the starboard plane, he could make out the final snag: if he could prise one of the handles of the cutter beneath the bare end at the same instant as the plane was brought back to rise the nip *could* be freed. If *Orcus* could be going astern at the same time he was certain the wire would clear – but he'd have to hurry for he was beginning to suffer waves of dizzyness. He'd drift backwards and tell Hicks to return to the boat, so that he could explain things to the captain: they must then reflood the tower and have its upper lid ready and open for Woolf-Gault's return when the job was complete.

It took him an eternity to get the message across, for Hicks was about all-in. Hicks then dropped down into the escape chamber. Woolf-Gault, using up much of his failing strength, helped to push the lid down upon its seating before swimming back to the plane. Jamming his right foot against the fairing and leaning against the stream, he managed to prise the end of the long handle of the cutting tool beneath the upper end of the severed wire. Bracing his back, he levered upwards, gently at first, then with all his strength.

The wire *might* have moved . . . If the plane could move upwards, if the boat could go astern *now*, he was ready for the final heave. Oh God, they must hurry, because an irresistible lassitude was creeping over him. Then he remembered the signal. He dare not move the long handle so that he could strike upon the hull with it three times. But yes, the plane *was* moving, creeping upwards, revolving on its axis. *Astern*, oh God, astern, make 'em go astern. He bore down on his heel, straightened his back. Suddenly, he realized that he was slithering forwards, his instinctive balancing against the stream now too pronounced. The boat was losing way. God! She was stopping and in seconds would be gathering sternway. He braced his back and heaved upwards on the handle of the cutter.

Woolf-Gault closed his eyes, gasping for the air which was keeping him alive. He exerted all his strength, yelling inside his mask with the effort. His body slumped and he fell backwards across the lip of the casing.

As his hands clutched at the steel, he felt the boat shuddering beneath him. There was a screeching of metal, a searing pain in the calf of his right leg. As he leaned forward to clear the handle, he saw that the wire had freed, whipping backwards to coil around the calf of his leg. The needle ends of the strands had pierced his suit and a cloud of blood was drifting upwards from his leg. The submarine was dropping away beneath him, a shadowy form vanishing into the abyss. He flailed with his hands, trying to wrench away from the coil. Then he was plunging downwards, spiralling to the sea bed, 520 feet below him.

Head down, feet kicking, the blood spurting from his severed artery, Lieutenant Woolf-Gault mercifully lost consciousness before the deep finally claimed him.

Bill Bowles' eyes were rivetted on the fore-plane indicator. At 1009 the first lieutenant in the fore-ends repeated the order to put the fore-planes in hand and to try applying five degrees of rise. Bowles held his breath: the tell-tale *was* moving, just budging, creeping from 'dive' to 'rise'.

Jimmy was shouting from for'd, 'Go astern!'

The tremor, the agonizing wait, and then, to Bowles' disbelief, the fore-planes were responding to the ten degrees of rise he was transmitting from his column.

Seconds later, as the boat's bows fell away, the planes were back in primary control: the captain ordered half ahead together to give his cox'n a chance to regain control. Bowles was sweating when finally he pulled her out at three hundred and ten feet, while the trimming officer pumped on Ms and trimmed heavily from for'd to aft.

'Stop starboard, slow ahead port,' Farge ordered from where he was standing between the periscopes. 'Sonar report at once any possible mine contacts – however doubtful.'

Bowles glanced over his shoulder at the man who held their lives in his hands. Farge still looked spruce enough, but the strain was beginning to register: there were grey shadows beneath his eyes and a muscle was twitching in the hollow of his left cheek. Apart from his obvious impatience to know what was going on for'd, he was wasting no time in taking *Orcus* clear of this minefield and across to the far side of the eastern channel. It was 1031 when Bowles saw Jimmy clambering through the doorway into the control-room.

'No chance, sir,' Prout said quietly. 'Lieutenant Woolf-Gault must be dead.'

'How d'you know?' Farge's voice, Bowles thought, sounded flat, listless.

'Hicks refused to drain down at once, sir. He signalled from the chambers for us to try the planes in hand again, while he watched Woolf-Gault from the lip of the upper hatch. Able Seaman Hicks banged on the tower with his saw: that's when I yelled for astern, sir.'

Bowles watched the tall, tired lieutenant-commander, with the tight, buttoned-up face, and the younger man, *Orcus'* second-in-command, who was cementing the respect which the ship's company held for him with each day that passed.

'Able Seaman Hicks saw what happened next, sir,' Prout went on. 'The wire began to slide free, but it catapulted off when the nip freed, the end coiling round Woolf-Gault's leg as the boat gathered sternway. Our bows dropped suddenly. The last Hicks saw of Lieutenant Woolf-Gault was his body spiralling downwards, ahead of the boat and dropping into the depths. Hicks then shut the lid, sir.'

'How is he?'

'I was about to drain down when the doc caught sight of Hicks through the port. May have to recompress him sir.'

'How long for?'

'The doc isn't sure yet, sir. He's watching Hicks now.'

The two men remained silent, the captain's dark, restless eyes sweeping round the consoles, checking, always checking.

'Will Hicks be all right?'

'He'll be lucky to avoid a touch of the bends, the doc says. 'Even if Hicks can stand the cold, sir.'

Farge nodded. 'I'm bringing the boat back now, Number One, to the far side of the lanes. Mines permitting, we should be in WP4 by 1430.' He plucked the broadcast mike from the socket on the deckhead. 'While I'm talking to the ship's company,' the captain said quietly, 'get me the latest battery readings.'

20

Washington, 16 May. Captain Trevellion spent the forenoon in the office of the Commander, British Navy Staff, Washington. Rear-Admiral Quarrie wore three hats: not only did he head the British team, he was also the liaison officer to SACLANT and the naval attaché in Washington. He was an astute judge of character and, where women entered the scheme of things, he could pick a good-looker from his Wren officers. The second officer who was his personal aide ran his office and inner sanctum impeccably.

Quarrie had darted off for a working lunch with his opposite number on SACLANT's staff, so Trevellion had snatched an hour's serenity before his ominous appointment at 1500 with Admiral Floyd, head of the American Navy and the First Sea Lord's counterpart. Trevellion and Quarrie had talked for an hour on the telephone this morning with Admiral of the Fleet, Sir Anthony Layde.

Though the perimeter forces, surface and submarine, were now disposed and having moderate success, the nucleus of Operation SDW was splitting apart. *Safari* was adrift from her Zulu waiting position, if the first Typhoon should break out at her earliest predicted sailing time: 0001 17 May. Satellite communications were disrupted for that area – and the less said about that the better. The Pentagon would neither confirm nor deny that five navsats and communication satellites had been destroyed in space. The President was clamping down on the issue, while the crucial days slipped by: the world was trembling in the balance as the protagonists waited upon the results of Operation SD. It was not surprising that tempers were becoming short – and, as Sir Anthony had rasped, 'The buggeration factor is high enough already, Pascoe.'

There was a tap on the door and the Wren second officer entered the room:

'Vice-Admiral Hart is in his car outside, sir. He says he won't come up because Admiral Floyd is back early from the

White House. The admiral would like you both in his office at once.'

Hart had warned Pascoe.

On Trevellion's first encounter with the American Navy's boss and Chairman of the Joint Chiefs of Staff, the admiral had seemed a smooth, distinguished officer at the height of his power. The silver, close-cropped hair, the taut, strong face and the ready smile all suggested a likeable, highly competent officer: an acid tongue, perhaps, if goaded, but the overall impression was one of slick efficiency and geniality.

But Hart had been right . . .

Admiral Floyd was striding to and fro in his office when they entered. There was nothing casual today about the tall, lean figure who, hands clasped behind his back, paced the soft carpet. He wore few ribbons on his well-cut, light-weight blue uniform. His face was an icy, expressionless mask. He did not invite them to sit, but nodded at the captain standing by the projector. The lights dimmed and a chart of the northern hemisphere of the Pacific Ocean shone on the far wall.

'I've just come from the Secretary of Defense, gentlemen. The President's been giving him hell. Right, John.' A motley of red and green crosses were superimposed on the chart.

'Count them, gentlemen,' Floyd said. 'That's CINCPAC's score to date: noon today.'

Trevellion saw that the crosses were bunched in three widely separated areas: three red crosses, the kills by CINCPAC's attack submarines, were sprinkled about the Kurils; one on the edge of the Chukchi Cap inside the Arctic Ocean; one off Komandor Island in the Bering Sea, and one at each end of the Aleutian Trench. Kills by the Pacific Fleet's ASW forces were coloured green and totalled five; three in the wide ocean between Midway and the Aleutians; one in the Great Pacific Basin off the Marshalls, covering Sydney; and one, north of the Marquesas, well within range of either Panama or Los Angeles.

'Eleven, total,' Butch Hart said.

The projector clicked and the North Polar chart glared at them. Then up came the red and green crosses: one red in the Yermak Ridge, another in the Nansen Deep. The only green cross must have been an SSBN on passage, caught by *Carl Vinson*'s Striking Force west of Spitzbergen.

Trevellion felt Floyd's eyes boring into him.

'Nato's bag?' the Chairman of the Joint Chiefs of Staff asked, his mouth a crimped line.

'Three,' Trevellion said.

'Two Yankees and a Delta I. SDE and SDW together total fourteen.'

The short silence was broken by the admiral's terse, clipped sentences

'We've been picking 'em off like a turkey shoot,' he said. 'When, for Pete's sake, is Nato going to deliver, eh?' His chin stuck out aggressively, as he stared at Trevellion. 'The President's impatient. He wants to know when the British are going to carry out their side of the bargain. He's using the hot line and, as he told the Secretary of Defense, he can't mollify the Kremlin much longer. We've told 'em we'll also take out their Typhoons and Alfas – why, for God's sake, are you Limeys being so goddam long about it?'

'Intelligence gives their first Typhoon's earliest sailing date as midnight tonight, sir.'

Admiral Floyd shook his head irritably. 'Put yourself in the President's place, captain. His argument collapses if we fail now. Fourteen SSBNS without a Typhoon just ain't good enough, gentlemen. The Soviet hawks are itching to pitch in, as soon as they can prove we've been bluffing. "We told you," they'll say. "Our Typhoons are inviolate, you haven't been able to sink 'em." Unless you can kill a Typhoon quickly, Captain, the Kremlin will know it can get away with it.'

'A bit more time, sir.'

'How long? The President's got to know.'

'It'll be all over by the twentieth or twenty-first, sir. One way or the other.'

'Seventy-two hours?'

'Yes, sir. The second Typhoon is expected for the twentieth. The President *must* wait, sir – in case we miss our first chance.'

The admiral smacked the back of his fist into the palm of his other hand. 'Okay,' he rapped. 'I'll tell the Secretary.' He rounded on Trevellion once more. 'If you Brits can't come up with the ante,' he snapped, 'you'd better let us in on the act.'

'I can only pass on your comments to the First Sea Lord, sir.'

'Do that, captain.' The admiral strode from the room.

Outside, in the sweltering, humid afternoon, Butch Hart laid his arm across Trevellion's shoulders:

'A Bourbon'll do us both good,' he said.

They walked together towards the senior officers' car park, each with his own thoughts. For the first time in his career, Trevellion felt unsure of the Service in which he served. He had never before had to apologize for the Royal Navy: he found the exercise acutely distasteful.

21

HM Submarine Orcus, 16 May. Although WP4 was only eight miles east of her mining emergency, by the time Farge had taken *Orcus* south to avoid the minefield danger, she did not bottom on the easterly edge of the outward channel until early afternoon. Farge was not the only man to breathe a sigh of relief when she settled again on the two-hundred-metre line. He felt satisfied too, because every outward bound enemy submarine, it seemed, must pass close to him. From midnight onwards, he could expect the Typhoon.

The enemy's surface activity continued to be intense but Farge was feeling a reaction to the strain of the last twelve hours. Leaving Prout in charge in the control-room with a reduced attack team closed up, he retired to his cabin and climbed on to his bunk.

The doctor had decided that he could not leave Hicks in the after ends much longer: in another two hours they would have to decompress him. Only then could Tomkins make a provisional diagnosis, but he would not rule out that Hicks might have suffered the bends.

Farge had been touched by the troops' reaction to Woolf-Gault's death. After the midday snack the cox'n had told him of how they felt. Woolf-Gault's act of gallantry had, in some curious way, bound the company more closely together. Many individuals felt twinges of shame and remorse at the way they had treated the poor guy – Farge included. The doctor and Bill Bowles must be the only men who could probably claim a clear conscience. *Orcus* had been lucky, but the might-have-beens were causing Farge moments of bitter self-reproach. He was dropping into a half-sleep when Sims tapped on his doorway.

'Contact, sir: a Victor II, bearing 250°, range eight thousand yards. She's diving.'

'Sure?'

'Confirmed, sir. Three shafts.'

'Same position, on the two-hundred-metre line?'

'Identical, sir. We'll get her course and speed when she passes abeam: refining is difficult with all this activity in the lanes.'

Sims was back ·again fifteen minutes later. An Alfa was diving in the same position. She seemed to be following the Victor II, now dived and steaming at twenty-five knots on a course of 050° up the same swept channel.

Farge's tired brain hardly registered the reports: the Victor II, a torpedo-firing fleet submarine, was the fastest nuke in the world after the Alfa who, with her forty-two knots, could outpace anything Nato could put to sea. They were probably northward-bound to do battle with those Nato boats deployed across the gaps.

If *Orcus* had not bottomed for most of the time, she would be out of amps by now; it was sixty-six hours since the last battery charge. The last readings confirmed his fears: thirty-nine per cent remaining. How much longer dare he continue without charging? For the hundredth time since embarking on this hair-brained mission, the image of the most precious person in the world drifted into his imagination. He did not even have a snap of her, no photograph he could prop on his minute desk, as did most submarine cos, yet she was unbelievably close to him, his Lorna with the smouldering eyes. What would she be doing back in Spinneycombe? Kicking off her muddy wellies in the porch after seeing to her lambs? Would she be working those beautiful acres of Exmoor which she cherished with such devotion, or walking along the banks of the brook chuckling past the farmhouse? And on the long dresser against the wall to the right of the open hearth would she have filled the earthenware jug and the small vase with flowers as she had promised? She'd keep them always fresh, she'd said: the jug for everyone in *Orcus*; the vase, for herself and him. She was sure to have bluebells which she pinched every year from his father's spinney bordering the two properties.

And how would she be coping? Worrying herself silly, or serene, committing their future to the God in whom she trusted, to whom she would be constantly praying? Farge wondered whether she told her mother of their secret, of the miracle which even now might be burgeoning within her. The taut lines about his mouth relaxed and he drifted into sleep, his fingers reaching beneath his shirt for the small cross which Lorna had slipped into his bag at the Carnburn Hotel.

'Captain in the control-room!'

Julian Farge rolled from his bunk. It was 1604 as he scrambled through the doorway of his cabin to find Tim Prout waiting for him by the periscopes, a grin on his face:

'*That's her*! Chris is certain, sir.'

Farge crossed to the sound-room, watched the sonar team refining the contact: nine thousand yards, bang in the centre of the channel. Sims' face glanced upwards, his eyes shining:

'Can't be anything else: shaft and blade counts all tally. The Typoon's signature, sir.'

'Certain?'

'Positive. The only boat with that many reactors.'

'Carry on refining.' Farge moved swiftly to the centre of his control-room. He plucked the broadcast mike from its socket:

'Captain speaking,' he announced briskly. 'Action stations, action stations. We're on to our Typhoon. We'll unstick now, take a look, then tail her. Remember, Ultra Quiet State.' He paused, listening to his men pouring from their bunks. 'And good luck, everyone. That's all – until we've finished the job.'

He watched them hustling to their action stations: the attack team, the cox'n on his planes, the wrecker, CPO Tom Grady, calmly competent at his panel. David Powys closed up silently behind him, the action oow.

'Break her out gently, chief,' Farge said. 'I *must* get an eyeball identification.'

'May I pump, sir?'

'On the way up to periscope depth. I'll stop at a hundred feet, for you to catch a trim.'

Farge's glance was everywhere, monitoring, checking, as they brought *Orcus* up from deep for the vital periscope sighting. Foggon took four minutes to correct his trim at one hundred feet, while the sonar team continued refining their prime contact. The first lieutenant, the attack team coordinator, stood behind his plotters, watching the display and presenting the picture to his captain.

'Happy, chief?' Farge asked. 'Don't dip me. If you break surface, you'll spoil our whole day.'

'Trim's fine, sir,' Foggon said.

'Periscope depth, sixty feet. Slow ahead together.'

Farge could feel the thumping of his heart as the submarine glided steadily upwards under Bowles' competent charge.

'Eighty feet . . . seventy . . .'

The picture from sonar and the plots was crystallizing in Farge's mind: five sweepers ahead of the Typhoon, range 4,200 yards; two destroyers astern, unidentified as yet. . .

Farge snapped his fingers, 'Up attack.'

The slender tube hissed from its well.

'Sixty-five feet.'

Farge opened the handles, pressed his forehead into the eyepiece, oblivious now to the murmured commands behind him.

'Put me on.'

'*On*,' the periscope reader called out. 'Red 165, sir.'

'*Breaking*.'

The grey-green undulations beneath the surface, the intensifying light . . .

'Fifty-eight feet.'

The lens broke through: there was the grey sky, the breaking wave crests.

'Bearing *that*. . . '

In those few seconds he caught sight of her a few degrees to port: a gigantic black whale, her long rectangular fin set well aft, a frothing wall of water pushing ahead of her rounded snout. Farge spun on his heel, his eyes transmitting to his brain the surface picture. He snapped shut the handles.

'Down periscope. Two hundred feet.'

'Fifty-seven feet, sir. Can I speed up?'

'*No*. Flood Q.'

'Fifty-six.'

'I'm 030° on her starboard bow. Five sweepers ahead of her, estimated range three thousand yards.'

He felt the bow-down angle coming on as Q took effect and Bowles planed her down.

'Sixty-two feet.'

'Stop flooding Q.'

'Seventy feet, sir.' The cox'n was pulling back on his column, controlling the bubble to prevent a stern break-surface.

'Seventy-five feet . . . eighty . . . eighty-five.'

'Blow Q.'

As the three and a half tons of additional seawater was blown from the emergency diving tank, he saw Bowles easing back on his column. The bubble began moving for'd.

'Stop blowing Q. Vent Q inboard.'

The roar of Q's foul air entering the boat overwhelmed everything, drowning the sonar reports; then came the calm, as the tank emptied. The cox'n, his eyes glued to his inclinometer, was easing back on his column. The silence was broken only by the murmured reports, the background hum of motors, the whisper of the ventilation. *Orcus* was gliding silently north-east at two hundred feet, the cox'n holding her while Farge nudged the boat ahead with short bursts on slow one.

'187, contact relative bearing red 95, sir.' The Typhoon was abeam and the sound-room had her taped. 'She's diving now.'

'Any other contacts?'

'Two destroyers, following up astern of her, on either quarter, probable Krivaks. Five Natya sweepers ahead, bearing red 40.'

'Our position, pilot?'

'Just entering the channel, sir. Time 1624. Ninety metres of water under us.' Following this monster, *Orcus* would be safe from the mine menace. Twenty minutes later, sonar reported:

'187, contact bearing red 50, range five thousand yards. Speed confirmed, fifteen knots.'

The Typhoon was drawing ahead and, presumably proceeding at her maximum effective sonar speed, was opening the range. Farge slicked back his black hair, rubbed the palm of his hand across his jaw.

'You can pump now, chief,' he said. 'I'll stay in the Krivaks' wakes until you've got your trim right. Slow ahead together.'

Eight minutes later the trimming officer was satisfied, the boat holding at three hundred feet while Farge grouped up and increased speed to twelve knots in the wake of the Typhoon.

By 1700, losing distance at the rate of three miles each hour, *Orcus* was already three and a half miles astern. Farge remained tense, hands in pockets, feet astride between the periscopes, watching his attack teams concentrating upon their work. The sound-room was methodically pumping out the data for the overall picture he needed: at a probable depth of four hundred feet the gigantic submarine was proceeding to her war station on a course of 050° at a speed of fifteen knots. With her reactors she could keep this up for months. *Orcus*, grouped up, with only thirty-seven per cent of battery power remaining, could not follow at this speed for long.

'The Krivaks are breaking away, sir,' reported Tim Prout. 'They're going on ahead and overtaking the sweepers who seem to be slowing down and turning to port.'

Farge eased down to allow the minesweepers to pass over *Orcus*. They cleared to port, and then he gradually worked up speed again to twelve knots. The Typhoon was on her own now, her escorting Krivaks cracking on ahead.

'Concentrate on the Typhoon,' he ordered. 'Don't lose her.'

Then at 1720 the 187 reported that the contact was drawing across to port. 'Relative bearing red 20, sir,' Sims called from the sound-room.

'She'll be altering to clear the minefield,' Murray said from his chart table.

'We'll have to risk cutting the corner,' Farge murmured. 'And we'll save distance. Port five.'

'Target's settled to her new course,' Prout said. '335°.'

'I'll keep fine on her port quarter, in case she streams a nasty. Steer 335°.'

The large minefield to the eastward was drawing clear astern when the 187 sonar reported that the Typhoon was altering course again and increasing speed. By 1830 she was four miles ahead and gaining with every precious minute which passed.

'Steer 340°,' Farge ordered wearily. 'We'll get in dead astern of her and hang on until as long as the battery holds out.'

He glanced around his control-room at the men who were nearing the end of their tether: already mistakes were occurring and his officers were strained to the limit, double-checking. Farge dared not increase to full speed. *Orcus* had been grouped up now for nearly two hours and he had ordered battery readings every half-hour; at 2000 only twenty-four per cent remained. Farge, sitting in his chair abaft the attack periscope, remained silent, sharing with his men the agony of despair.

The picture was clear enough now: the Typhoon was drawing away and there was nothing more that *Orcus* could do.

It was a matter of guesswork when the monster would start to disappear from the sonar plots. Her course seemed unlikely to take her to her war station, for she was heading for the centre of Spitzbergen. Somewhere ahead of her must be the two Krivaks but they had vanished from the plots. The best that Farge could do was to signal this miserable state of affairs before he either lost her or ran out of amps.

Three-quarters of an hour later, Sims was slithering across the deck, his strained face trying to conceal any signs of elation: they were all becoming wary of false hopes.

'Her blade and shaft counts are decreasing, sir.'

Murray called across:

'Her 2100 position puts her on the edge of the two-hundred-metre line, sir.'

Farge rose wearily from his chair and moved across to the chart table.

'Here, sir, on the tip of the bank.'

Farge traced the spur of shallower water protruding to the north-west. In another eighteen miles the Typhoon would be rounding the tip.

'She's settling again to fifteen knots,' Sims called from the sound-room.

By 2100 the Typhoon was twelve miles ahead and the sonar was having difficulty in holding her. Despair quickly replaced the optimism in *Orcus*' control-room.

'She's altering to the north, sir,' Sims called from the sound-room.

'That's it,' Farge murmured. 'This is the best we can do. She's rounding up clear of the shallow bank. We'll lose her soon. Sims, refine as best you can, and ask the chief radio supervisor to report to me.' He turned to Murray. 'How far off is she now?'

The tall figure of the Chief RS approached from the radio-room.

'Chief, we'd better prepare our flash report,' Farge said.

During the next hour, while the sound of the Typhoon faded to the northward, the sonar team produced the most accurate state report of which they were capable: the only other contact was distant and bearing 350°, ten degrees to port of the Typhoon. They could not classify, except to identify the contact as fast-revving and probably geared-turbine. At 2205 *Orcus* crossed the Typhoon's track.

'Group down,' Farge ordered, trying to conceal his weariness. 'Slow ahead together.' He brought his submarine round to the north-east for a final refinement. Typhoon had not altered course or speed.

'No contacts, watcher,' the sound-room reported. 'Target bearing still appears to be the same.'

'Typhoon's course 010°, sir,' Prout confirmed. 'Speed fifteen knots.'

'The submarine is returning to periscope depth,' Farge announced. 'Stand by to raise the W/T mast.' He glanced towards the Chief RS who was propped against the door of his radio room.

'Ready, chief?'

'All set, sir.'

'Stand by to raise ECM mast.'

'No contacts, sector seventy-seventy,' the 187 sonar reported. 'Target bearing still the same.'

'Ten up,' Farge ordered the cox'n. 'Fifty-eight feet.'

Their mission was nearly completed: transmit the flash report and *Orcus* could creep away on her last amps to the westward and the open spaces for her vital charge. Then home, if the enemy did not pick up the W/T transmission. It was up to Janner Coombes now.

'150 feet . . .'

'Sector sweeping, seventy-seventy, no contacts.'

Farge felt a sudden anti-climax. It was nearly over, the tension, the days of twitch. He'd snatch a quick look while the masts were up. If the sea was still rough, there'd be no risk of a mast sighting. He'd go deep, slide out, send the troops to watch-diving to catch up on their zeds.

Bowles was as rock-like as ever, planing her up: Foggon had her, was flooding normally, compensating for her bodily trim.

'Seventy feet.'

'Raise W/T and ECM masts. Up search.'

He watched the masts and the periscope sliding upwards, gleaming in the white lighting. Wearily he opened the handles, shoved his forehead into the eyepieces.

'Breaking.'

'Make the flash report,' Farge commanded.

He swung round on his low-power periscope, covering the whole horizon. From behind him, he registered the whirring and the crackling from the radio-room, as the Chief RS pushed out twice the vital signal, the message which would bring *Safari* in from deep field, the flash for which Coombes would be waiting – even though the enemy had sailed twelve hours earlier than expected.

'ECM, scanning contact red 20.'

Farge flicked to high power. 'Put me on.'

The lens swung to port, was held steady by the reader.

'On.'

'Flash report passed,' the radio-room reported. 'Good signal strength.'

Farge felt his Adam's apple mounting in his gorge: in his field of vision three dots showed, low on the horizon.

'Bearing *that*,' he snapped.

'Red 45.'

Farge tried to keep his voice level as he snapped shut the handles:

'Down all masts,' he ordered. 'Three hundred feet.' He watched in silence as the tubes slid down into their wells.

'Port ten, steer 240°,' he commanded. 'We'll slip away to the south-west.' He turned and faced his first lieutenant:

'Ultra Quiet State remains in force, Number One,' he said. 'Three helicopters are on that bearing.'

22

HM Submarine Safari, 16 May. They were playing Beat That
at the end of the wardroom table while they waited for their
captain to rejoin them in their interrupted round of Liars. It
was 2225 when Janner Coombes finally returned from *Safari's*
control-room to this after-dinner ritual which he was loath to
miss: to his way of thinking, this half-hour was a safety-valve
which did nothing but good. He took his place on the pilot's
left: Farquharson was a crafty player. Coombes had already
lost two lives this evening, his two matches in the centre of the
table proving the point. Number One, Lieutenant-Commander Stuart Hamilton, led off, rattling the poker dice in one
of the pots.

Coombes enjoyed this moment, one of the interludes during
patrol when he could get to know his officers. Malcolm Gunn,
Safari's indefatigable MEO, had only this evening felt able to
leave his manoeuvring-room since the steam-leak breakdown.
All was well and *Safari* had been cracking along at thirty knots
until 1900 when Coombes reduced to twenty while approaching North Cape. Since the enemy had invaded northern
Norway, hydrophones were suspected off the area.

Though Coombes had remained on a course of 081°, the
breakdown had lost precious hours: even at full speed he could
not possibly make Position Zulu by midnight tonight. He was
trying to make the area on time, but *Safari* could not be nearer
than 180 miles south-west of Zulu by 2400. At 0500 17 May she
would still be sixty miles due south of the position, but this last
minute alteration by cutting the corner was a calculated risk he
had taken.

Coombes felt frustrated to the tits: not only was he adrift on
his waiting position, but coming up for the W/T routines was
reducing his speed made good. From midnight onwards, *Orcus*
could be coming on the air; again his thoughts wandered to
Farge and his chances down in the inlet . . .

'Your throw, sir,' Farquharson was saying, passing him the

two pots. 'Kings on tens.'

'Sorry,' Coombes said, accepting the call and glancing at the MEO on Farquharson's right. 'What did you give him, Malcolm?'

'Kings on nines, sir,' Gunn said, grinning and looking his captain straight in the eye. Coombes tipped up the edges of the pots.

The chuckles round the table ceased as Luke Wesley, the signal communications officer, hurried into the wardroom and stopped by Coombes' elbow:

'Flash report, sir,' he blurted as he passed the message pad into Coombes' outstetched hand.

PRECEDENCE: FLASH
SECURITY CLASSIFICATION: SECRET
FROM: CINCEASTLANT
TO: SAFARI
INFO: SACLANT, COMSUBLANT, COMSUBEASTLANT, COMSTRIFOR, COMSTRIGRUTWO
DTG: 162228 (ZULU) MAY

TYPHOON 70° 48′ NORTH 33° 36′ EAST AT 162219 (ZULU) MAY. COURSE 010° SPEED 15. MESSAGE ENDS.

Shoving the pad across to his first lieutenant, Coombes exploded:

'Bloody hell! She's sailed half a day early!'

His chair fell backwards as he hurried into the control-room, his officers following him. Ignoring the sound risk from the possible hydrophones off North Cape, Coombes took *Safari* immediately up to thirty knots.

'Course direct for Zulu?' he called across to Farquharson at the chart table. Then he turned towards the scc, 'Port five.'

As he reached for the intercom, Farquharson called across:

'066°, sir. I'm laying off Typhoon's track, giving her fifteen knots.'

'Steer 066°,' Coombes ordered.

He wished to reach every man in his ship's company, from the cox'n in the control-room to the JR tucked away in the remotest corner of his fighting machine. He flicked the switch and spoke into the mike of the broadcast system:

'Captain speaking,' he rasped. 'We're on to our man – twelve hours early. The Typhoon has sailed and is heading north. We're pushing along now after her. I've altered course to intercept her, but we can't possibly be within sonar range before dawn, even if she sticks at fifteen knots. I'll be going to action stations during the morning watch. I'll be asking a lot of you, so get your heads down and get in a good meal. That's all.' The intercom snicked and he stretched up to replace the mike.

'I've laid off our tracks, sir,' Farquharson said.

Coombes crossed to the chart table. The navigator had traced out the two tracks and the hourly distances: by 0600 tomorrow morning, the Typhoon should be thirty-five miles ahead. Coombes crossed to the scc and spoke to the scow:

'Stay on "George",' he said, 'and shake me at 0400.'

23

HM Submarine Safari, 17 May. CPO Scanes, MEAOW, checked the lower-level watchkeeper and, after handing over his watch to the MEAOW of D watch, was thankful to get the hell out of it. He was sweating from the heat of the lower level and his ears were singing from the scream of the turbos. He craved a shower before snatching an early breakfast. But before going for'd to the SRS' mess on 2 deck, he'd have a word with the wrecker. CPO Hank Botham, third in the ratings' hierarchy in the propulsion department, looked after things for'd of the tunnel. He was a friend of Scanes' from training days and often helped out when Scanes needed to switch the junior stokers. Botham liked to be near the SCC now that the Old Man had closed up the cox'n, Bull Clint, on the planes.

The captain was pushing it and the boat was batting along at thirty-plus. There had been an atmosphere of subdued excitement throughout the boat since the skipper's broadcast at 0400. When he eased down to twenty knots, sonar had immediately picked up a faint contact dead ahead to the north-east. However it was so faint that the operator of the searcher had decided it was spurious – and, anyway, the contact was fading to the northward. Scanes negotiated the tunnel and passed through to the for'd end. He'd sneak in to the control-room to see what was on.

The twitch syndrome was certainly evident in the ship's overcrowded nerve centre. Orders crackled through the control-room and by the way Coombes was prowling about his cage, his fingers twirling his moustachios, things were hotting up – some unfortunate sod was catching the rough edge of the Old Man's tongue.

'Shouldn't go any further, chief,' murmured Luke Wesley, the signal communications lieutenant. 'It's dangerous.'

'What's going on, sir? Back aft, we heard that sonar's picked up something.'

The two men were standing on the starboard side of the

control-room, by the ladder down to 2 deck and next to the cage protecting the masts. To the right of them was the snort system and for'd of it the chart table sprawled over by Farquharson's lanky frame. Above the navigator's head was his SINS, its dials and instruments projecting to the bulkhead door and the passage leading for'd. The captain was standing between the two athwartship periscopes and waiting for the boat to lose way. His arms hung loosely from his massive chest; his fiery beard masked the form of his face from which his piercing, blue eyes flicked around the control-room. Coombes was concentrating upon the diving panel in front of which Hank Botham was seated, serenely coping with the situation. On Botham's left, Bull Clint was on the planes, his hands off the column as 'George', the automatic hydroplane control, kept *Safari* ten feet either side of the ordered depth, her fore-planes locked, as she thrashed along. 'George' was safer than Clint on the planes: if he sneezed *Safari* would loop the loop at this speed. Luke Wesley was leaning towards Scanes.

'The sound-room picked up two contacts at 0500, chief, when the captain reduced for a listen. Both were fine on the port bow. They merged, but were definite and at about fifty miles. We're easing down now for another listen.'

Scanes saw that it was 0612 by the clock on the diving panel. The SCOW, standing behind Botham, had his eyes glued to the log – twenty-four knots and still walking back as the submarine lost way.

'At six, go six,' Coombes rapped, his large head canted as he waited impatiently for the first sonar reports. 'Steering in hand.' The hooter blared as the SCC rang on the revolutions for twenty knots – and Scanes felt the kick in his guts when the sound-room came in with its report from the main sonar.

'2001 new passive contacts, bearing red 52 and red 47.'

The tension became electric as the sonar team called out their bearings. Scanes saw the stiffening of the plotters' backs where they were tracking on the displays on the port side, abaft the cox'n. To their left was the action information console, in front of which the three operators were silently tracking the sonar reports which the AIC computer analysed from the data streaming in from the sensors. Standing behind them was the AIO, Lieutenant Kenneth Whalley, watching points while alongside him was the Fire Control Officer: Lieutenant-Commander Simon Grenville, lean and deceptively nonchalant, as he supervised his two operators, a new able seaman whom Scanes did not know, and the smiling Joe Robinson, the good-natured West Indian whom everyone liked. Their displays glowed in front of them, blue-green circles, served by the fire control computer which accepted the processing of the tracking from AIO. And behind them all stood the immobile figure of the first lieutenant, Lieutenant-Commander Stuart Hamilton, quiet, authoritative, the exact complement to their ebullient captain. Hamilton was a respected Jimmy and, as attack co-ordinator, was skilled in presenting the tactical picture to his captain.

The clock showed 0627 before the plots produced their sit-rep page numbers, 332, 333 and 334, though the last, well to the north and very faint, was being disregarded.

'Sector on the net,' Coombes ordered. 'Come right, steer 080°.'

'Coming right, 080°.'

The refining continued until at 0632 the captain was satisfied. He brought *Safari* left again, recrossing 332 and 333's tracks. For a brief moment he stood back, then his head jerked up as he made his decision:

'That's the Typhoon all right, Number One: the right number of shafts and the correct signature. She must have speeded up since the flash and track 333 must be an escort. They never told us about her.'

'Confirmed Victor II, sir. No doubt about it: three shafts. She's ten miles astern, on the Typhoon's port quarter.'

'How far's the Victor ahead of us?'

'Twenty-one miles at 0600.'

'We'll overtake at fifteen knots, if I crack on again.'

'Affirmative. At 0700, she'll be at twelve thousand yards.'

Scanes saw that the captain had already made up his mind: though *Safari*'s prime target was a Typhoon how the hell was *Safari* to get at her without being picked up first by the Victor II?

'Come left, steer 090°,' Coombes ordered. 'Reactor plant to full power state.'

'Manoeuvring – control,' the scow repeated. 'Assume the full power state.'

'Manoeuvring . . . roger. Assume the full power state.'

Seconds later the manoeuvring-room came back, and Coombes swung towards the SCC:

'Steering in auto. Revolutions for thirty knots.' He turned to his first lieutenant:

'Send the hands to breakfast, Number One. We'll be within twelve thousand yards of the Victor by 0700.' He grinned as he stretched up for the intercom. 'Their Lordships won't like it,' he murmured, 'but we've got to sink this bugger first.'

Scanes turned abruptly and began shinning down the steps to two deck: he'd have to hustle if he was to eat before the Old Man went to action stations.

Janner Coombes, in clean shirt and tie, hands in pockets, feet astride, stood back from his attack team. The first lieutenant, Stuart Hamilton, was silently checking the operators concentrating over their instruments. The FCO, Simon Grenville, as rigid as a statue, was watching his console and his two operators; the Action Information officer, who was also *Safari's* TASO, Kenneth Whalley, was checking the refining of the past hour's sonar-ranging on the Victor II. Coombes had veered *Safari* back and forth to provide broad tracking and now the computer was presenting its final solution.

Coombes felt confident: if the Victor had not picked him up by now – she was 11,500 yards at this instant – he was certain he could sink her. He had worked up *Safari* to his satisfaction and felt master of this superb fighting machine. His team was part of him now, instinctively anticipating his thinking: a restrained calm pervaded the control-room of his hunter-killer as she swooped silently into the attack on her unsuspecting prey. . . . The SCOW, Luke Wesley, was in the bandstand supervising Hank Botham, on the SCC. Bull Clint was for once silent, his arms folded, his eyes fixed on his instruments, as he supervised the auto-trimming. The fore-planes were locked, the after-planes automatically keeping the submarine within ten feet of the ordered depth of six hundred feet, while she hurtled northwards. *Safari* was one of the most silent, most efficient hunter-killers in the world, Coombes was sure of that.

'The Victor's weaving back to starboard, sir, range 11,000.'

Coombes nodded, calm now, his reactions geared to as fine a

pitch as they would ever be, the tactical picture etched on to his mind. In two minutes' time the Typhoon would be sixteen miles ahead; the Victor II 10,500 yards ahead of *Safari* and eleven miles astern of the Typhoon's port quarter. The Victor was weaving to keep clear of her consort's wake and *Safari* was working relentlessly into her attacking position inside the two wakes. The Victor was being overhauled at a relative speed of fifteen knots though, to keep in station under continuous weave, she was obliged to steam faster than the Typhoon : the CEP was continually confirming the Victor at twenty knots.

'0730, sir,' the navigator was calling across: 'Range 10,300 yards.'

Coombes could wait no longer: the Victor might at any moment pick him up and retaliate.

'Action stations! Plant at half-power state. Revolutions for twenty knots. At twenty, go twenty.'

Luke Wesley repeated his captain's command through the intercom and seconds later the bulkhead doors were shut, each compartment sealed off from its neighbour.

'No buggering about, Number One: I'll go straight in. Stand by Tigerfish attack.'

'Track 333 is target,' Stuart Hamilton reported as Coombes leaned forward to watch the command display, the cathode ray tube upon which the target's noise was visually projected. As the next fifteen minutes slipped by, the sonar reports and the monitoring of the plotters mounted to a crescendo while the two spots on the displays converged. Coombes swung *Safari* across the Victor's position for the last time, to present the sonar with the best ranging opportunities.

'Bring numbers one and two tubes to readiness state one,' Grenville, the FCO, ordered.

In the tube-space, the crew were opening the valves and making their final checks: and then the tube-ready indicators were glowing red in the fire control console. So far, so good: track 333 was down to 6,400 yards.

'At fifteen, go fifteen,' Coombes rapped. 'Fore-planes and steering in hand.'

'AIO checks correct,' Kenneth Whalley, the AIO, reported.

'Fire control checks correct,' from Grenville.

'Try the final solution,' Hamilton snapped. 'Course 085°,

speed twenty-six, range 5,900 yards.'

Coombes had been through the drill so often before, coaxing, bullying his team to as near perfection as he could get them. But now . . . the tension was almost tangible as the moment dragged closer. At five thousand yards he would fire. At six hundred yards to go Hamilton's final solution was coming up correctly. The computers were confirming the last refinements and the sonar reports were streaming in, a familiar background, as Coombes watched the glowing displays: the spokes and crosses were slowly converging, but range was the crux. Simon Grenville was stretching out his arm, his finger poised above the fire button.

'Contact 333, red 10. Range, five thousand yards.'

'Ready to fire, sir.' Stuart Hamilton was ice cool as he made his final report.

'Stand-by to fire,' Coombes snapped, his eyes on the fire control console.

'Cut a firing bearing,' Whalley commanded his team.

'Sonar cut!' The sonar controller's reply was immediate.

A few seconds to check the cut and then Coombes commanded briskly:

'*Fire!*'

Grenville's finger stabbed at the fire button.

Five seconds . . . five, four, three . . . then the unmistakable *phumph*! as the water slammed behind the torpedo in its tube. The boat shivered.

'At ten, go ten,' Coombes ordered. He'd ease her down, just in case. The clock showed 0747. All eyes were on the fire control console and its operators while they guided the Tigerfish towards its target.

'Weapon under guidance,' Grenville reported. In the tense silence, only his brisk commands and the voices of the guidance operators could be heard while the seconds ticked away: five minutes at the torpedo's running speed should do it. . . .

The boat was now at a two-degree bow-down angle; Bull Clint was easing back on his fore-planes while the boat began to lose way.

'Step the weapon to a course of 357°,' Hamilton commanded crisply, his eyes glued to the spokes glowing on the screens before him.

'2001, contact 357°, range 4,600 yards,' the sonar controller reported.

'Arm the weapon,' Hamilton snapped – and seconds later: 'Select "activate".'

'Weapon has acquired and is attacking,' Grenville rapped.

Coombes glanced at the clock: 0749, another three minutes. They'd chopped the wire: the fish was homing on its own . . .

At that instant the plot cut in brusequely:

'Target track 333 altering outwards to port. Turning towards . . . range 4,200 yards.'

Coombes caught his breath: the Victor had picked up the noise of the Tigerfish.

The digital clock was remorselessly ticking away the seconds . . . then, at 0750 the unmistakable reasonance of an 'active' transmission blasted their world.

'2001, active contact 355°, range 4,600 yards.'

The reverberations hummed in their ears as the enemy's pinging struck home.

'Weapon has missed . . . is slowing left for re-attack,' Hamilton called out. The spokes had drawn apart on the scans, steadied, converged again.

'Weapon has re-acquired and is re-attacking,' Hamilton reported, his voice steady.

'God,' Coombes whispered to himself. 'The torpedo is wrong for depth – it's passing over the top of the Victor.'

'Loss of guidance commands on the weapon,' Grenville reported.

Coombes closed his eyes: at any moment, the Victor would be firing her own torpedoes.

'Six down,' he rapped. 'Assume reactor full-power state, revolutions for thirty knots! Deep diving stations, one thousand feet. Lock the fore-planes; after-planes in auto. Take her down, Number One.'

'Loud explosion on the target bearing,' the sonar controller announced. 'Implosion sounds on target bearing, 354°.'

Coombes could not resist his own contribution to the cheers echoing in the control-room.

'Quiet,' he shouted. 'She can still have fired her fish.'

As *Safari* planed swiftly down to the depths, they could all hear the hideous sounds of the enemy breaking up and collapsing beneath the pressures of the ocean: the buckling bulkheads, the screech of tortured steel, the exploding tanks. The cheers ceased as suddenly as they begun.

It was 0801 when *Safari* reached her ordered depth. The breaking-up noises gradually faded – and the silence in the control-room was broken by Coombes asking quietly:

'Range of track 332, please, the Typhoon? Switch to sector.'

'2001, tracking . . .'

He was surprised at the length of time the sound-room was taking to find the monster. Then the sonar controller came in:

'2001, track 332 very faint, 358°. Estimated range 37,000 yards and fading.'

Coombes moved back to his position by the periscopes.

He turned towards Hamilton: 'We can't let the Typhoon slip away: six up. Five hundred feet.'

Safari flew up to five hundred feet, sweeping upwards like an aircraft.

'2001, contact fading on 008°. Last counts give thirty-plus.'

The sound-room held the contact for seven minutes longer. By 0819 the Typhoon had vanished from the displays.

In sinking her first opponent *Safari* had alerted her prime target: the Typhoon was lost, tearing away to the northward. Elation turned to despair as Coombes took his submarine up to maximum safe speed after his invisible foe. He could do nothing but hold on, hoping that something would slow the enemy down. Whatever happened, he must resist calling for more power: a propulsion failure now through excessive revs would be fatal, not only for the success of the mission, but to *Safari*'s own safety.

Because of his blind impetuosity, all that *Orcus* had endured, all that Julian Farge might have risked, all that the old O boat might now be enduring, was for nothing. He sent the hands to watch-diving, then strode angrily to his cabin.

24

HM Submarine Orcus, 17 May. Julian Farge was too weary for
sleep. He lay stretched on his bunk, his eyes closed, his mind
flitting from problem to problem, incapable of concentration.

Since that chopper sighting at 2108 when *Orcus* turned to the
south-west after the flash report, life had become surprisingly
calm. Enemy ASW forces must have been in the area to the
north-west but, apart from the ECM contact, there had been
nothing. *Orcus* was creeping away steadily on a course of 240° at
slow one to conserve her precious amps. He'd hold on until he
could delay the decision no longer – the air was becoming foul
and the battery was down to a dangerous level – for every hour
he could gain towards the vastness of the Norwegian sea
increased *Orcus'* chances of evading the enemy's inevitable
retaliation. Both he and FOSM had understood the suicidal risk
of *Orcus* sticking up her masts on the Soviet doorstep. The flash
report was bound to be picked up and fixed within seconds of
the transmission being whacked out. But if *Orcus* could endure
only a few more hours . . .

He had ordered half-hourly battery checks: the 0100 reading
gave eight per cent remaining. He had been unable to snort
since he'd got the box up off Vardø, at 2000 on 13 May, over
seventy-six hours ago. If he had not bottomed almost
continually, he would never have made it, particularly after
tailing the Typhoon, grouped up for two and a half hours, at
full speed during the last burst. This final caning of the battery
had reduced things to this twitch level – but what was worrying
him more than the running down of the battery was the parlous
state of the life-support system.

Orcus was running short of candles, the vital element for
oxygen replenishment, the burning of which supplied the
oxygen and eliminated the lethal carbon monoxide. She was
also down on her CO_2 absorbent, and its rationing was causing
splitting headaches. The air was foul and breathing was
becoming an effort. If he had not at the outset banned

unnecessary talking, movement and all cooking, they would now be in a mess. But the cold was getting them down most, with no heating and minimal heat from the reduced lighting.

'Captain in the control-room!'

He slid from his bunk in answer to the traditional summons. Sims, the oow, was leaning against the door to the sound-room:

'Watcher's got a contact, sir: 350°, steam turbine and closing on a steady bearing. We're classifying.'

Farge went back to his cabin for his sweater and by 0136 sonar came up with the disquieting news that the counts were confirming the signature of a Leningrad ASW carrier. Five minutes later, the sound-room picked up three more contacts on the same sector, probable destroyers, all at slow speed.

'An ASW hunting group,' Farge murmured. 'Chris, shake Alastair, Number One, the Chief and WEO, please. I have the ship.'

Ten minutes later, Farge and his key officers were grouped round the chart table, Chris Sims again taking over the watch. David Powys had spread his battery graphs across the chart table.

'We're down to 6·7 per cent. The curve falls away sharply at the end.' His fingers followed the falling curve, traced the sharp dip to zero.

'At this discharge rate, how long have we got?' Julian asked quietly.

'Difficult to say, sir.' Powys was fiddling with his pocket calculator. 'Perhaps five hours, sir. We're hardly using anything at these revs, slow one, grouped down.'

'What speed are we making good, Alastair?'

'Four knots – and we've still got a bit of westerly set under us,' Murray said.

'Happy with your DR?'

'Reasonably so, sir. We switched SINS off after the flash report.'

Farge reached up for the dividers. 'Five hours at four knots,' he murmured. 'Twenty miles at the most, gentlemen.' He measured off the distance from the latitude scale. Sticking one point of the dividers in the 0136 DR position, he traced out an arc to the west and south.

'Twenty miles short of Vardø,' he indicated, 'and . . .' The point of the dividers swung southwards, then began crossing the shallower bank where they had sighted the Norwegian fishing-boats aeons ago. A spur of the bank stretched north-west with soundings of 165 metres and less.

'Five hundred feet and less,' he said softly, leaving unspoken the thought in their minds. 'Everywhere else, it's deep water.' He looked up and met his senior officers' glances. Then he traced out a course to the centre of the spur. 'I propose we make for that bank,' he said. 'If we can reach it with what's left of the battery's capacity, we can try to snort there – as safely as anywhere else. We might suck in enough air to sit it out a bit longer on the bottom, while the heat passes over. If we're left in peace we might be able to stick it out until tomorrow's twilight.'

'Will you tell the troops of your intentions?' Tim Prout asked.

'Not yet,' Farge said. 'Nor the other officers. No point in worrying them.' He grinned ruefully. 'Miracles can still happen – and thanks, all of you.' He moved back into the centre of the control-room.

'Port ten,' he ordered Sims. 'Steer 206°. Remind the hands that Ultra Quiet State remains in force.' He walked slowly around his control-room, checking the gauges, having a word with the planesman and the watch-keeper on the panel. He turned to Sims:

'You have the ship, officer of the watch. Shake me if you're worried, and at 0400.' He stuffed his hands in his pockets and, shuffling in his slippers from the control-room, retired to his cabin.

Exhaustion brought Farge a fitful sleep but at 0315, with the two-minute reports from the sound-room filtering into his consciousness, he finally quit his bunk. Rubbing his eyes and smoothing back his hair, he sat himself at his desk. Pulling up his chair, he extracted his leather writing holder from his personal drawer, took out a few sheets of writing-paper and arranged them neatly in front of him. He held his pen poised for a moment as he closed his eyes. He could see her so vividly in his imagination, her fair curls, her laughing eyes, her soft smile. Then he bent over his desk and began to write.

'We should be crossing the bank now, sir,' Murray reported. 'Time, 0502.'

'Nothing from the sound-room?'

'Only the distant contact, sir. Still very faint,' Sims said.

Farge stood between his periscopes, hands behind his back, waiting for his men to reach their action stations. He could hear them struggling through the boat, many swaying as if they were drunk while they fought for breath.

'Take a quick sounding, pilot.'

The trace appeared, enought to show that *Orcus* was in 490 feet of water.

'Depth recorder switched off,' Murray reported.

Farge reached for the intercom:

'Captain speaking.' He kept his voice low, matter-of-fact. 'We've nothing much left in the box,' he said, 'and as you all realize, there's not much air. I haven't risked coming up before this, because a detection would definitely have been bad news. So we've got the choice: either sit on the bottom here at 490 feet and slowly snuff it, or risk sticking out our necks by getting in a quick snort. We've heard nothing for over nine hours – only a faint contact to the north. With luck, we may get in a bit of a charge and, what matters most, recirculate the air.' He paused. 'We're only twenty-five miles from the coast, but I reckon the risk is worth it. A quick charge is all we want, enough to take us north-west into the deep field again, where we can snort to our heart's content.' He said carefully:

'I don't want to raise your hopes. Vardø, Norway's main port up here, is our nearest point of land, but the Russians are in control of the coastline, as you all know. Pockets of the Royal Marines are still resisting in the mountains; remnants of 45 Commando are, I know, organizing resistance groups among the Norwegians.' He cleared his throat. '*Safari* should have received our enemy report on the Typhoon, so we've done what's expected of us. I don't know what's waiting for us up top, but so far we've been lucky. Of one thing you can be sure: I shan't sacrifice the boat needlessly. If I'm forced to, I'll surface to give us a chance to bale out. Be ready for anything. Obey your officers; keep your heads; and don't hang about, because I'll be scuttling the boat if it comes to it. With God's help, we'll get out of this.' He turned to Bill Bowles. 'And thanks, cox'n, and all of you,' he ended quietly. 'No captain's ever been served by better men.'

He replaced the mike and turned to Prout:

'I'll come straight up,' he said briskly. 'Sixty feet.'

Bowles drew the column towards him. The bubble slid forward. The terse commands of the trimming officer and the distant whine of the motor were all that could be heard in the control-room.

'Stand by to snort, generating both sides,' Farge ordered. He had to hold her at a hundred feet for the completion of the snort drill, an opportunity to catch a trim which Eddie Foggon did not miss: *Orcus* was light and when the trimming officer had flooded Ds, the engine-room came through on the intercom:

'Ready to snort, generating both sides.'

'Periscope depth,' Farge ordered briskly. 'I shan't raise the snort mast until I've had a look.' He moved backwards from the gauges and took up his position between the periscopes. Still nothing from sonar.

'Eighty feet, seventy-five.'

'Up attack.'

The friendly hiss of the steel tube, sliding upwards again from its well . . . he opened the handles as the eyepieces came level.

'Sixty-two feet . . .'

He pushed his face into the eyepieces, heard behind him the MEO restraining the cox'n and his bubble.

'Sixty feet. *Breaking!*'

The darkness merged swiftly with the grey underneath of the surface – daylight– and, as the smeared lens cleared, he saw the yellow-green tinge of the mud-stained sea, its creamy wave-crests curling towards him. He swung on his heel, taking in the horizon line of the southern sector – he could see no land to the eastward – then round to the north, to the north-west and –

'Bloody hell!' he shouted. '*Down periscope!* Stop snorting. Flood Q. Three hundred feet. Don't speed up, for God's sake.'

As he stood back from the periscope, the image of three, clumsy-looking Hormone helicopters etched indelibly in his mind, the control-room exploded into action. At sixty-five feet the first active pinging from the ASW helicopters blasted against the hull. At eighty feet, *Orcus*, still at slow one, but three and a half tons heavy with Q flooded, was sinking like lead.

'Shut off for counter-attack,' Farge shouted above the controlled chaos. 'Blow Q.'

The engine-room was coming through:

'Induction hull valve and emergency hull valve shut.'

Foggon was tapping Bowles' shoulder and pointing at the bow-down bubble.

'Can I speed up, sir?' The MEO's mouth was a hole in his pale face: he had over-flooded Ds on the way up.

'Yes,' Farge snapped. 'To hell with the amps.'

'Group up, half ahead together,' Foggon ordered. Then, as the cox'n gained control again, the bubble slipping for'd, the boat began to porpoise.

'Two hundred feet.'

'Hard-a-dive on the fore-planes,' Foggon was shouting above the din.

Farge watched Bowles forcing for'd on his column, calm determination on his face as the boat began swooping down again. Then, seconds after another active ping from the attacking helicopters, a shattering explosion rocked the submarine. Farge glimpsed the curved frames springing toward him, felt the pressure on his lungs. Glass tinkled around him from the broken gauges, men slithered to the deck, hurled from their seats. A nuclear depth-bomb, not too distant. . . ?

'Fore-planes jammed hard-a-dive,' the cox'n called out.

'Hydraulic pressure gone,' the wrecker shouted. 'Switching to secondary.'

'Fore-planes in hand,' Farge snapped. But with the broad-cast system off the board and the bulkhead doors shut down for counter-attack, his orders could not be repeated by voice. 'Open bulkhead doors,' he shouted.

'340 feet – 380.' The bubble was against the stops.

'Blow one, two, three main ballast.'

As he held on to the pipes above his head, his feet slipping from beneath him, he heard the high pressure air screaming along the line to the ballast tanks for'd.

'410 feet – 420.'

In seconds *Orcus* would be smashing herself into the bottom. Holding his breath, Farge watched the depth-gauge pointer racing round the dial.

158

'Bubble's coming off, sir,' Bowles called out as the air emptied from the for'd main ballast tank to bring up her bows.

'430 – 425 – 420. Bubble's moving for'd.'

'Stop blowing main ballast. Group down, stop together.'

The wrecker shut his master blows. The screaming ceased in the air lines. Grady's voice broke through the sudden calm:

'Hydraulic pressure's on the line.'

'Planes are in power, sir.' Bill Bowles reported as he pushed his column for'd, while the bows continued to soar upwards: twelve degrees bow-up and still porpoising wildly. Farge *must* rid the tanks of any trapped air while the turmoil persisted:

'Open main vents.'

He heard the clunk from for'd as the mushroom-headed valves jumped open.

'One, two, three main vents checked open,' the report came back from for'd.

The boat was still cocked upwards at eleven degrees, but her rate of ascent was decreasing swiftly. She steadied at 240 feet; and then the depth started to fall away again. The MEO glanced over his shoulder at his captain:

'She's very heavy, sir.'

Farge nodded, acknowledging the trimming officer's mis-judgement on the way up from deep.

'Open D port and starboard Kingstons,' Foggon ordered.

'270 feet.'

The panel lights blinked as the Kingston valves were monitored 'open'.

'Blow D, port and starboard,' Foggon continued, his eyes on the panel.

Farge was listening to the hiss of the high pressure air as Grady opened his blows, when another active ping reverber-ated through the hull, a nerve-twitching, eerie sound. As the noise died away, the sound waves disappearing into the distant ocean, the control-room suddenly split asunder.

An appalling shock hammered the boat at the exact moment that Grady was set to shut his HP air blows. Foggon yelled at Grady but the CPO had been flung backwards, his seat wrenched from the deck by the explosion. The submarine was being picked up by a giant's hand and hurled upwards. In seconds her bows were leaping towards the surface, the bubble against the stops. Men were scrabbling about the deck, trying to regain their feet, their hands streaming blood where they clawed among the slivers of glass and perspex from the gauges and instruments.

Farge glimpsed Foggon hauling himself upwards, grasping at the metal frame of the wrecker's seat. Pushed from behind by Sims, the MEO was snatching at D's HP air blows, desperately trying to shut them.

The cox'n lifted his hands from his column, his voice inaudible as Farge shouted for Q to be flooded. The depth-gauge pointer was flying backwards behind its splintered glass, 160 feet and still swooping upwards. . .

Sims somehow opened Q and to the pandemonium was added the roar of its inboard venting as someone used his initiative. The angle must be over 60° bow-up, but for some reason she was steadying: 155 – 155 – 147 – 135, then began dropping fast. God, why weren't the bows coming down, with that extra three and a half tons right for'd in Q? And with D Kingstons. . . ?

'Shut D Kingstons. Shut main vents,' Farge shouted above the diminishing chaos. 'Vent Ds inboard. Stand by to blow Q.'

The submarine was now dropping backwards, sliding into the depths stern-first. The depth pointer was slewing fast round its dial as she hurtled towards the bottom. 390 feet, 410: still she remained at this terrifying angle, the hands standing against the vertical surfaces as Grady fought his way back to the panel, to be held there by Sims and Grant.

'Blow seven, six, five main ballast,' Farge yelled above the din, as he tried to lift her stern. 'Group up, full ahead together.' Nothing was holding her now and the angle was not coming off. She was desperately heavy aft. 'Blow Q.'

Somehow Grady reached the blows and Farge heard the glorious sound of the HP air in the lines. The three men struggling at the panel had their eyes fixed on Farge while he gave the after main ballast tanks all the air he dared – but he continued blowing, listening for the rising whine of the main motors, feeling with the soles of his feet for the angle to come off, watching for a decrease in depth. He could waste no more of the precious HP air. 'Stop blowing main ballast.'

Someone was shouting:

'D Kingstons jammed open!'

'Stop together,' Farge commanded.

'475 – 480.'

'Hold on – *down on the deck!*' Farge yelled at the top of his voice. 'Protect your heads!' He flung himself to the sloping deck.

'490 feet.'

Surprisingly, he felt a gradual deceleration as the submarine ploughed to a halt, the hull trembling throughout its length. She remained for a few seconds at her terrifying angle, then Farge felt her bows subsiding. As he hauled himself upright by the periscope rods he felt her stem come up all-standing on something hard. The depth pointer was fixed at 487 feet.

After the shocked seconds of relative calm, he heard shouting through the open doors as men scrambled along the plates of the engine-room, the curses of his control-room team while they struggled to their stations. The unnerving active pings were growing louder as the enemy strove to regain contact.

'All compartments make your reports.' Farge ordered, on his feet again, leaning against the steel tube of the search persicope. 'Begin from aft.'

And in those next few minutes, Farge's worst fears were realized: the after-planes, the rudder, both propellers – all inoperative. She had stuck her after-ends deep into the mud.

'Control – engine-room.'

'Control?'

'Water flooding into the gland space.'

'Roger.'

'Captain, sir,' Foggon said. 'Number two HP air accumulator is almost empty. Both pumps are failing to cut in.'

'Is number one reservoir empty?'

The MEO nodded.

'Control – engine-room.'

'Control?' Farge shouted aft through the engine-room door.

'Six and five main vents jammed open. We can't shift them in hand.'

Foggon met Farge's glance, then shook his head slowly.

'No point running the compressors on atmosphere, sir.' He was gasping for the air which was not there, as another active ping blasted the boat.

'Everybody for'd,' Farge rapped. 'Into the fore-ends and for'd accommodation space.' He glanced at Tim Prout:

'Number One, take charge in the fore-ends. I'll take the accommodation space.'

The captain stood aside, watching his men streaming through the engine-room bulkhead door: some with flesh wounds and bloodied faces, others smeared with grease, clothes sodden, helping each other as they struggled up the slippery deck which had settled at a forty-degree angle. The comedians were chiakking each other, even now.

Farge had lost track of time. He knew only that *Orcus* was crippled, unable to move. With the after main vents jammed open he could not blow his after main ballast, even if he could produce HP air by running the compressors on atmosphere to a slight vacuum – there was precious little atmosphere remaining. The jammed after main vents explained the disastrous angle. His propellers were damaged, the shafts probably distorted if water was streaming into the gland space. Then he heard, above the noise of the last of the hands clambering through the control-room, the whisper of a destroyer's propellers passing overhead. How often had he heard that sound reproduced in the simulator. . . ? He cocked his head to one side, listening, as the wardroom steward poked his head through the door. Riley, a handkerchief at his mouth, was crimson in the face, coughing and gasping for air:

'There's gas, sir,' he choked. 'Coming up through number two battery boards.'

Riley was pushed aside and Prout's head appeared between the legs of the last stoker clambering through the doorway:

'Chlorine, sir.'

Farge nodded: the battery cells must have been damaged and seawater from the flooded Ds was seeping into the battery bilges. He waited until the reverberations from another active blast disappeared, then faced Prout

'What's the keel depth in the fore-ends?'

'454 feet, sir.'

'We've got a chance, then.'

'Yes – if everyone keeps his head.'

'Abandon ship: prepare for a rush escape,' Farge commanded brusquely. 'You take the fore-ends.'

'Aye, aye, sir. Able Seaman Hicks is missing: the doc turned him in in the after messdeck.'

Farge turned to his cox'n who, the last man in the control-room, was waiting patiently by the panel.

'Go aft, please, cox'n. Check that everyone's for'd.'

Bowles was already slithering downwards to the engine-room door. Farge watched him disappearing into the shadows of the machinery space as the first lieutenant shoved the last stoker through the for'd door:

'Better get dressed, Tim. Don't flood up until I give the order.'

'Right, sir.' Prout met his captain's eye. 'Good luck, sir,' he said. 'See you in Vardø.' He turned briskly and disappeared for'd up the passageway.

Waiting for Bowles to return, Farge was on his own. He could smell the faint tang of chlorine. He'd better grab a suit and start dressing. He reached up to the deckhead lockers and pulled out escape suits for Bowles, Hicks and himself. Amazingly, he felt quite serene as another active blast invaded his boat. He could do no more.

The enemy was having a field day . . . and fleetingly he wondered whether the Russian captains would machine-gun survivors in the water. In peacetime, they behaved as sailors the world over. They'd just sunk their submarine; they'd not wallow in blood. If only some of *Orcus*' company could survive, even a few, to tell 'em in *Dolphin* what *Orcus*, the old lady of the squadron, had tried to achieve – perhaps they'd install her shield in the Submariners' Church, with all those others who had never returned. At least, she'd carried out her mission. Janner Coombes could be on to his prey, might even have sunk the Typhoon by now?

Farge closed his eyes, his thoughts rushing onwards, glimpsing in a flash of clarity a vision of peace which was at this moment within the grasp of humanity. And he prayed to the God whom he had discovered at this last moment. From far away he heard the approaching chatter of the torpedo's propellers, the racket of the weapon which submariners were trained to recognize. It came from the port quarter, louder, until the propeller beats merged into one single, deafening roar. He grabbed at the periscope rods; for God's sake, hurry,

Bowles . . .

A thud, a blinding flash: the explosion, remarkably unimpressive after the previous upheavals, shook the old
submarine's hull. He was deafened momentarily by the sound
of cascading water in the engine-room as the bulkhead door
slammed shut on its hinges, torn from its clips. He picked
himself up at the foot of the bulkhead, reached up and swung off
on the quick-acting wheel, watching the dogs dig home into
their sockets. Gasping for air, he fought his way upwards to the
for'd door of the control-room, fell through it, grasped at the
outstretched hand reaching for him.

As they hauled him upright and began slipping his feet into
the legs of the escape suit, he half turned towards the
passageway leading to the fore-ends:

'Shut bulkhead doors,' he gasped, choking from the first
whiffs of the lethal gas. 'Flood up the fore-ends. *Rush escape!*'

25

USS Carl Vinson, 17 May. Though midsummer was only five weeks away, his wind-cheater, fur hat and gloves did little to keep out the biting cold. Must be my age, Vice-Admiral Lincoln Jessup, Jr, thought to himself as he paced his small admiral's deck above the main conning position on *Carl Vinsons*'s island. He needed the air after this long day, the most gruelling twenty-four hours he had endured since his appointment as commander of Carrier Striking Force, Atlantic. It was good to see his ships out there, dispersed across the horizon, on the edge of the pack-ice: the cruisers, destroyers and frigates and, jutting above the horizon-line to the north-east, the spiky topmast of the other carrier, the old lady, *Constellation.* His force packed a punch, but even with *Constellation*'s contribution, his own aviators were flying round the clock.

The admiral's Striking Force was steaming 140 miles to the west of Isfjord, Spitzbergen's main inlet on its western coast. If Nato had not reacted so swiftly in Spitzbergen, when the enemy invaded Norway four months ago, Jessup wouldn't have been here now: Spitzbergen was a vital link in the West's periphery of defences. The radar early warning and sosus chains were making it possible for SACLANT to challenge the Soviets' assumption of proprietorship in the Barents Sea . . . a helluva day, since the receipt of *Safari*'s flash report at 0835 this morning. To maintain the Force's LRMPs his carriers' Phantoms, Tomcats, Hornets and F-18s were flying at extreme limits round the clock to maintain even an hours' umbrella above the LRMPS.

Jessup moved to the for'd end of his bridge, where the wind was buffeting the slab face of *Carl Vinson*'s tiered island. He held on to the frosted rail, watching her gigantic flight deck below him, stretching forward eight hundred feet from the point at which he stood. Even this huge carrier was moving about in these dreary, green seas; *Carl Vinson*'s bows were pitching rhythmically, wisps of spray drifting upwards and turning to ice before slatting against the steel upperworks of the island. The aviators were taking these harsh conditions in their stride, operating a thousand miles from their carriers, refuelled in flight by tankers. The arduous weather was claiming more casualties among his airmen than was the curiously negative response of the enemy.

Yes, Operation SDW was certainly putting to the test those years of peacetime training, those Goddam years of pinching and scraping to keep the fleets in being while Uncle Sam picked himself up again after the Vietnam syndrome, a malaise ably exploited by Soviet subversion throughout the free world. Jessup's eyes were watering as he peered into the icy wind: the deck-handlers were hard put to it in these conditions, but the spirit among *Carl Vinson*'s 6,400 men was improved now that there was a purpose to the eternal flogging of the Atlantic: the Phantom and Tomcat squadrons were landing on and taking off with admirable precision. He wondered how he himself would cope with these sophisticated flying machines with speeds of mach 2·5-plus: his flying days were over, but he still yearned for his old Corsairs. Flat-tops were fun in those days, less intense: airplanes did not cost millions of dollars apiece; pilots did not take years to train; and the atom did not drive the carriers . . . Thank God it would soon be over. The President had been briskly curt this morning on the telephone, before passing Jessup over to the Secretary of the Navy: SACLANT had been given another twenty-four hours to bring the operation to its conclusion. Tomorrow at midnight Nato's disposition deployments must be withdrawn from the Barents – the Kremlin was now thoroughly suspicious and running out of patience. SACLANT must not be caught with his pants down when, or if, the Kremlin carried out its threats.

But until Operation SD proved its point, the Kremlin was still retaining faith in its last resort, second strike capability, the SLBMS fired from their invisible SSBNS. The world was still one step away from the holocaust, and Nato had failed to sink the SSBNS it had boasted it could. The total score of fifteen still fell short of the twenty commanded by the President to clinch deterrence and to bring back peace. Destruction of the Typhoon remained the key, but the despair beginning to be felt by Jessup's staff was difficult to combat as they monitored *Safari*'s abortive chase.

Jessup twitched back the sleeve of his wind-cheater: 2105. His staff had been deploying and monitoring Nato forces like pieces on a chessboard since 0900. It was time for him to rejoin his hard-worked team, if only as a dismal witness to the escape of their quarry: the elusive Typhoon would soon be lost under the polar ice. He turned and elbowed his frame through the starboard screen. The door banged shut behind him, as he made his way down to the anti-submarine control centre.

The first watchmen were already installed, the plotters going smoothly about their business of monitoring the movements of all deployments, past, present and future. Whereas earlier there had been an ill-concealed pessimism in the control centre, Jessup, standing before the displays, detected immediately that the atmosphere had altered: there was a bustling confidence which had been absent when he quit to snatch his breather. He dropped into his chair and watched as the computers flipped their data on to the screens. His staff captain had taken charge, a sure sign that something was developing – but first, Jessup needed to recap on the day's events. He swept his eye over the 'past' screen, focussing on the red and blue tracks, the enemy's and Nato's respectively.

Based on *Safari*'s report, the Typhoon's red track started well south at 0800 (estimated). The monster was presumed to have speeded up to thirty-five knots, an estimate confirmed at 1210. Every naval commander merited an element of luck and Jessup acknowledged his fortune when at 1030 the sosus chain on the Perseus Bank had picked up, then identified, the Alfa close south of the shallower water. What had aroused Jessup's suspicions was her relatively slow speed, even after clearing the bank. The Alfa was capable of forty-two knots, but she was heading north-east at only twenty before increasing to thirty-five when reaching the deeper water. Her illogical progress alerted Jessup to the possibility of her acting as an escort ahead of the Typhoon – and the earlier presence of a Victor II (sunk by *Safari*) as a rear escort underlined his suspicions.

Since 0900 there had been jubilant moments in the control centre, instants of intense excitement, as well as despair. The first was the confirmation of the Alfa's signature, course and speed; the second, when his staff's hopes were confirmed: at 1207, sosus picked up the Typhoon. Jessup immediately flew off another Viking patrol and alerted the RAF's Nimrods.

The Typhoon, having steamed at speed sine 0800, must have altered to 056° at 1100 to avoid the Perseus Bank and, by SOSUS again, was confirmed as following the Alfa at twenty knots while skirting the shallows. The Typhoon had cracked on to thirty-five knots at 1600, once she was clear of Perseus. But the high drama of the day still lay ahead.

Jessup would long remember the first Nimrod's flash report: the excitement mounting in the anti-submarine control centre as the movement of every unit in his force was immediately co-ordinated; the data streaming in; the scrambling Phantoms, Tomcats and F-18s; and finally the relentless passive refining from the Vikings' and Nimrods' sono-buoy fields. It had been a model hunt, culminating in the torpedoing of the Alfa who, even if she had not been bounced by the LRMPs, would have steamed straight into the four SSNs waiting on their patrol line stretching between Graham Bell Land and the Northern tip of Novaya Zemlya.

The sinking of the Alfa had altered the whole picture: the Typhoon, only sixty miles astern, must have been alerted by the Alfa – or might have heard the sinking – because at 1740 the Typhoon altered course to 332°, a course shaving the other SOSUS bank.

Safari, controlled directly by COMSUBEASTLANT, was steaming at full speed on 0100 since losing her quarry: since noon, the forlorn plan had been to try and force the Typhoon back towards the Spitz–Alexandra Land gap. Nato's four SSNs were standing by to scare her northwards, and after *Carl Vinson*'s Viking sank the Alfa at 1730 the LRMPs were moved to the south-eastward to achieve the same result. *Safari*'s track was now converging on the Typhoon's. At 2000, an hour ago, when the enemy fined up to due north for the deep water off Cape Mary Harmsworth, *Safari* was tantalizingly close astern: only thirty-five miles separated the two submarines. Since then tension had heightened, despite the despairing realization that nothing now could prevent the enemy from reaching the ice. The time was already 2101 and she was outpacing *Safari* at the rate of five knots: in only two hours, if the Typhoon forged onwards through restricted sea room and depth at this desperate speed, she would be approaching the edge of the polar ice.

Jessup had considered using his LRMPS earlier to locate the Typhoon after she turned north. He wished now that he had ignored the advice of the submariner on his staff who reminded him that the inaccuracies of navigation in these high latitudes increased the possibility of wrong identification by aircraft to a degree which might risk the destruction of *Safari* by Nato's own torpedoes or NDBS. It was also suspected that Soviet SSNS were concentrating in the area and a terrible mistake could so easily take place – but Jessup knew that when the party was over and the records analysed, his decision to allow *Safari* to continue the chase, instead of his aircraft, would be judged to have been a fundamental error on the part of the Commander of the Striking Force. There remained now only one slim chance: to move in each of the SSNS waiting on either side of the Cape Platen and Arthur Island gap. Again, faulty identification and the risk of tragedy was only too real. . .

'Admiral, sir,' the staff captain was calling across from the command display, 'Victoria Island SOSUS reports the Typhoon has reduced speed to twenty knots.' The grin on the captain's face was a tonic which Jessup badly needed.

'She's not got enough sea room, sir,' the staff submariner added. 'She's too close to the shallow bank to the west of the cape.'

The admiral jumped to his feet:

'How far astern is *Safari*?'

'Thirty-eight miles, sir – overtaking now at a rate of ten knots.'

Jessup scratched the grizzled hair at the side of his head, as he interrogated his submarine officer:

'If you were commanding the Typhoon and did not suspect that you were being tailed, once you were clear of the cape, would you increase speed again?'

The young officer shook his head. 'Not in these waters, admiral. Not in these shallows and approaching the edge of the polar ice.'

The admiral nodded. 'Okay. Pass *Safari* a sitrep,' he said briskly. 'Call off all our dogs of war and tell *Safari* she has no restrictions.' He turned to the wall display, glanced at the wavy line marking the polar ice. 'It's up to her now,' he murmured. 'Let's hope the Limeys are on the ball.'

26

HM Submarine Orcus, 17 May. "Swain, 'swain, for God's sake, give me an 'and!'

Buchanan's desperate cry and the ice-cold water swirling to Bowles' knees brought the cox'n round from semi-consciousness.

'Can't move 'is legs, 'swain.'

Bowles' head was still reeling, but he and MEM Buchanan together managed to drag the paralysed diver from the side of the bunk to which he was clinging. Buchanan shoving and Bowles heaving, they slithered the helpless Hicks up the sloping deck of the after-ends towards the after bulkhead door of the engine-room.

'Hold on,' Bowles gasped, 'while I get the door open.' The diver's terrified eyes rolled in their sockets as he followed Bowles' movements up the steel plating.

In those brief moments, the cox'n tried to collect his disorientated thoughts together, endeavoured to reconstruct the happenings since the noise of the torpedo's propellers. His wrist watch had stopped at 0541, but how long had he been lying there since the explosion? His head was splitting and the whole of his left side felt as if it had been kicked in . . . the bulkhead was still a few feet away, but in the gloom of the emergency lighting he could already see the water spilling from the lower lip of the oval door. He propped himself upright and shoved against it with his shoulders. He could not budge it: the engine-room must be flooded.

Fighting for breath in the foul air, Bowles hurled himself at the actuating wheel, wrenched at it until the lugs were notched home into their sockets; then he lay back, exhausted, against the door. They were trapped – but they couldn't now be overwhelmed by a deluge from the engine-room. The water was up to the hatch of the engineers' store, but the level seemed to have stopped rising; mere luck – or was the atmospheric pressure in their constricted space now equalizing with the sea pressure outside? Bad air under pressure could kill.

That was when Bowles decided to take no chances. Painfully and slowly, he and Buchanan dressed Hicks into an escape suit, then donned their own – but, God, how long ago had all this happened?

Two further explosions had wracked the boat, both at the for'd end – must have been hours ago. He and Buchanan shared the strain of supporting the paralysed Hicks, propping him into a half-sitting posture against the door of the after heads. Listening to the sound of beating propellers from craft overhead, Bowles refused to be hustled into an impetuous and possibly fatal decision. He'd persuade Buchanan and Hicks to sit it out, to wait for the enemy to quit the area before they attempted their escape through the chamber above their heads.

They were, after all, still alive; they were breathing good air at the right pressure, though for how long was problematical. The after depth-gauge had showed 487 feet: they had been trained to escape from five hundred, admittedly under the somewhat artificial conditions of the diving tank at Dolphin. Though Bowles was optimistic that they could make their escape, he was worried most by what might be waiting for them up top. He did not relish being chopped up on the surface by racing propellers, or shot. Taken prisoner by Ivan? Some sixth sense was telling him to hold on, to wait. He handed Hicks over to Buchanan and leaned back, trying to ease his cramped limbs.

How much longer should he risk delay? It seemed an eternity since the last surface noise had faded to silence. Perhaps three hours? Could be six, even. The enemy would certainly watch *Orcus*' grave for hours – but how many? Four, before pushing off? Had they marked the sinking with buoys? Perhaps they'd shoved off to chase *Safari*? Four hours, then – and the hunt must have taken another couple of hours – and add another two for luck . . . Four plus four, eight; add another three . . . eleven in all. Adding that to the time his watch stopped, made it 1641. The evening of 17 May? But in this God-forsaken waste there was no darkness, no real night in May, no mantle of invisibility. Hang on a bit longer. Stick it out for as long as we can and the better chance we'll have. . .

His companions looked pretty rough. Hicks' eyes were

closed; Buchanan was reeling where he hung on to the slumped body of the diver . . . but God, how can we get the poor fellow into the escape tower?

In the hours which followed Bowles gradually came to his decision: the two younger men would tackle the first ascent, Hicks lashed to Buchanan, while the MEM opened the valves and the upper hatch. Their escape suits would take them up safely, provided they could discipline themselves to breathe normally. As for himself, he'd flood up on his own, the last man out. It had been done before.

The time to go could not be far off . . . it was quiet up top – and silent down here, save for their breathing. He leaned towards Buchanan and signalled that it was time for him and Hicks to prepare for escape. The MEM's grotesque head wagged atop the orange suit and, lashing the diver to him, he clambered up into the chamber. It was a long time before Buchanan signalled that he was ready: then, the MEM heaving and Bowles shoving with the last of his failing strength, they somehow managed to slide Hicks through the lower hatch and into the chamber.

They paused again to recover and then Buchanan was levering the diver up to a sitting position, his knees to his chest. Hicks was responding to Buchanan's efforts. The MEM held up his fist, nodded and shipped the lower lid. Then Bowles was on his own, the two men locked above in the escape-tower. Through the sighting port, Bowles could see Buchanan opening up the flood, and then the water-level climbing up their legs.

Bowles felt the thud above him when Buchanan opened the upper lid. Then through the port, he saw the lower part of the MEM's legs floating upwards: Bowles held his breath, waiting for the cramped bundle that was Hicks to follow upwards. But the man was stuck, Buchanan's legs threshing. The lashing joining the two men jerked, whipped – and then Hicks was slowly rolling upwards, suddenly vanishing. Thank God . . . and Bowles slumped backwards, leaning against the heads door. The two men must be on their way to the surface, or they would have dropped back into the chamber. The upper hatch would be left open, so it was his turn now. He'd shut the upper lid, give 'em a few minutes, then follow . . . *Orcus'* company were certainly contributing with the most precious commodity of all. He supposed their deaths *could* be justified, but only if the sacrifice helped to prevent the appalling alternative with which England was threatened by the Soviets.

Bill Bowles and his Hilda were simple people; they had found support in their faith . . .

Hilda'd always been true to their marriage, he knew that, despite his long absences, and the spate of separations and desertions which decimated the lives of so many of their service friends and acquaintances. He could see Hilda still, as she was at eighteen, twenty years ago. For him, though twice he had been tempted, she was now more attractive, even more desirable than during those first passionate months. Hilda, his Hilda . . . he wasn't going to give up now – but if he didn't make it, well, the kids would look after her . . . Flood up and get on with it, Cox'n Bowles: the chamber was drained down.

He reached up and twisted the upper hatch control handle to 'idle'. He checked that he had his vent cap. Then he climbed into the dripping tower and, using the lanyards, lifted the lower lid into place. For an instant he paused, alone in the dark tower; this depth produced a pressure of three hundred pounds per square inch – thank God, these modern suits were designed to compensate automatically. Breathe naturally: the gas bottle in the suit did the rest. Here goes . . . and deliberately he zipped up his suit. He opened the flooding valve and then the water was licking around his feet, swirling and frothing. In seconds, the sea was up to his navel, icy cold, shrivelling him –and he shivered inside his suit when the water reached the top of the vent. He smacked the vent cap over the top of it and then felt the water deluge starting to ease. The swirling surface was up to his chin, over his mouth, then his head was under water, his world pitch black as the pressure equalized. Panic now, Bowles, and you're done for: drill, drill, remember what they taught you, lad. . .

He felt the cold circumference above him, traced the circular hatch, stood beneath it, breathing regularly, hearing the clicking of his exhaust valve . . . *save me God*. With a swift movement he reached upwards and opened the lid, pushing it with all his strength.

He felt the surge, the pain in his ears: heard the roaring

above him as the air bubble lifted him crashing through the hole. He ignored the pain on his shoulders, as he scraped upwards in the darkness and sensed the sudden leap upwards. *Breathe normally*, that's what they said: in . . . out . . . there was enough air in his suit to last the ascent. Thirty seconds for a five-hundred-foot escape; how long to go now? He tugged at his apron to control his attitude. He clamped his feet together, trying to halt the somersaulting, felt the water rushing past him as he threshed up towards the life-giving surface.

The pressure was building up in his suit, pressing on his lungs; then he felt its automatic-venting compensating to prevent his lungs from bursting . . . but how long, oh God, how long? He closed his eyes with the pain, screaming, for he could bear no more of this agony. His mind began to swim as the roaring overwhelmed him, then there was a gradual lightening around him, paler, brighter.

He flew upwards, shooting from the surface like a fish, his lungs about to burst asunder. He felt the shock of the waves beneath him, heard their rhythmic music – and then he was on his back, turned over by his suit . . . just before he lapsed into semi-consciousness, he remembered to pull the toggle. The compressed air hissed. His survival suit inflated, blowing up like a balloon to keep the back of his head to the breaking seas. As he floated up on the crests, he glimpsed an off-shore fishing-boat, a canoe-sterned craft, chugging towards him, then another and another.

27

HM Submarine Safari, 17 May. With his navigating officer, Coombes was poring over the chart of the Barents Sea. The red and blue tracks, the Typhoon's and *Safari's*, had formed an elongated triangle, with its northern apex converging between Cape Mary Harmsworth and the shallow water to the eastward of Victoria Island. The Typhoon was still steering 335°, to which she had altered an hour ago.

'She's heading for the Nansen Deeps, sir,' Farquharson murmured. 'In an hour and a half she'll be under the polar ice.'

'Thank God the weather's moderated,' Coombes said, 'or we'd lose her. It'll be quiet under the ice in this calm.'

It had been a long chase since 0830 and by 2300 both men were feeling the strain.

'If she reaches Nansen,' Coombes went on, 'we're finished. She'll bottom on the edge and we'll never get at her.' He glanced again at the sounding lines: Nansen was over two and a half miles deep. The Typhoon with her titanium hull could reach four thousand feet. If *Safari* lost her now, she'd never pick up the monster again in that vast Arctic basin. Coombes reread COMSUBEASTLANT's flash which *Safari* had received when she came up for the 2130 routine. The Typhoon was then a faint but definite contact at thirty-seven miles' range. Sonar had already confirmed that the quarry had reduced speed to twenty.

PRECEDENCE: FLASH
SECURITY CLASSIFICATION: TOP SECRET
FROM: CINCEASTLANT
TO: SAFARI
INFO: SACLANT, COMSUBLANT, COMSUBEASTLANT, COMSTRIFOR, COMSTRIGRUTWO
DTG: 172130 (ZULU) MAY

TYPHOON 80° 19′ NORTH 41° 02′ EAST. COURSE 360° SPEED 20. ALL OWN FORCES WITHDRAWN. YOU HAVE NO RESTRICTIONS. MESSAGE ENDS.

The day, one of frustrations and vacillations, was ending better than it had begun: the balls-up over the atmosphere specification was a mistake which Coombes certainly could have done without. He couldn't blame the watchkeeper for the failure of the oxygen generator during *Safari*'s attack on the Victor II, but the momentary slackness had compounded trivial errors to a point where *Safari*'s mission could possibly be jeopardized.

The oxygen specification had slipped too low before the defect was noticed. The resulting drowsiness among the ship's company had produced an over-correction in the proportion of oxygen: a fire broke out in one of the freon refrigeration machines. The buggeration factor then ensured that at the same time there should be a freon gas leak; the resulting small discharge of the killer gas, phosgene, had not been immediately detected during the Victor II drama. They had switched to the secondary life-support system while trying to rectify the atmosphere specification (the freon gas was automatically sucked up). Since the emergency, the atmosphere, though breathable, had become distinctly foul.

For Coombes, the life-support system in modern submarines was as great a miracle as that of the nuclear power – but whereas battery capacity was the Achilles heel of the conventional submarine, the provision of good atmospheric air was the worry always at the back of an SSN captain's mind. Coombes crossed his fingers, trusting that *Safari* would not be forced to periscope depth at this critical moment to recycle the air – though *Safari* would be in a mess if, once committed under the ice, he had not first got the air right.

With Farquharson beside him, Coombes went over the day's events, taking the good news first: the uninterrupted communications with Northwood came at the top of the list. There had been no break in the VLF communications: COMSUBEASTLANT had monitored *Safari* for the past twelve hours towards the prime target. Admittedly, having to come up for the half-hour routines had tried Coombes' limited patience. but that exercise was in the past, since *Safari* had picked up the Typhoon.

The sinking of the Alfa by STRIGRUFOR's aircraft had altered things. From then onwards, as *Safari* batted northwards at thirty knots, their hopes had risen. At 1730 the Typhoon altered to the north-west and, spurred on by the wiles of the aircraft astern of her, converged with *Safari*. But elation in the British boat soon evaporated when it was confirmed that, still steaming faster than *Safari*, the Typhoon would pass ahead. This, the bad news, was only rectified by the 2130 flash. Since then, the enemy had reduced to twenty knots to feel her way through the Victorian Island–Alexandra Land gap – perhaps also sensitive to possible sosus detection?

The culmination of *Safari*'s hopes occurred at 2035 when, slowed for her routine, she picked up the Typhoon at thirty-seven miles. But once again their elation was dashed: at 2100 the plotting team confirmed that Typhoon was outpacing *Safari* at the rate of five knots, the range having increased to thirty-nine miles. Despair was only dispelled by the sitrep from *Carl Vinson*, since when *Safari* had been overtaking. Now, at 2310, the enemy was only seventeen miles ahead, and presumably still unaware that she was being tailed, was continuing at twenty knots. *Safari*'s navigating officer, his sins working impeccably, had taken her through the gap at three hundred feet, fifteen miles to the west of Cape Mary Harmsworth, without reducing speed. The passage had been one during which they talked little: there wasn't much sea room at this speed.

'How far to the edge of the ice?' Coombes asked his navigator for the umpteenth time.

'Now, sir? Thirty-seven miles.'

'And the target?'

'Twenty-one. She must ease down soon.'

'And go deep,' Coombes muttered. 'We're sixteen miles astern and overhauling at ten knots. But how long dare we go on without being detected? She must hear us soon.'

'Will you be reducing, sir?' Farquharson asked. 'For the ice?'

'I'll have to,' Coombes snapped. 'Bloody fool question, pilot.'

'I want to set up sins, sir.'

'We'll wait and see.'

Coombes stretched, then lumbered into the centre of his control-room. He nodded at his first lieutenant:

'Go to action stations, Number One,' he ordered. 'Remain at Ultra Quiet State.'

28

HM Submarine Safari, 18 May. The fore-endies, CPO Scanes thought, certainly have the advantage of variety. Back-endies were a different breed – the sheer repetition of the propulsion department's routine needed men of stoical stuff because, whatever happened in the control-room and the fore-ends, life back-aft ground on day after day: the inexhaustible nuclear kettle was an insatiable mistress. He was paying his daily visit to the control-room to keep abreast of things and to see how Hank Botham was getting on – they'd only managed to have a few words together because the Old Man decided to go to action stations half an hour ago. With nothing to do off-watch, Scanes tucked himself into his favourite corner by the starboard side of the mast cage.

The tension could be felt in the control-room. The captain stood behind the attack co-ordinator, their unflappable Jimmy, Stuart Hamilton, who, hands in pockets, was overseeing the fire control and action information consoles. His team had been closed up for two hours already but, judging by their brisk reports, the climax of the chase could not be far off. Grenville, shifting his weight nervously from one foot to the other, stood glaring over the heads of the two operators at his fire control console, waiting to start the attack. To his right, the ops officer, Kenneth Whalley, was murmuring to his three men at their action information displays. The navigator, Farquharson, was the only officer raising his voice, as he supervised the harassed plotters on the CEP: upon them and the sonar people *Safari*'s survival and the success of her mission now depended. Who would fire first, the Typhoon or *Safari*?

If their lives did not depend on the outcome, Scanes would have enjoyed this final drama. The impending battle would be a test of nerve between the captains of the two submarines: a trial of cunning, of stealth, the prize survival, and perhaps peace.

'The Typhoon's easing down, sir.' Stuart Hamilton turned

his craggy, lined face towards the captain. 'She may be going deep.'

'What's her range?' Coombes asked.

'Sixteen thousand yards.'

Scanes glanced at the clock. 0005, Sunday ... and his thoughts flashed to the Dartmoor village of Meavy, where Beryl was staying with mum until he got back.

'How far to the ice for us, pilot?'

'Fourteen miles, sir.'

'And for the target?'

'Six miles.'

Scanes felt his gut tauten. He longed to shout at that brawny skipper of theirs, yell at him to ease down. The ice edge was only 28,000 yards – the Typhoon only sixteen thousand yards ahead. No one knew precisely where the edge of the polar field began and yet that red-bearded captain was continuing to hurtle onwards towards the hazard, and risk being picked up by the Russian. Coombes stood there rock-like, fingering his flaming whiskers:

'Stand-by Tigerfish attack. Two torpedoes, two hits,' he commanded briskly. 'Tell me when the ice is at ten miles.'

The next ten minutes dragged, the tension relieved only by Bull Clint who, grinning in the cox'n's seat, his hands on his lap, had blurted out, 'Ringo-dingo,' his favourite expression, while *Safari* hurtled onwards at full speed. His fly-whisk was swinging with the angle of the boat as she swooped to either side of four hundred feet, the ordered depth. Lieutenant Wesley, standing silently in the bandstand and supervising the delicate trimming, was not amused. Scanes jumped when the navigator shouted:

'Ice, range ten miles, sir.'

'Assume half power state,' Coombes snapped. 'Revolutions for twenty knots.' His arms hung downwards, his shirt-sleeves too long and becoming grubby at the cuffs.

'Target course 335°, sir,' Farquharson announced from his CEP. 'Estimated speed, ten knots.'

Scanes tried to calculate: the Typhoon was six miles ahead and only four from the ice. Overtaking her at a rate of ten knots *Safari* would very shortly be within range, providing her quarry did not escape, screened by the noise from the ice. To be so close and to lose the target now would be a disaster.

'Target range twelve thousand yards, bearing dead ahead,' the 2001 sonar reported a few minutes later over the intercom.

The speed was coming off and at twenty-two knots the captain ordered the after-planes in hand. Bull Clint took over the column.

'At twenty, go twenty,' Coombes snapped. 'Six down, five hundred feet.'

Scanes felt the angle increasing, watched the pointer on the gauge falling away. Thank God the Old Man was taking no risks with the ice. The tension could be felt, Botham's voice and the subdued reports of the plotters being the only interruptions when at 0035 *Safari* neared the edge of the polar ice. Only the motors hummed in the control-room for at action stations the doors were shut, each compartment a sealed world on its own.

'Track 334 is target,' Hamilton reported.

'Bring number one and two tubes to readiness State One,' Grenville ordered.

Scanes could hear his own breathing as he waited, watching the drill. In the tube-space the bow caps would be opening, the attack team tubes' crew opening the valves, flooding numbers one and two tubes. The silence in the control-room was broken by reports from the sonar controller and then, in the speakers, Scanes heard the first sounds of the ice grinding above them, moving mazily in the Arctic swell.

The sinister sound always gave Scanes the creeps: he had never yet discovered anyone who enjoyed this mysterious world beneath the polar cap: it was deep here in the Arctic Basin, too deep for comfort. But what made the adrenalin spurt were the invisible, uncharted dangers, hazards which had to be risked if *Safari* was to remain undetected. . .

The captain and the navigator had spent the afternoon studying the ice patrol reports. The buzz suggested that this was a bad year, the icebergs more numerous than usual after the hard winter. Silent, gigantic, their bases piercing the depths for hundreds of feet, these isolated monsters were a constant menace to submarines. Scanes clearly heard the creaking, then the distant booming – if only *Safari* could use her active sonar, at least she'd pick up the fang-like protrusions of the icebergs, detect the ice pillars which could stretch down from the surface to the sea bed. Another distant boom echoed sepulchrally up ahead and Scanes caught the glance which flickered between the captain and the first lieutenant.

The sonar was picking up the peeking sounds of fish – Scanes had sometimes heard the 'chukking' of dolphins, a joyful sound after the weird creakings of the ice. Scanes was thankful that *Safari*'s sonar controller was one of the most senior chief ops in the Navy: not much got past him. During the last patrol, he had allowed Scanes to listen in on the sonar – the joyful twitterings, the chief said, were the sounds of shrimps making love.

'AIO checks correct, sir,' Whalley, the ops officer, called.

Grenville hesitated, then followed with his report.

'Fire control correct.'

'Try the following solutions,' Hamilton rapped, 'Course 335°, speed ten, range 8,200 yards . . .'

The captain was bending over the command display, twitching at his beard:

'Pilot,' he snapped at the navigator. 'How close is the ice?'

Why's the Old Man worried about the depth above us? Scanes wondered.

'May I run the upper echo-sounder?' Farquharson asked, surprise on his face as he half turned. The detection hazard, Scanes knew, was great: the Typhoon might pick up the reverbs from the sounder's echoes – presumably Coombes had calculated the risk:

'Yes. Be quick about it.'

'Range 8,100 yards,' Hamilton said.

Scanes heard the faint ticking of the overhead sounder, a few transmissions. . .

'Least distance 464 feet, sir,' the navigator reported, flicking off the sounder.

'Try the following solutions,' the attack co-ordinator was continuing. 'Course 330°, speed ten, range 6,900 yards.' Hamilton seemed as unconcerned as always.

Scanes, watching the attack developing, was fascinated by the precision, the result of months of training. They might have been in the simulator, the way they were going on.

Hamilton was trying his next solution, refining, always refining when at 0500 the sonar controller cut in brusquely:

'Track number 334 – bearing drawing left.'

'How long's she been held?'

'Two minutes. She's speeding up. sir.'

At 0053 the attack co-ordinator gave the target's course as 240°, her speed fifteen. The captain bounced back into the centre of the control-room:

'Stream the decoy,' he snapped, 'Stand by to fire!'

The controller cut in, for the first time excitement in his voice:

'Track 334 – torpedo discharged! Range 5,400 yards, port beam.'

The captain turned back to his command display, his eyes glued to the spokes. Already Scanes could hear the noisy chatter of the enemy's torpedo, the fastest in the world, speeding towards them.

'Switch on the decoy,' Coombes rapped.

Scanes prayed that the device had been streamed in time . . . then controlled pandemonium broke loose:

'Stand by to fire!' the captain shouted. 'Steer 090°.'

The intercom broke in:

'Decoy streamed and switched on.'

Scanes heard it, a loud clattering reverberating throughout the hull as the foxer broke into its chorus, thousands of yards astern. Thank God . . . but the enemy's torpedo had been running for how long?

The ops officer cut his firing bearing. The sonar controller called over the intercom:

'Firing bearing cut!'

'Fire one!' the captain snapped, his eyes on the display. Then the *phumph* seconds later as the first Tigerfish threshed forwards in its tube.

'Fire two!'

Coombes ordered, 'Planes and steering in auto: starboard fifteen. Assume full power state. Revolutions for thirty knots.'

'Both torpedoes running, sir.' Grenville was crouched over the shoulders of his two aimers, watching each man calmly guiding his Tigerfish towards the Typhoon.

'Enemy torpedo, 4,500 yards,' sonar chipped in.

'Got a bearing?'

'Port quarter, 3,800. Target is streaming decoy, bearing red 120, sir. Range 4,100 yards.'

Coombes was watching the spokes of his display. The mark of the racing enemy torpedo was growing more intense as the noise from its propellers showed up on the cathode ray screen.

'Coming in on seven o'clock, sir,' Hamilton announced.

'How long for ours to hit?' Coombes asked him.

'Two and a half minutes, sir.'

'Weapons under guidance,' Grenville called.

Hamilton took over: 'Step weapon one to a course of 310°. Step weapon two to a course of 290°. Arm both weapons. Select active.'

Grenville was trying to control the excitement in his voice. 'Both weapons in contact and attacking.'

Sonar cut in:

'Target has streamed decoy, bearing red 140.'

'Range of enemy torpedo?'

'2,700 yards astern sir. Track 334 bearing 240°, speeding up.'

Coombes glanced at the log: *Safari* was at full speed and the enemy fish was having to overhaul. 'Six up, two hundred feet,' he rapped.

Scanes held on when the submarine swooped upwards savagely. Coombes was throwing her about, taking evasive action; Scanes clung to the mast grille as she banked.

Then he distinctly heard the click-click of the enemy torpedo's hydroplanes. Any second now. . .

'Torpedo altering away, range nine hundred yards.'

Scanes jammed his fist into his mouth to suppress his yell of relief as the bloody thing veered away, lured by *Safari's* decoy. An instant later, the rap of an explosion clanged against the hull. The boat shivered, trembling throughout her length.

'Torpedo and own decoy destroyed,' sonar called out.

'Stream another decoy,' the captain snapped. 'Midships, six down, seven hundred feet. Starboard five, steer 100°.'

Grenville half turned, his face a study of despair:

'Number one weapon has failed to acquire. Turning right.'

'Number one weapon has failed on its first pass,' Hamilton reported calmly. 'Is making its second pass now!'

The first Tigerfish had been wrong for depth, Scanes realized, and was having another go. To have a torpedo failure after all this, would be the end. He pushed the horrid doubt to the back of his mind: the Navy disliked leaving the vital servicing of its torpedoes in the hands of civilians, but the wires had been chopped and there was nothing more to be done. Both Tigerfish were on their own, homing on their target.

Then, just as sonar reported that the Typhoon had discharged her second torpedo, Scanes felt a tap on his shoulder:

'Come aft, chief,' the pale-faced stoker blurted. 'You're wanted on the lower level. Distiller's giving trouble.'

Crouching over his command display, *Safari*'s captain was watching two torpedo tracks: one, his own, diminishing in intensity, the Typhoon's, intensifying with each second that was ticking away. The racing of the enemy torpedo's propellers was only too audible.

'It's going like hell,' he blurted, his eyes flicking to the clock: over half a minute since he'd ordered the streaming of *Safari*'s seond decoy.

'Get a move on with the decoy,' he shouted, 'or it'll be too bloody late. Switch to active, even if it's half-streamed.' And he listened to Grenville's anxious voice while *Safari*'s second Tigerfish turned again to make its second pass

'Number two weapon in contact and attacking!'

Coombes felt remote, a powerless spectator ever since the guiding wires of the weapon were chopped on command by its FCO. Its umbilical cord severed, *Safari*'s second Tigerfish was on its own now, homing in on the gigantic enemy submarine. The Typhoon's captain would not allow *Safari* a second opportunity. The Russian's retaliation would be massive: the existence of everyone in the British submarine hung precariously in the balance, their lives depending upon the ingenuity of the Tigerfish's designers and upon the diligence of the civilians who serviced the torpedo. . .

The sonar controller's reports were streaming in, his voice as calm as if he was conducting exercises off Portland:

'Track 334, bearing 264°, range 3,800 yards. Target's torpedo approaching port beam.'

Coombes could feel his heart pumping beneath his shirt. The Typhoon's captain had been swift on the draw.

'Torpedo approching, sir, 3,100 yards . . .'

The torpedo's track was thickening, clear and distinct on the display, racing towards *Safari*.

The sound-room cut in:

'Searcher holding the torpedo, 261°.'

At the same instant, the attack co-ordinator said:

'Tigerfish has re-acquired and is attacking.' Hamilton stood rigid, his eyes fixed on the Tigerfish's track.

Grenville shouted from his fire control console: 'Loss of guidance commands on the weapon,' and immediately there was a faint clang from somewhere aft.

'Loud explosion bearing 255°. Implosion sounds on target bearing 255°,' the sonar controller reported.

Even without the benefit of sonar, Coombes heard the breaking-up noises on *Safari*'s starboard beam – and then, drowning them, the racket of the enemy's torpedo growing louder, louder as it homed in on to *Safari*.

'Six down, seven hundred feet!' he rapped. He must summon every scrap of guile, every grain of experience he'd amassed over the years to evade this savage beast now hurtling towards *Safari*: he'd drive *Safari* to her limits to evade the torpedo which had sniffed him out. Bull Clint was sitting tensed in his seat, his eyes fixed on the indicator of the after-planes, ready to take over should the auto fail.

'Got a bearing?' Coombes called out.

'Torpedo port quarter, fifteen hundred yards.'

'Starboard ten. Steer 180°. Hold on everyone.' The angle was jerking down: her bows fell away and Coombes felt the elation he always experienced when putting his submarine through her paces. *Safari* behaved like a fighter aircraft, responding positively and immediately to her controls. He was flying her down at thirty knots to seven hundred feet, at a rate of six hundred feet a minute. As she banked to the turn, he grasped the mast cage to keep his balance.

'Torpedo coming in on five o'clock,' sonar reported; 'twelve hundred yards.'

'Roger.'

'540 feet – 560 – 580 –'

'Decoy half-streamed and switched on, sir,' Hamilton called.

'Too flaming late,' Coombes murmured. Things were moving so fast: he'd hardly hoisted in that he'd hit the Typhoon. His total concentration was bent upon saving *Safari* from this torpedo speeding in on his starboard quarter.

'Midships,' he commanded, 'port five. Come left to 090°.'

The boat flung upright, steadied, then canted over, banking into her opposite turn.

'640 feet – 660 – 680 –'

The torpedo must be overtaking at a relative speed of over twenty-five knots – he could hear the cacophony of its propellers even above *Safari*'s wake. There was still a remote chance by swinging the decoy across its homing head – but *Safari*'s decoy was only partially streamed. He'd be hearing at any second the click-click of the torpedo's hydrophones as they drove the weapon down to *Safari*'s depth.

'Seven hundred feet, sir.'

'Roger.' He staggered to keep his balance as *Safari* swooped upwards, counteracting her angle to settle on her ordered depth.

'Torpedo's moving left, searcher!'

The sonar was still in contact, but was the Typhoon's torpedo *really* turning, lured by *Safari*'s decoy? The spoke had defined clearly on his PPI, the mark intense, now, no mistaking it. Dear God, it was turning away.

'Torpedo right astern, searcher – it's merging with the decoy.'

Coombes held his breath, his eyes mesmerized by the pin-point of light crawling across the face of the display

'Course, sir, 090° . . .'

Then events moved fast.

'Starboard ten: steer 180°.'

A hammer clanged against the hull. The boat trembled the length of her.

'Explosion astern, searcher! Decoy noise ceased,' the sonar controller called. 'Weapon has stopped running. No contact, searcher, on that bearing.'

Coombes heard the whisper of relief soughing through his control-room – but the cheer which followed ceased as abruptly as it had erupted.

'Seven hundred feet, sir,' the scow reported, satisfied that *Safari* was under control at her ordered depth.

'Control – manoeuvring,' cut in an anxious voice from the manoeuvring-room.

'Control?'

'Manoeuvring: hull valve.' The MEO's words were curt, difficult to distinguish above a roaring noise coming over the speakers: 'Circulating inlet valve is off its seating.'

Coombes snatched at the intercom:

'How bad, chief?'

'Full emergency, sir! Major flooding.'

'How long can you give me?' Coombes demanded, feeling the adrenalin spurting. At seven hundred feet the deluge in the engine-room must be devastating.

'Take her up. Fast.'

Blowing main ballast would be too slow: the HP air was insufficient for emergency blowing at this depth.

'Stand by to surface!' Coombes rapped. 'Fifteen up. Planes in hand. Give me all the revs you can, chief. Emergency full ahead.' The roaring ceased as the intercom died.

The boat was swooping upwards. Bull Clint, his arms stretched rigidly before him, his hands gripping the column, was planing her upwards – the bubble was against the stops, but the boat must be at a forty-degree bow-up angle. The control-room teams were desperately clinging to any projection they could.

'Six hundred feet, sir – 580 – 560 –'

'Depth of the ice, pilot?' Coombes shouted.

Farquharson had anticipated and was already running the overhead sounder

'No deep ice, sir: surface is 590 feet.'

'540 feet – 520 –'

At sixty feet a minute, another fifty seconds at excessive revs from the engines and she would be up . . .

'Shut main vents,' Coombes ordered, trying to keep his cool. 'Blow all main ballast.'

He listened to the marvellous music of the HP air screaming along the line. The wrecker was working feverishly, his hands flickering over the switches on the ship control console.

'Three hundred feet.'

'Surface!'

The first lieutenant was holding Coombes upright, pushing him with all his strength towards the periscopes. No time for sonar clearance: straight up. But above the din the sonar controller was cutting in above the bedlam:

'No contacts on sector, 187.'

'*Surfacing now!*' Coombes shouted. He heard the doors opening, sensed the bridge team gathering beneath the lower lid of the tower. Drill, drill, drill – thank God his men were trained up.

'Blowing on all main ballast!'

'150 feet.'

'Permission to open the lower lid?'

'Open the lower lid. Stop blowing main ballast,' Coombes called out above the racket. 'Prepare the blower for running.'

'Hundred feet.'

'Course, sir, 180°.'

'Man the tower,' Coombes ordered. 'Assume the half power state. Revolutions for ten knots.' He heard the thumping on the lower lid, saw the legs of a man scrambling into the tower.

'Mast drained down . . . snort valves shut.'

'Sixty-five feet. *Breaking!*'

'Up ECM mast, up search periscope.'

Coombes forced his back against the barrel of the attack periscope, gripped the handles of the search periscope as it swept upwards.

The lens pierced the surface as he was flung backwards, his feet sliding across the deck while the submarine rocketed upwards, her bows rearing high before plumping downwards with the momentum of thirty knots behind them. A curtain of spray leapt into the sky as her 4,500 tons crashed back into the waves.

As he slithered round on his heels, he heard his men picking themselves up from the deck. Nothing in sight: a grey, dismal sky, and from horizon to horizon a waste of patchy pack-ice.

'Open bulkhead doors,' he snapped. 'Signals officer, is the flash report ready?'

'Ready to send out, sir.'

'Make it immediately.'

Coombes stood back from the periscope as the MEO reported from the manoeuvring-room: 'Captain, sir?'

'Yes, chief?'

'Can't tell yet, but I think the valve's only lifted off its seating. The pumps are winning at this depth.'

'Can you steam?'

'Slow only, sir. The excessive revs may have damaged the engines.'

'Thanks, chief.' Coombes paused. He desperately needed time to think. 'Can you repair the valve?'

'Can you stay on the surface, sir? We may have to rig a cofferdam and the least depth the better for us. We took quite a thump from the explosion back aft. I'll report on the damage as soon as I can.'

'Roger, chief. There's nothing up top but miles and miles of pack ice. I'll start recirculating the air while we push out our flash report.' He hesitated before asking, 'You all right, back-aft?'

'No one hurt,' Malcolm Gunn replied, his soft Scottish voice steady and reassuring. CPO Scanes got a wetting, that's all.' Then the chief added as an afterthought, 'I'd appreciate as much warning as possible if you have to dive.'

'Roger. ECM is clear at the moment. Well done, you back-endies.' Coombes twitched at his whiskers as he switched off the intercom. Whether *Safari* could remain on the surface depended upon Ivan. It was senseless to harass Malcolm Gunn further: he was a first-rate MEO and realized only too well the decisions facing his captain.

'Open the lower lid,' Coombes ordered. 'Officer of the watch on the bridge.' He briefed the OOW then turned towards Hamilton. 'Bring her to full buoyancy. You have the ship, Number One. I'm going up top.'

'I have the ship, sir.'

The PO steward stepped forward from behind the masts, his captain's heavy-weather clothing in his arms.

'Thanks.'

Then, clad in his warm clothing, the hood tied about his head, fur mitts on his hands, Coombes entered the tower. Far above, the small circle of daylight showed; he grasped the wet, slippery rungs of the ladders and began climbing upwards towards it.

After nearly a fortnight's existence below in the comfort of *Safari*'s constant atmosphere, the intense cold on the minute bridge was a shock to Coombes' system. The steel was alread crisped with frost; the lookouts were stamping their feet and beating their muffed hands together to keep their circulation going. . . .

Coombes stared over the lip of the fin, his mind sluggish, mesmerized by her whale-like snout butting steadily through the pack ice; he listened to the cracking as it parted asunder to hiss down *Safari*'s rounded sides. To the north visibility was shutting down where sea smoke was forming, caused presumably by the icy wind sweeping across the relatively warm surface. The intercom snicked on:

'Bridge – control.'

'Bridge.'

'ECM reports reconnaissance aircraft frequency, bearing 020°. Distant, sir,' and Coombes detected a trace of anxiety in Hamilton's voice.

'Roger. Anything further from sonar?'

'Nothing more since 0200, sir. But there's a Mayday on radio distress frequency from the same bearing, sir.'

'A Mayday?'

'Yes, sir, strength six.'

'Roger. Keep me informed of all ECM contacts.' Coombes turned, watched the ECM warner mast swivelling slowly above his head. This was the third contact since *Safari* surfaced three hours ago. She had got away with it so far, but she was chancing her luck, even up in this God-forsaken ocean. How much longer before the chief was finished with the hull-valve? And would the damn thing hold, even at periscope depth? He turned impatiently, cursing softly to himself.

The exhilaration of having sunk the Typhoon rapidly evaporated as he realized that *Safari* was struggling for survival. And now ECM was picking up Maydays originating from a source close to the Typhoon's breaking-up position: though she was crippled in deep water just outside the edge of the polar ice, there must be survivors. How else could one of her combined indicator and radio beacon buoys have succeeded in reaching the surface?

At 0130 Coombes had followed up his first flash with an amplifying sitrep which was immediately acknowledged by CINCEASTLANT. It was comforting to know that the home team were aware of *Safari*'s plight: unable to dive as yet, she continued to steam at ten knots on the surface, heading for the shelter of the glacial but friendly Nordaustland, that vast chunk of island with its two thousand foot cliffs, north-east of Spitzbergen. It was also comforting to have received the signal half an hour ago that part of *Carl Vinson*'s Striking Force had been alerted and was racing northwards to the area. *Safari* was still ninety miles from safety – the shallow water, in case of catastrophe. *Safari* was ordered to signal her eventual diving position and to transmit on every hour, a procedure which Coombes was observing reluctantly. His radio transmissions *must* soon bring down reprisals upon *Safari*. What the hell was holding up the chief? It was all Coombes could do not to pester Malcolm Gunn with bloody-fool enquiries. Talk of the devil, that was him on the intercom:

'Bridge – control.'

'Bridge.'

'MEO here, sir. The hull valve's reseated, if you'd like to take her down slowly. Give me five minutes to clear things up, will you?'

'Bloody good-o,' Coombes shouted. 'Five minutes, then?'

'Please. Slowly, mind you, in case it doesn't hold.' The Scottish voice paused. 'We ought to stay at periscope depth, sir, until we get back to base. I don't want to push our luck.'

Coombes couldn't believe it. Almost home and dry: the Typhoon sunk, *Safari* still afloat and homeward bound. Selfish bugger, he mused. How was Julian Farge getting on? And what about those poor sods, those still alive, a thousand feet down in the crippled Typhoon? He grabbed the mike:

'Diving stations,' he called. 'Diving in five minutes time. Ask the navigating officer to speak to me.'

'Pilot here, sir.'

'Give the communications officer our position and tell him to push out our diving signal: time 0356.'

Coombes grinned at his bridge team, unidentifiable in their bulky arctic clothing. 'Take your last look,' he told them. 'Next stop, Faslane.'

The sea smoke to the north-east was shutting down fast, wreathing in sinuous trails along the surface: hundreds of miles of whiteness, wiped bare of life by this merciless, icy wind.

'Bridge – control. Diving signal passed.'

'Roger. Finished with the wireless mast. Captain coming below.' Coombes nodded at the bridge oow, then shouldered his own bulky torso through the upper lid to clamber down the ladders to his control-room.

They unpeeled him from his warm clothing while he prepared to take his last check through the search periscope. Number One was muttering behind him:

'ECM's picking up that frequency again, sir – 018°. Pulse shifting and seems stronger.'

Coombes said nothing. He swung to the bearing: nothing, only the sea smoke.

'Clear the bridge – clear the bridge,' he commanded, feeling the turmoil in his gut. 'Come below. Shut the upper lid. I have the ship.'

He swept the horizon again, an unease pricking at him, as the diving drill continued around him.

'Bridge is clear, sir,' from the oow; and then the lookouts were slithering down the ladders, bringing the compass repeat and the bits and pieces with them. He heard the resonant echoing from the hammering as they fastened home the bolts. Coombes faced the ship control console to check that the HP air and hydraulics were on the line.

'Upper lid shut, two clips, two pins,' a voice called down from the darkness of the tower.

'Lower and secure ECM mast.' The damn thing was only causing twitch.

'Boat diving now,' Coombes said.

'Diving now, diving now,' the SCC repeated.

'Open three and four main vents.' He looked at the clock: 0401. Eight minutes to get down, for invisibility. Thank God for that. If the hull valve held, no problem. The ECM mast was hissing behind him, on its way down.

'Three and four main vents indicated,' the SCC reported, monitoring the tell-tales in the console.

'Report the bubble,' Coombes snapped.

'Bubble moving for'd, three degrees,' Bull Clint said, pushing up *Safari*'s nose to clear the for'd tanks of residual air.

'Open one and two main vents.' Coombes had dived this boat innumerable times, but never before had he been so relieved to feel the surface mantle of invisibility spreading above him.

'Bubble coming off, sir,' Clint called.

'Six down, eighty feet, back to fifty-eight.'

Coombes sighed with tiredness: he'd better take a final look.

'Bubble moving aft, sir,' the cox'n said.

Coombes began his last search by sweeping westwards, then slowly through south across the endless white waste merging formlessly with the dead sky. He shivered, whether from the cold or from the effect which this desolate ice-scape was having on him he did not know. All he had left now was the northern sector and that would be it. . .

The sea smoke was drifting across the northern horizon and reducing visibility to five miles.

He felt his heart leap as into his circle of vision the silhouettes of two aircraft parted the sea smoke, two sleek Soviet bombers end-on, growing larger with every second. They were low, clipping the ice, and streaking towards the half-dived submarine.

'Action stations, action stations,' the captain shouted from his periscope. 'Shut all bulkhead doors.'

Glued to the eyepieces, he watched them, less than a mile now, one a few feet higher and to the side of the other. In the lower half of his lens, the dark mass of *Safari*'s half-submerged hull was still looming above the surface. Two wisps of smoke spurted from beneath the wings of the first aircraft: then two more, from the other.

'Down periscope,' Coombes blurted. 'Blinder bombers. They've fired their rockets. *Hold on!*'

'All hatches dry, sir,' the scc reported, calmly continuing the drill. 'Lower lid shut and clipped.'

'Forty feet, sir,' Bull Clint shouted. 'Two down.'

'Six down –' But as Coombes spoke the rockets struck, blasting two holes through the pressure hull in the for'd escape compartment.

Seconds later *Safari* was hurtling down, her fore-ends flooded, at a thirty-degree bow-down angle. She struck the bottom at 0406, in a depth of 297 feet. She hung for a moment, her stern slowly subsiding; she settled then, almost level, crippled in the mud of the sea bed.

As Coombes picked himself up from the deck of th

control-room, the intercom snicked above his head:

'Control – manoeuvring.'

He stagged towards the mike: 'Control.'

'Hull valve's just holding. We're okay back-aft.' Coombes could hear Gunn gasping as he fought for breath. 'I may have to scram, sir.'

Coombes was reeling, shocked by the suddenness of disaster.

'All compartments make your reports,' he commanded, searching for words. 'Starting from for'd.'

He was swaying on his feet, holding on to the periscope rods, as the control-room crew struggled back to their stations.

There was no reply from the for'd escape compartment, the JRS' accommodation space or fridge spaces: the whole of the fore-ends for'd of the main bulkhead was flooded. If the reactor was scrammed the submarine would lose all power.

'Oh God,' Coombes muttered to himself. 'I must have time to think or we're buggered.'

29

USS Carl Vinson, 18 May. It was 2105 when *Carl Vinson* turned the corner fifteen miles north of Phippsoya, the diminutive and most norferly of the outlying islets protecting Spitzbergen. Vice-Admiral Jessup stood sheltering on the leeward side of his bridge were, even in this giant ship, he was forced to flex his knees as he great carrier pounded east at full speed into the worsenir gale. *Constitution*, five miles on *Carl Vinson*'s port quarter, as barely visible, shrouded by the icy spray. Both carriers' scorts, the DDGS, were pin-points astern of them on the wesrn horizon, unable to keep up in this appalling weather He felt the judder of the ship as she splunged again into theng, ice-green swell. Peering upwards at Old Glory flapping self to tatters, he relinquished the lip of his bridge, then stared through the screen door and into the warmth of the car's citadel. Unzipping his wind-cheater, he hurried down te anti-submarine control centre where he plumped into hiair in front of the admiral's display. The glowing PPI sc was slowly presenting a logical picture. Jessup took thoceedings State which his flag-lieutenant was hold ing tow him.

'Th Dan,' Jessup said. Methodically he perused day's nings. Goddamit, had it all started only twent hours First there had been *Safari*'s flash report:

DTG 06 (ZULU) MAY

TYI SUNK 81° 15′ NORTH 38° 54′ EAST DEPTH
ME ENDS.

They *had* done it at last – and thank thou sup. SDW had succeeded, as far conc though it was too early to kno supe were stepping back from the brin hold reath while the Kremlin delibe next ad deflated the earlier exhilar

AMPLIFYING SITREP. WATERTIGHT INTEGRITY AFFECTED BY ACTION WITH TYPHOON. PROCEEDING SURFACED COURSE 216° SPEED 10 TO CLOSE SHALLOWS NORTH-EAST NORDAUSTLAND. INTEND REPORTING ON THE HOUR. MY POSITION 81° 2′ NORTH 38° 40′ EAST. MESSAGE ENDS.

Safari was then 240 miles to the eastward of STRIFOR's advanced screens and Jessup had immediately detached three guided-missile destroyers. They raced through the heavy seas and were due to reach the British submarine by 030 if the weather did not deteriorate further. Jessup also scrambled a fighter patrol and flew off two stand-by Vikings. He decided not to move his force until the situation clarified. The two carriers, *Constitution* and *Carl Vinson*, remained crsing 150 miles west of Isfjord.

Shortly after her amplifying report, *Safari* signall that she was picking up Maydays on international distress frequency from the Typhoon's last known position. At 0216 Viking *Lima*, homing on the transmissions, sighted the Typhoon red and white beacon marked with the letter 'H' – the Russ system for donating a submarine bow marker. Viking *Hotel* and *Lima* 237 but, though the beacon continued to trait, there sign of life from the monster submarine lystricken own below the edge of the polar ice. as after ted the RAF for further LRMP suppthat the peration changed abruptly.

ent talked directly to Jessup Kremlin
a Typhoon could be ng. The
but the President w tiously
nded delighted *Safari*'s
thless bunch, admiral
was no new of *Orcus*.
r the Br
wased. She
nd, was
Vas then
rou 456: the
transs – but
ted po Jessup's
at the Br marine

960 FEET.

God for that,
as Nato was
whether the
The world was
rated. But *Safari*'s
ation.

indicator buoys had homing capability – and at 0500 *Safari* failed to report.

CINCEASTLANT transmitted the SUBSMASH at 0504 and soon after Jessup's force was ordered to proceed with utmost despatch to Isfjord. Two DSRVs, already earmarked for Operation SDW, were being air-lifted from Prestwick, ETA Isfjord 1000.

The next five hours were memorable. The two carriers' dash eastwards into the head seas developed into a race, the ageing *Constitution* losing by only a short head. Both ships arrived forty minutes after the DSRVs landed. The destroyer screens, unable to keep up, waited outside for the carriers' turnaround. The helo-lift began at 1130, *Avalon 3* landing on *Carl Vinson*'s flight deck at 1205. Then fell the most cruel of blows.

At 1142 the helo carrying the main body of DSRV *Avalon 4* suffered a tail rotor failure. The DSRV, its crew and that of the helo were lost in eight hundred feet of water. STRIFOR proceeded with *Avalon 3* at full speed for the SUBSMASH datum position 'X'.

Then came some welcome news from CINCEASTLANT: the Soviet command was sailing a rescue task force to the Typhoon's position. The Kremlin was requesting co-operation and assuring the President that STRIFOR would not be harassed. Jessup was to maintain full alert and air cover. He was to inform the Russians of all his intentions.

It was a hard flog all right, the wind whipping up to Force 9. Blizzard conditions existed during the afternoon and even the great carriers were forced to reduce speed. At twenty-five hours' steaming *Carl Vinson* expected to be at position 'X' tomorrow at 0500 – Monday, 19 May.

Jessup laid the Proceedings State to one side. It was 2130 already, twelve hours since the destroyers had been on station over *Safari*'s position – and he was glad that *Safari* had not been told that only one DSRV was now available. He wondered how the DDGs were faring, though the wind was beginning to ease. He yawned and stretched, yearning for his bunk. Tomorrow would be another hectic day – and patience was not one of Jessup's qualities. He did not know how he could endure another ten hours of waiting for *Carl Vinson* to reach 'X' – th position which, due to the terrible weather, was likely become *Safari*'s watery tomb. As a professional, Jessup used to facing facts – and he could not dodge this one.

30

USS Carl Vinson, 19 May. Jessup watched the three DDGs bucking into the seas while trying to keep station on *Safari's* buoy. For Jessup it was the worst moment during the whole of SUBSMASH. The buoy was the vital communication link, indeed the only one: the DDGs were lying off, waiting for the cable of the buoy to part at any moment. They had established contact on underwater telephone last night at 1030, but the bad weather during the rest of the night rendered underwater communication very difficult, the squelching distorting all speech. But during the early hours of this Monday morning, the wind miraculously began to moderate, to leave a long swell, the surface ice streaked slate-green where the leads of open water stretched like fingers to leeward.

Jessup enjoyed these snatched interludes on his bridge, for a brief moment trying to escape his heavy burden. In half an hour *Carl Vinson* would be in position, ready to launch *Avalon 3*, the DSRV. The swell would make the helo's task hazardous but apparently the drop evolution had been exercised in worse conditions.

The admiral stood in the lee, marvelling at the skill and confidence of his chopper pilots: no problem, they had said, to lift that massive sausage-shaped load over the side and to dump it gently into this long swell, the troughs of which must be twenty feet below the crests. He turned as the screen door slid on its tracks. His staff captain, baggy half-moons beneath his eyes, was saluting:

'There they are, admiral – starboard bow.' They lifted their binoculars – yes, the first crosses of the Soviets' mastheads were etched against the leaden sky.

'Funny old world, Tom. Twenty-four hours ago, if someone had dreamed this up, we'd have laughed our arses off.'

'Their first units located the Typhoon buoy at dawn, sir. ⌐his lot's their heavy mob, complete with diving bell and lifting ⌐r.'

The screen door slid back again and the communications officer, still in his shirt sleeves, stepped out on to the bridge:

'The Soviets are on the air, sir. They're asking to speak admiral to admiral, using their interpreter.'

'They've kept their word, sir, since the President's call,' the staff captain added 'They've been co-operating all down the line.'

'Yeah,' Jessup murmured. 'When we lost *Avalon 4* and the helo, I sure appreciated their message. And I reckon they meant it: Gorshkov's traditions will die hard in their navy.' The two officers stood aside as the admiral moved towards the screen door:

'Keep the fighter coverage going, Tom,' he said, 'and the Force at Readiness State One.' His bushy eyebrows rose, as he peeled off his jacket. 'Some guy has to make the first move after a quarrel,' he said in his slow, Southern drawl. 'I'll talk to 'em, Tom: reckon it should be interesting.'

31

HM Submarine Safari, 19 May. There was barely sufficient light percolating through from the control-room for Janner Coombes to read his own handwriting. His first decision after being forced to scram the reactor was to switch to emergency lighting. The cold gleam of the single white light bulbs were having a depressing effect on morale: deprived of the evening film show, the hands found boredom difficult to combat, with reading difficult under the lighting conditions. There was a sepulchural gloom about the compartments when the first lieutenant did his rounds with the cox'n. The canteen manager and sixteen others were drowned in the deluge which overwhelmed the fore-ends when the missiles struck. Nothing could be done about the bodies, because three compartments were flooded for'd of the main bulkhead.

Even the effort of sliding his chair towards his desk made Coombes fight for air. He inhaled a long draught, felt the scarce oxygen reaching to the depths of his lungs, then tried to focus his thoughts as he picked up his pen. He *must* complete this final day of his patrol report so that FOSM could know what happened. He leaned backwards, trying to pin-point the sequence of events, and painstakingly jotted down the times for his rough draft – detailed times after *Safari* plunged into the mud were impossible to recall.

The first entry in the log was at 0412 when the chief was forced to scram the reactor six minutes after their first attempt at shifting the submarine. And that was when he, Janner Coombes, made his serious misjudgement in the crisis of the moment – understandable, but criticial: he blew main ballast. He then went full astern on the egg-beater, the battery-driven vertical shaft and propeller which, in emergency, could be lowered like an outboard motor to drive the boat at four knots. Hundreds of tons heavy, the 4,500 ton submarine was stuck t. He *tried* not to overdo the discharge on the minute battery oing astern too long – it was difficult to judge, but now they could be paying with their lives for his error.

At 0500 he'd gathered his senior officers into the wardroom (yesterday, wasn't it, 18 May?). It did not take long to reach their decision: they knew that the indicator buoy had reached the surface and that its homing beacon was transmitting satisfactorily: it would only be a matter of time before the LRMPs picked up the signal. It was best to stay put, taking all prudent measures: conserve what was left in the battery; burn up as little air as possible by banning cooking, by turning-in, not talking and by using the CO_2 scrubbers. If conditions became desperate, they could attempt a controlled escape: 297 feet was easily within limits.

Their decision was proved to be the right one when two hours later, at 0640, the first of a Viking's active transmissions pinged against the hull. Hope soared and it was difficult to stop the infectious chatter which was burning up the limited oxygen. At 0930 morale rose even higher when the noise of propellers from the first of the destroyers was picked up by the watcher sonar. Communications with the surface was then established through the underwater telephone – and Coombes began to anticipate with enthusiasm the routine calls from that distorted, burbling, American voice of the destroyer CO.

From that moment onwards, 1040 18 May, Coombes' patience had been tested to the limit: his junior officers steered well clear, but Number One and the chief had demonstrated once again their calming influence. The increasing condensation in the submarine as the temperature dropped; the enforced, fitful, disturbed sleep woken violently by nightmares; the periodic contact with the destroyer through the telephone until the gale made speech unintelligible – a full night and day dragged by. Dawn on 19 May had brought the abatement of blizzard conditions up top.

At 0835 Coombes could once more understand the destroyer captain's words: *Carl Vinson* and *Constitution* should be seven miles off by 0900; *Avalon 3* would be lowered immediately into the water and should start her first descent at 1030. That, Coombes calculated, would make it thirty hours since *Safari* scrammed. The jubilation was contagious: it was difficult to restrain the optimistic whisperings through the boat, ar excitement fanned by Bull Clint who, fly-whisk in hanc accompanied Number One through the boat to make their final count. Once the DSRV began its descent, the hands would start to muster aft, because *Avalon 3* would be docking over the engine-room escape hatch. The DSRV could lift twenty-four men per trip – so, subtracting the number of dead for'd, three lifts should do it. The air was still good and hopes were high.

At 1130, the destroyer captain was on the underwater telephone:

'Hi, commander,' the distorted voice burbled. 'How you doin'?' He sounded as jubilant as Coombes.

'Okay down here.'

'Good – that's fine.' The American voice paused, waiting for the 'squelching' to subside. 'Are you in good shape? Life support okay?' His heartiness was irritating: why didn't he get on with it?

'We're fine: all set and ready to go.'

'Commander – we've a little problem up here.' He seemed to hesitate. 'How much longer can you hold on? Life support – how many hours?'

'Difficult to estimate – we're okay at the moment – twelve hours, maybe.'

'Twelve? Good, good. Wait one, please.' Several minutes elapsed before he was on the line again:

'Could you wait a bit longer, commander? We'd like to start the first descent at about 1730.'

Hell, Coombes exploded to himself. 'What's the trouble?' he asked curtly over the phone.

'The Typhoon is sunk at 960 feet. Forty-six of her men are trapped. They're in bad shape. The Russians are co-operating with us, but they don't have time for a rescue with their diving bells: the water's too deep and the weather's not yet fined up sufficiently for their support vessel.'

'So?' Coombes asked, glancing at his officers grouped around him.

'They're asking us to help with *Avalon 3*: apparently their hatches are designed for our DSRV fit. The admiral's asking if you can wait a bit longer, commander, while *Avalon 3* makes two lifts to save the Russian survivors?'

'Can't you use *Avalon 4*?' Coombes asked.

'Wait one.'

Another long interval. Then:

'Commander: *Avalon 4* was lost yesterday in a helicopter crash.'

The hopes of the men grouped about the telephone evaporated as suddenly as they had arisen. It was Coombes' turn to ask for time to consider:

'Wait one.'

At 1140 he and his officers made their decision: they'd *have* to wait, wouldn't they? Submariners were much the same the world over, even the Soviets. . .

'Okay: we'll expect you at 1730,' Coombes told them on the surface. 'My life-support guesstimate is 2300, repeat 2300.'

'Roger. Thanks, commander – out.'

Coombes spoke to the troops over the broadcast and they accepted the disappointment as he expected – but the smiles vanished from that moment onwards.

Life now, at 1700, was bloody unpleasant, in spite of the destroyer captain's hourly efforts at jocular encouragement. Coombes was kicking himself for putting altruism before the safety of his men – but he was not to know how rapidly the air conditions were to deteriorate. Each breath was now an effort and everyone was suffering acute headache.

Fortunately, lying crippled on the ocean bed required little working of the boat; mens' minds were becoming fuddled, and it was too easy to report a valve shut when it was open, a dangerous symptom from which World War II submariners suffered when the atmosphere of their boats became pressurized, but lacked oxygen.

Coombes lifted his head wearily, met Trix's gentle smile from her photograph, and stared at the clock in front of him. 1709: in twenty minutes recovery should begin and that should be the beginning of the end of a rotten dream.

'Captain, sir?' Hamilton was leaning against the doorway, his chest heaving. 'The destroyer's asking for you.'

Coombes pushed the sheet of writing-paper from him and dragged himself into the control-room. Luke Wesley handed him the telephone.

'Commander?' The American was much easier to understand, the speech almost normal with improvement in the weather.

'How's things, commander?'

'Short of air. We're standing-by.'

'Commander, I hate to tell you: we've another problem.'

Coombes felt the surge of anger rising. 'What now, for God's sake?'

'*Avalon's* recovered the Russian survivors,' the voice from the surface said. 'The DSRV has been lifted back to *Carl Vinson* for a battery change.' The American sounded cagey.

'Yeah?'

'The swell's bad, commander. There's a sea running.'

'For God's sake,' Coombes muttered to himself, glancing at Hamilton, 'get on with it, man.'

'*Avalon's* undercarriage has been damaged during the lift – sorry, commander. We've signalled for spares, but delivery will take time.'

It was unreasonable, Coombes knew, to begin to hate that fruity, casual voice from the surface.

'How long for the spares?' He was trying not to shout. 'I can't hold out much longer – a few hours at the most.'

'Fifteen hours – mebbe.'

'Cancel the whole damn thing,' Coombes told him. 'Stand-by for my controlled escape.'

'The weather's not too good. The ice is jumping about – listen, commander, Goddammit, let me finish –'

'I've made my decision. I'll contact you when I'm ready for the first ascent. Out.'

He was handing back the instrument to Wesley when the American came in again, exasperated also, by the tone of his voice:

'You've gotta listen: the Russians are offering to help. They're steaming as fast as they can towards me: thirteen miles off now.'

Coombes battened down on his smouldering wrath. He asked stiffly:

'What do you propose, then?'

'As soon as the weather's okay, they'll let go two anchors close to you. Their divers and the two bells are jacked up, ready for lowering.'

'When are they starting? What's required of us?' Coombes

was cooling down: they were doing their best up top and, if they were quick about it, it would still be more prudent to accept a bell escape, than to chance a free ascent.

'They have two six-man bells, commander, with an escape hatch fit.'

'Wait one, please.'

This time he'd rely upon no one's but his and his officers' judgement.

Since then, for the past three hours, *Safari* had been waiting, waiting while Coombes sat at his cabin desk trying to pass the painful hours. Number One was installed in the control-room chair, completing his patrol report. At 2245 they heard the first Russian anchor rattling to the bottom close alongside.

Coombes tried to ignore the excrutiating ache pulsing in his forehead as he did his best to marshal his erratic thoughts. Breathing was a painful struggle: the deep inhalations of oxygen-starved air to the depth of his lungs were giving less and less relief – and he began to wonder whether he'd left it too late for a rush escape. If he hadn't stupidly exhausted the HP air during the emergency plunge, at least they would have had longer to live by using the emergency breathing system through the HP air ring main.

His own thinking was becoming hazy, so how about the others, those who'd put in more demanding physical effort? he'd endure another hour, then order a rush escape, before it was too late. Better to die under the open sky, sliced up, perhaps, by the ice than to snuff it out in this grisly fashion. He slashed a final line across the bottom of his patrol report: FOSM would have all the evidence, anyway – and now Trix, bless her, deserved the few lines he was determined to write her, just in case . . .

He supposed historians might pronounce that Operation SDW was significant in the scheme of things: but was the loss of his men and perhaps Farge, too, a price worth paying? His moustaches twitched with a sardonic smile. He didn't know whether this sinking of the Typhoon had convinced the Kremlin that their game was not worth the candle. The operation was somewhat of a confidence trick, anyway, wasn't it? And he slumped back in his chair, worn out, sick of it all, caring no more for the follies of the distant world above. He and his men were at the sharp end: if the West had woken up earlier, would *Safari* be stricken here in 297 feet of water, crippled and dying? Coombes wondered whether, through the mystery of divine planning, the ideals of the multi-lateral disarmers could now be realized?

He slumped towards his desk, picked up his pen again and began to write:

Monday, 19 May

Trix, my darling wife,
By the time you get this, you will be recovering and longing to leave hospital. How I wish I could be with you to welcome you home with the children!
But I'm afraid it's not to be, as I'm otherwise engaged at the moment, as you know. I've been pretty busy so haven't been able to write my few daily lines to you – nor the children. Try to explain to Luke why I haven't been able to draw him his usual picture of *Safari*!
This, dear Trix, is a difficult letter to write – and if you receive it, you'll know that (as we once talked together) I'll be waiting for you on the 'other side'. We've had a wonderful marriage. And you'll have the sprogs to comfort you during the first difficult years – Luke is already proudly looking after you when I'm away, even now, isn't he? But I must get back to my work. . .
Thank you, darling. May God bless you and our children – and a great big hug for Sarah and Luke too.

He signed his letter with a flourish, sealed it in an envelope and carefully buttoned it into the hip pocket of his trousers. And now it was time to talk to his men. He reached up and extracted the small book from the shelf above his desk.

When the crunch came, every man called upon his God – Christian, Moslem, Buddhist, the lot – yes and probably the Soviet communist submariner as well. Coombes flicked the pages of the Naval Prayer Book: Forms of Prayer to be Used at Sea. He'd begin: 'Thou hast promised that when two or three are gathered together,' then read the General Confession. He'd read the traditional prayer: 'Oh Eternal Lord God, who alone spreadest out the heavens, and rulest the raging of the sea; who hast compassed the waters with bounds until day and night come to an end . . .' The powerful, majestic words, solemn splendid prose, fashioned by men who really placed their faith in God, would lift the men's spirits, and he'd finish with the Lord's Prayer.

Coombes canted back on his chair and called through to the scow in the control-room.

'Inform the First Lieutenant and the ship's company that I'll be talking on the broadcast in five minutes' time.'

'Aye, aye, sir.'

Coombes let the curtain drop back into place and wearily climbed to his feet. Knackered though he was, he'd bloody well fight this terrible lassitude to the end. By God, we're not done yet: perhaps He would see them through, if it was His will.

He tightened his tie and shuffled across the few yards of the deck to his customary position between the periscopes.

He reached for the mike, heard his men gasping as, silently, they struggled to their feet. Robinson was at his place in front of the CEP; Number One, silent, head bowed; Bull Clint, by the planesman's seat, was leaning forward because of the curving hull; the wrecker stood in front of his panel. Coombes switched on the intercom.

'Captain speaking,' he began, struggling for breath. 'Wherever you are throughout the boat, I invite you to join us in prayer for our families and our country, asking for God's mercy, asking Him to save us, if it be His will.' He cleared the phlegm in his throat.

'The prayer of Saint Chrysostom,' he began. 'Almighty God, who gives us grace at this special time with one accord to make our common supplications unto thee; and dost promise that when two or three are gathered together in thy name, thou wilt grant their requests.' He had to stop, fighting for breath. In that brief silence, his men around him, shivering in the clammy chill, heard the rattling of an anchor cable echoing against the hull. Coombes looked up, then flipped over the page to where he had marked the confession. As he concluded the supplication he heard Sims calling for him to man the underwater telephone.

'Tell 'em to wait up top,' Coombes said. 'I'll take the call when we've finished.'

Safari had been crippled for forty-three hours: a few minutes to end with the Lord's Prayer and their tribulations would be almost over.

Washington, 19 May. For the past two days the British staff had been at immediate notice, constricted to their homes and hotels. Trevellion was on his hotel bed, trying to keep awake, when Rear Admiral Quarrie's secretary came through on the extension.

'The meeting's convened for 1600 at the White House, sir,' she said. 'Our car's on its way to pick you up.'

Trevellion had time to run a razor over his gaunt face: crescent shadows hung beneath his eyes and the lined hollows in his cheeks were dark with stubble. Forty-seven hours since the momentous news came through of the Typhoon sinking; two days of brinkmanship supreme, America and the free world daring not to breathe, while their citizens streamed from the cities into the countryside. For the second time that day, Trevellion offered a silent prayer of thankfulness that Rowena and Ben were safely tucked away in Cornwall, though Culdrose, presumably a prime target, was too close for comfort.

It had been 1715 yesterday when SACLANT came through with the news – 0100 Moscow time. Apparently, at the other end of the hot line, the Soviet leader had been as surly as his Motherland's national mascot, refusing to believe the President's claim: the Kremlin was waiting for C-IN-C Northern Fleet's reports. Meanwhile the threat of a nuclear first strike still hung over the West. And that, so the reports from the ops people went, was when the Soviet leader hung up. And now the telephone was purring from Trevellion's bedside. His car was waiting at the hotel entrance.

Rear-Admiral Quarrie was already in his seat when Pascoe Trevellion was ushered into the Situation Room, which Trevellion reckoned was the most elegantly and comprehensively equipped ops room he had yet encountered. But he was becoming blasé, having spent much of his time here during the crisis. A vacant seat was separating Quarrie from 'utch Hart who had befriended Pascoe since Trevellion first arrived in Washington.

'Hi, Butch,' Trevellion grinned, accepting the seat which Hart indicated. 'He's back from the hills, then?'

Hart nodded his grey head, his distinguished features breaking into a slow smile. 'Could be good news, Pascoe. They wouldn't have allowed the President back, otherwise, would they?'

'The first eleven's here, I see,' Trevellion added, glancing round the room packed with senior officers from the three services.

'Uh?'

'Cricket,' Trevellion explained. 'Forget it.'

The screen along the wall glowed as the maps were projected: the usual one of the Pacific area; the other, the North Atlantic. The red and green crosses were dotted as before, concentrated in the critical areas – but now three blue crosses showed, two in the Pacific off the Kuril Islands, one north-west of Murmansk.

'Two of ours and one of yours,' Hart said.

Trevellion inclined his head, but remained silent. Though the Kremlin was claiming a sinking off Vardø, Nato refused to confirm that *Orcus* was missing. FOSM still had no news of her since her signal giving *Safari* the vital enemy report. A hard price to pay. The double-circled red cross of the Typhoon kill on the edge of the polar ice somehow failed to compensate, now that an end to this sea war was in sight.

'Gentlemen, the President.'

They stood up and the American leader, flanked by his Secretary of Defense and the Chairman of the Joint Chiefs of Staff, Admiral Floyd, entered through the door leading from the White House. The President looked as fit as ever, but the strain of the terrible load he bore was beginning to show in his craggy face. He glanced round at them all with his humorous, shrewd eyes, bade them, with a casual wave of the hand, to be seated, then strode to the lectern on the raised platform. He waited for the Secretary of Defense and Floyd to settle in front of him. He nodded at the aide and the lights dimmed.

'Well, gentlemen,' the President began laconically, 'you've allowed me back from the hills, so I'd better not keep you waiting.' He pointed to the wall maps. 'There you have it, the

2

irrefutable evidence, gentlemen. You've achieved in three weeks what I demanded of you: Operation SD has killed twenty-one of the enemy's SSBNs.'

'One a day,' Hart murmured into Trevellion's ear.

'. . . culminating at 0100 yesterday, Sunday morning, with the kill I was waiting for: the enemy's untraceable, unsinkable monster submarine, one of their Typhoons.' He paused, searching amongst his audience until his glance lighted upon Quarrie. 'Gentlemen, we've got the Royal Navy to thank for ramming home the final nail in the coffin.' And as he smiled, a murmur of assent ran round the room. Trevellion remaining half turned, twitched a smile at Butch, as the President continued:

'SD's been a success, but since the destruction of the Typhoon, I've missed more sleep than during the preceding three weeks of waiting. For the past two days, I've been negotiating with the Soviet leader. The threat of failure, blackmail some would call it, is a powerful bargaining counter, gentlemen.' He paused to sip from the glass of water on the lectern. The President was firstly a politician, and his audience, the most hardened and sophisticated in the world, hung upon his words.

'Twenty-one of the enemy's ballistic missile submarines sunk in twenty-one days: the Soviet leaders cannot accept that loss-rate. The Kremlin is now convinced that the Soviet navy will be annihilated if the sea war continues.' He paused, then added sombrely:

'The Soviet leader called me twenty minutes ago. He assured me that he has cancelled his ICBM threat. All Russian forces are being ordered to withdraw from Northern Norway. The Soviet government wishes immediately to discuss practical ways of bringing about *real* détente, lasting peace. The Soviet leader, gentlemen, even professed interest in my insistence on his taking his armies out of Eastern Europe and so removing his threat of overrunning the West. As you all realize, gentlemen, it is *that* menace which forces us to have any nuclear arms at all.'

This announcement produced a momentary, stunned silence, a silence suddenly shattered by waves of cheering. The President waited for the jubilation to subside, then added quietly:

'By demonstrating our world-wide capability, I emphasize "world-wide", gentlemen, the enemy has been convinced, sobered by the brutality of the means we have been forced to adopt, that he cannot win. The success of our submarines, complementary in both oceans, has clinched the policy of deterrence which we have followed during these dangerous years.' Turning again to the wall displays behind him, he added laconically, 'Before we disperse, you should know that Vice-Admiral Jessup has just been on to me. His Striking Force has rescued the forty-six survivors from the Typhoon. The Soviet navy is co-operating whole-heartedly and is at this moment endeavouring to recover the survivors from the British submarine, *Safari*. We'll let you know, of course, as soon as we hear anything further.'

He stepped down from the podium. As the audience rose to its feet, Trevellion saw an aide scurrying towards Admiral Floyd, a telephone extension in his hand.

'Mr President,' Floyd called gruffly. 'One moment, Mr President.'

Trevellion watched the President halt in his tracks, turn, then speak briefly on the extension. Raising his voice, he announced from the crowded floor:

'You'll be relieved to know that the Soviet rescue ship has started to lift *Safari's* crew. The first diving bell was locked on satisfactorily to the submarine's hatch ten minutes ago. It's nice to know,' he added, turning to leave the room, 'that they're human, after all.'

There was for Pascoe Trevellion a dream-like quality about the scene as they wrung his hands, pressed their congratulations upon Quarrie and himself, the warmth of American spontaneity suddenly spilling over. Then, discreetly leaving Quarrie to the circle of delighted officers, Trevellion slipped away to the communication complex which was at the end of the long corridor.

'Ministry of Defence, London,' he asked the operator. 'First Sea Lord, please.'

The voice he knew so well could have been next door.

'First Sea Lord here.'

'Trevellion, sir.'

'Well?'

'It's all over,' Trevellion said quietly. 'SD's worked, sir. They're getting out of Norway.'

'And the nuclear threat?'

'Cancelled, sir.'

Trevellion could hear only the crackling in the phone. Then Anthony Layde said quietly:

'They've sunk *Orcus*. The Russians recovered thirty-four survivors.'

'Farge, sir?'

'The Norwegian resistance picked up several dead, Farge among 'em. His body's been identified.'

'Thanks, sir,' Trevellion said. 'He was my PWO in Icarus.'

'Better come home, Pascoe,' Layde said gruffly, 'to the haven where you would be.'

The instrument clicked. Trevellion walked outside, blinked in the afternoon sunlight, noted the vivid colours of the garden. The cut lawn smelt sweet: a beautiful day, spring in Washington. The avenues were framed in colour, clouds of rose and yellow, pink and white, where the ornamental trees blossomed. Down the highways the traffic streamed, a jet-liner roaring overhead. A beautiful world, fragile, precariously balanced. Trevellion straightened his lanky frame. He'd walk back to his hotel this evening, back to the real world where humanity bustled; where men and women earned their daily bread, free to make their own decisions, to lead their lives the way they chose, to live in peace. What was it that President Roosevelt had told the world, before taking his country into World War II?

Trevellion, walking towards the hustling crowds on the sidewalks, retrieved those words of hope from the recesses of his mind:

'We look forward to a world founded upon four essential freedoms. The first is freedom of speech and expression – everywhere in the world. The second is freedom of every person to worship God in his own way – everywhere in the world. The third is freedom from want . . . the fourth is freedom from fear.'